Sir Edward Bulwer Lytton

Eugene Aram

A Tale: Vol. I.

Sir Edward Bulwer Lytton

Eugene Aram
A Tale: Vol. I.

ISBN/EAN: 9783337081829

Printed in Europe, USA, Canada, Australia, Japan

Cover: Foto ©Andreas Hilbeck / pixelio.de

More available books at **www.hansebooks.com**

NOVELS

OF

SIR EDWARD BULWER LYTTON

Library Edition

ROMANCES

VOL. II.

EUGENE ARAM

A Tale

BY

SIR EDWARD BULWER LYTTON, BART.

[10.]

LIBRARY EDITION—IN TWO VOLUMES

VOL. I.

WILLIAM BLACKWOOD AND SONS
EDINBURGH AND LONDON
MDCCCLXI

" Our acts our angels are, or good or ill,
Our fatal Shadows that walk by us still.
. . . . . .
. . . All things that are
Made for our general uses, are at war,—
Ev'n we among ourselves !"

JOHN FLETCHER, upon *An Honest Man's Fortune.*

SIR WALTER SCOTT, Bart.

ETC. ETC.

Sir,

It has long been my ambition to add some humble tribute to the offerings laid upon the shrine of your genius. At each succeeding book that I have given to the world, I have paused to consider if it were worthy to be inscribed with your great name, and at each I have played the procrastinator, and hoped for that morrow of better desert which never came. But, *defluat amnis*, the time runs on—and I am tired of waiting for the ford which the tides refuse. I seize, then, the present opportunity, not as the best, but as the only one I can be sure of commanding, to express that affectionate admiration with which you have inspired me in common with all your contemporaries, and which a French writer has not ungracefully termed "the happiest prerogative of genius." As a Poet and as a Novelist, your fame has attained to that height in which praise has become superfluous; but in the character of the writer there seems to me a yet higher claim to veneration than in that of the writings. The example your genius sets us,

VOL. I.   *a*

who can emulate ?—the example your moderation bequeaths to us, who shall forget ?   That nature must
indeed be gentle which has conciliated the envy that
pursues intellectual greatness, and left without an enemy
a man who has no living equal in renown.

You have gone for a while from the scenes you have
immortalised, to regain, we trust, the health which has
been impaired by your noble labours, or by the manly
struggles with adverse fortunes, which have not found
the frame as indomitable as the mind.   Take with you
the prayers of all whom your genius, with playful art,
has soothed in sickness—or has strengthened, with generous precepts, against the calamities of life.*

> " Navis quæ tibi creditum
>   Debes Virgilium————
>   Reddas incolumem ! " †

You, I feel assured, will not deem it presumptuous in
one who, to that bright and undying flame which now
streams from the grey hills of Scotland,—the last halo
with which you have crowned her literary glories,—has
turned from his first childhood with a deep and unrelax-
ing devotion ; you, I feel assured, will not deem it presumptuous in him to inscribe an idle work with your
illustrious name :—a work which, however worthless in
itself, assumes something of value in his eyes when thus
rendered a tribute of respect to you.

THE AUTHOR OF " EUGENE ARAM."

LONDON, *December* 22, 1831.

* Written at the time of Sir W. Scott's visit to Italy, after the
great blow to his health and fortunes.

† O ship, thou owest to us Virgil—restore in safety him whom
we intrusted to thee !

PREFACE TO THE EDITION OF 1831.

SINCE, dear Reader, I last addressed thee, in *Paul Clifford*, nearly two years have elapsed, and somewhat more than four years since, in *Pelham*, our familiarity first began. The Tale which I now submit to thee differs equally from the last as from the first of those works ; for, of the two evils, perhaps it is even better to disappoint thee in a new style than to weary thee with an old. With the facts on which the tale of *Eugene Aram* is founded, I have exercised the common and fair licence of writers of fiction. It is chiefly the more homely parts of the real story that have been altered ; and for what I have added, and what omitted, I have the sanction of all established authorities, who have taken greater liberties with characters yet more recent, and far more protected by historical recollections. The book was, for the most part, written in the early part of the year, when the interest which the task created in the author was undivided by other subjects of excitement, and he had leisure enough not only to be *nescio quid meditans nugarum*, but also to be *totus in illis !* *

* Not only to be meditating I know not what of trifles, but also to be wholly engaged on them.

I originally intended to adapt the story of Eugene Aram to the Stage. That design was abandoned when more than half completed ; but I wished to impart to this Romance something of the nature of Tragedy— something of the more transferable of its qualities. Enough of this : it is not the Author's wishes, but the Author's books, that the world will judge him by. Perhaps, then (with this I conclude), in the dull monotony of public affairs, and in these long winter evenings when we gather round the fire, prepared for the gossip's tale, willing to indulge the fear and to believe the legend, perhaps, dear Reader, thou mayest turn, not reluctantly, even to these pages, for at least a newer excitement than the *Cholera*, or for a momentary relief from the everlasting discussions on " *the Bill.*" *

LONDON, *December* 22, 1831.

* The year of the Reform Bill.

PREFACE TO THE EDITION OF 1840.

THE strange history of Eugene Aram had excited my
interest and wonder long before the present work was
composed or conceived. It so happened that, during
Aram's residence at Lynn, his reputation for learning
had attracted the notice of my grandfather—a country-
gentleman living in the same county, and of more in-
telligence and accomplishments than at that day usually
characterised his class. Aram frequently visited at Hey-
don (my grandfather's house), and gave lessons, probably
in no very elevated branches of erudition, to the younger
members of the family. This I chanced to hear when I
was on a visit in Norfolk, some two years before this
novel was published, and it tended to increase the interest with which I had previously speculated on the
phenomena of a trial which, take it altogether, is perhaps the most remarkable in the register of English
crime. I endeavoured to collect such anecdotes of Aram's
life and manners as tradition and hearsay still kept
afloat. These anecdotes were so far uniform that they
all concurred in representing him as a person who, till
the detection of the crime for which he was sentenced,
had appeared of the mildest character and the most

unexceptionable morals. An invariable gentleness and patience in his mode of tuition—qualities then very uncommon at schools—had made him so beloved by his pupils at Lynn, that, in after life, there was scarcely one of them who did not persist in the belief of his innocence. His personal and moral peculiarities, as described in these pages, are such as were related to me by persons who had heard him described by his contemporaries: the calm benign countenance—the delicate health—the thoughtful stoop—the noiseless step—the custom, not uncommon with scholars and absent men, of muttering to himself—a singular eloquence in conversation, when once roused from silence—an active tenderness and charity to the poor, with whom he was always ready to share his own scanty means—an apparent disregard to money, except when employed in the purchase of books—an utter indifference to the ambition usually accompanying self-taught talent, whether to better the condition or to increase the repute ;—these, and other traits of the character portrayed in the novel, are, as far as I can rely on my information, faithful to the features of the original.

That a man thus described—so benevolent that he would rob his own necessities to administer to those of another, so humane that he would turn aside from the worm in his path—should have been guilty of the foulest of human crimes—viz., murder for the sake of gain ; that a crime thus committed should have been so episodical and apart from the rest of his career, that, however it might rankle in his conscience, it should never have hardened his nature ; that, through a life of some duration, none of the errors, none of the vices, which would seem essentially to belong to a character capable of a deed so black from motives apparently so sordid,* should have been discovered or suspected ;—all this presents an anomaly in human conduct so rare and surprising, that it would be difficult to find any subject more adapted for that metaphysical speculation and analysis, in order to indulge which, Fiction, whether in the drama or the higher class of romance, seeks its materials and grounds its lessons in the chronicles of passion and crime.

The guilt of Eugene Aram is not that of a vulgar ruffian : it leads to views and considerations vitally and wholly distinct from those with which profligate knavery and brutal cruelty revolt and displease us in the literature of Newgate and the Hulks. His crime does, in fact, belong to those startling paradoxes which the poetry of all countries, and especially of our own, has always delighted to contemplate and examine. Whenever crime appears the aberration and monstrous product of a great intellect, or of a nature ordinarily virtuous, it becomes not only the subject for genius, which deals with passions, to describe; but a problem for philosophy, which deals with actions, to investigate and solve :—hence the Macbeths and Richards, the Iagos and Othellos. My regret, therefore, is not that I chose a subject unworthy of elevated fiction, but that such a subject did not occur to some one capable of treating it as it deserves ; and I

---

* For I put wholly out of question the excuse of jealousy, as unsupported by any evidence—never hinted at by Aram himself (at least on any sufficient authority)—and at variance with the only fact which the trial establishes—viz., that the robbery was the crime planned, and the cause, whether accidental or otherwise, of the murder.

never felt this more strongly than when the late Mr Godwin (in conversing with me after the publication of this romance) observed that "he had always thought the story of Eugene Aram peculiarly adapted for fiction, and that he had more than once entertained the notion of making it the foundation of a novel." I can well conceive what depth and power that gloomy record would have taken from the dark and inquiring genius of the author of *Caleb Williams*. In fact, the crime and trial of Eugene Aram arrested the attention and engaged the conjectures of many of the most eminent men of his own time. His guilt or innocence was the matter of strong contest ; and so keen and so enduring was the sensation created by an event thus completely distinct from the ordinary annals of human crime, that even history turned aside from the sonorous narrative of the struggles of parties and the feuds of kings to commemorate the learning and the guilt of the humble schoolmaster of Lynn. Did I want any other answer to the animadversions of commonplace criticism, it might be sufficient to say, that what the historian relates the novelist has little right to disdain.

Before entering on this romance, I examined with some care the probabilities of Aram's guilt ; for I need scarcely perhaps observe, that the legal evidence against him is extremely deficient—furnished almost entirely by one (Houseman) confessedly an accomplice of the crime, and a partner in the booty ; and that, in the present day, a man tried upon evidence so scanty and suspicious would unquestionably escape conviction. Nevertheless, I must frankly own that the moral evidence appeared to me more convincing than the legal ; and, though not without some doubt, which, in common with many, I still entertain of the real facts of the murder,* I adopted that view which, at all events, was the best suited to the higher purposes of fiction. On the whole, I still think that if the crime were committed by Aram, the motive was not very far removed from one which led recently to a remarkable murder in Spain. A priest in that country, wholly absorbed in learned pursuits, and apparently of spotless life, confessed that, being debarred by extreme poverty from prosecuting a study which had become the sole passion of his existence, he had reasoned himself into the belief that it would be admissible to rob a very dissolute, worthless man, if he applied the money so obtained to the acquisition of a knowledge which he could not otherwise acquire, and which he held to be profitable to mankind. Unfortunately, the dissolute rich man was not willing to be robbed for so excellent a purpose : he was armed, and he resisted—a struggle ensued, and the crime of homicide was added to that of robbery. The robbery was premeditated, the murder was accidental. But he who would accept some similar interpretation of Aram's crime must, to comprehend fully the lessons which belong to so terrible a picture of frenzy and guilt, consider also the physical circumstances and condition of the criminal at the time : severe illness—intense labour of the brain—poverty bordering upon famine—the mind preternaturally at work, devising schemes and excuses to arrive at the means for ends ardently desired. And, all this duly considered, the reader may see the crime bodying itself out from the shades and chimeras of a horrible hallucination—the awful dream of a brief but delirious

* See Preface to the Edition of 1851, p. xviii.

and convulsed disease. It is thus only that we can account for the contradiction of one deed at war with a whole life—blasting, indeed, for ever the happiness, but making little revolution in the pursuits and disposition of the character. No one who has examined with care and thoughtfulness the aspects of life and nature, but must allow that, in the contemplation of such a spectacle, great and most moral truths must force themselves on the notice, and sink deep into the heart. The entanglements of human reasoning; the influence of circumstance upon deeds; the perversion that may be made, by one self-palter with the fiend, of elements the most glorious; the secret effect of conscience in frustrating all for which the crime was done—leaving genius without hope, knowledge without fruit—deadening benevolence into mechanism—tainting love itself with terror and suspicion; such reflections—leading, with subtler minds, to many more vast and complicated theorems in the consideration of our nature, social and individual—arise out of the tragic moral which the story of Eugene Aram (were it but adequately treated) could not fail to convey.

BRUSSELS, *August* 1840.

PREFACE TO THE EDITION OF 1851.

If none of my prose works have been so attacked as *Eugene Aram,* none have so completely triumphed over attack. It is true that, whether from real or affected ignorance of the true morality of fiction, a few critics may still reiterate the old commonplace charges of "selecting heroes from Newgate," or "investing murderers with interest;" but the firm hold which the work has established in the opinion of the general public, and the favour it has received in every country where English literature is known, suffice to prove that, whatever its faults, it belongs to that legitimate class of fiction which illustrates life and truth, and only deals with crime as the recognised agency of pity and terror, in the conduct of tragic narrative. All that I would say farther on this score has been said in the general defence of my writings which I put forth two years ago; and I ask the indulgence of the reader if I repeat myself :—

"Here, unlike the milder guilt of Paul Clifford, the author was not to imply reform to society, nor open in this world atonement and pardon to the criminal. As it would have been wholly in vain to disguise, by mean tamperings with art and truth, the ordinary habits of

life and attributes of character which all record and remembrance ascribed to Eugene Aram, as it would have
defeated every end of the moral inculcated by his guilt
to portray in the caricature of the murderer of melodrame
a man immersed in study, of whom it was noted that he
turned aside from the worm in his path, so I have allowed
to him whatever contrasts with his inexpiable crime have
been recorded on sufficient authority. But I have invariably taken care that the crime itself should stand
stripped of every sophistry, and hideous to the perpetra-
tor as well as to the world. Allowing all by which attention to his biography may explain the tremendous
paradox of fearful guilt in a man aspiring after knowledge,
and not generally inhumane—allowing that the crime
came upon him in the partial insanity produced by the
combining circumstances of a brain overwrought by intense study, disturbed by an excited imagination, and
the fumes of a momentary disease of the reasoning faculty,
consumed by the desire of knowledge, unwholesome and
morbid, because coveted as an end, not a means, added
to the other physical causes of mental aberration—to be
found in loneliness, and want verging upon famine ;—all
these, which a biographer may suppose to have conspired
to his crime, have never been used by the novelist as
excuses for its enormity ; nor, indeed, lest they should
seem as excuses, have they ever been clearly presented to
the view. The moral consisted in showing more than
the mere legal punishment at the close. It was to show
how the consciousness of the deed was to exclude whatever humanity of character preceded and belied it from
all active exercise—all social confidence ; how the knowledge of the bar between the minds of others and his

own deprived the criminal of all motive to ambition, and blighted knowledge of all fruit : miserable in his affections, barren in his intellect—clinging to solitude, yet accursed in it—dreading as a danger the fame he had once coveted—obscure in spite of learning, hopeless in spite of love, fruitless and joyless in his life, calamitous and shameful in his end ;—surely such is no palliative of crime, no dalliance and toying with the grimness of evil ! And surely, to any ordinary comprehension, any candid mind, such is the moral conveyed by the fiction of *Eugene Aram*." *

In point of composition *Eugene Aram* is, I think, entitled to rank amongst the best of my fictions. It somewhat humiliates me to acknowledge, that neither practice nor study has enabled me to surpass a work written at a very early age, in the skilful construction and patient development of plot ; and though I have since sought to call forth higher and more subtle passions, I doubt if I have ever excited the two elementary passions of tragedy—viz., pity and terror—to the same degree. In mere style, too, *Eugene Aram*, in spite of certain verbal oversights and defects in youthful taste (some of which I have endeavoured to remove from the present edition), appears to me unexcelled by any of my later writings, at least in what I have always studied as the main essential of style in narrative—viz., its harmony with the subject selected, and the passions to be moved ; while it exceeds them all in the minuteness and fidelity of its descriptions of external nature. This, indeed, it ought to do, since the study of external nature is made a peculiar attribute of the principal character whose fate colours the narrative.

* " A Word to the Public," 1847.

I do not know whether it has been observed that the time occupied by the events of the story is conveyed through the medium of such descriptions. Each description is introduced, not for its own sake, but to serve as a calendar marking the gradual changes of the seasons as they bear on to his doom the guilty worshipper of Nature. And in this conception, and in the care with which it has been followed out, I recognise one of my earliest but most successful attempts at the subtler principles of narrative art.

In this edition I have made one alteration, somewhat more important than mere verbal correction. On going, with maturer judgment, over all the evidences on which Aram was condemned, I have convinced myself that, though an accomplice in the robbery of Clarke, he was free both from the premeditated design and the actual deed of murder. The crime, indeed, would still rest on his conscience and insure his punishment, as necessarily incidental to the robbery in which he was an accomplice with Houseman ; but finding my convictions, that in the murder itself he had no share, borne out by the opinion of many eminent lawyers, by whom I have heard the subject discussed, I have accordingly so shaped his confession to Walter.

Perhaps it will not be without interest to the reader, if I append to this preface an authentic specimen of Eugene Aram's composition, for which I am indebted to the courtesy of a gentleman by whose grandfather it was received, with other papers (especially a remarkable "Outline of a New Lexicon "), during Aram's confinement in York Prison. The essay I select is, indeed, not without value in itself as a very curious and learned illustration

of Popular Antiquities, and it serves also to show, not
only the comprehensive nature of Aram's studies and
the inquisitive eagerness of his mind, but also the fact
that he was completely self-taught ; for in contrast to
much philological erudition, and to passages that evince
considerable mastery in the higher resources of language, we may occasionally notice those lesser inaccura-
cies from which the writings of men solely self-educated
are rarely free ; indeed, Aram himself, in sending to a
gentleman an elegy on Sir John Armitage, which shows
much but undisciplined power of versification, says : " I
send this elegy, which, indeed, if you had not had the
curiosity to desire, I could not have had the assurance to
offer, scarce believing I, who was hardly taught to read,
have any abilities to write."

THE MELSUPPER AND SHOUTING THE CHURN.

THESE rural entertainments and usages were formerly
more general all over England than they are at present ;
being become by time, necessity, or avarice, complex, confined, and altered.   They are commonly insisted upon by
the reapers as customary things, and a part of their due
for the toils of the harvest, and complied with by their
masters perhaps more through regards of interest than
inclination.   For should they refuse them the pleasure of
this much-expected time, this festal night, the youth especially, of both sexes, would decline serving them for the
future, and employ their labours for others who would
promise them the rustic joys of the harvest supper, mirth
and music, dance and song.   These feasts appear to be

the relics of Pagan ceremonies, or of Judaism, it is hard
to say which, and carry in them more meaning and are
of far higher antiquity than is generally apprehended. It
is true, the subject is more curious than important, and I
believe altogether untouched ; and as it seems to be little
understood, has been as little adverted to.   I do not remember it to have been so much as the subject of a conversation. Let us make, then, a little excursion into this
field, for the same reason men sometimes take a walk. Its
traces are discoverable at a very great distance of time
from ours—nay, seem as old as a sense of joy for the benefit of plentiful harvests and human gratitude to the eternal Creator for his munificence to men. We hear it under
various names in different counties, and often in the same
county ; as *melsupper, churn supper, harvest supper, harvest home, feast of in-gathering,* &c.   And perhaps this
feast had been long observed, and by different tribes of
people, before it became perceptive with the Jews. However, let that be as it will, the custom very lucidly appears
from the following passages of S. S., Exod. xxiii. 16 :
" And the feast of harvest, the first fruits of thy labours, which thou hast sown in the field."   And its
institution as a sacred rite is commanded in Levit. xxiii.
39 : " When ye have gathered in the fruit of the land,
ye shall keep a feast to the Lord."

The Jews, then, as is evident from hence, celebrated
the feast of harvest, and that by precept ; and though no
vestiges of any such feast either are or can be produced
before these, yet the oblation of the Primitiæ, of which
this feast was a consequence, is met with prior to this, for
we find that " Cain brought of the fruit of the ground
an offering to the Lord," Gen. iv. 3.

Yet this offering of the first-fruits, it may well be supposed, was not peculiar to the Jews, either at the time of
or after its establishment by their legislator ; neither the
feast in consequence of it.   Many other nations, either
in imitation of the Jews, or rather by tradition from their

several patriarchs, observed the right of offering their Primitiæ, and of solemnising a festival after it, in religious acknowledgment for the blessing of harvest, though that acknowledgment was ignorantly misapplied in being directed to a secondary, not the primary, fountain of this benefit ;—namely, to Apollo or the Sun.

For Callimachus affirms that these Primitiæ were sent by the people of every nation to the temple of Apollo in Delos, the most distant that enjoyed the happiness of corn and harvest, even by the Hyperboreans in particular, Hymn to Apol., Οι μεντοι καλαμην τε και ιερα δραγμα πρωτοι ασταχυων, "Bring the sacred sheafs, and the mystic offerings."

Herodotus also mentions this annual custom of the Hyperboreans, remarking that those of Delos talk of ʹΙερα ενδεδεμενα εν καλαμη πυρων εξ Ὑπερβορεων, "Holy things tied up in sheaf of wheat conveyed from the Hyperboreans." And the Jews, by the command of their law, offered also a sheaf : "And shall reap the harvest thereof, then ye shall bring a sheaf of the first fruits of the harvest unto the priest."

This is not introduced in proof of any feast observed by the people who had harvests, but to show the universality of the custom of offering the Primitiæ, which preceded this feast. But yet it may be looked upon as equivalent to a proof ; for as the offering and the feast appear to have been always and intimately connected in countries affording records, so it is more than probable they were connected too in countries which had none, or none that ever survived to our times. An entertainment and gaiety were still the concomitants of these rites, which with the vulgar, one may pretty truly suppose, were esteemed the most acceptable and material part of them, and a great reason of their having subsisted through such a length of ages, when both the populace and many of the learned, too, have lost sight of the object to which they had been originally directed. This, among many other

ceremonies of the heathen worship, became disused in
some places and retained in others, but still continued
declining after the promulgation of the Gospel. In
short, there seems great reason to conclude, that this
feast, which was once sacred to Apollo, was constantly
maintained, when a far less valuable circumstance, *i. e.*,
shouting the churn, is observed to this day by the reapers,
and from so old an era ; for we read of this acclamation,
Isa. xvi. 9 : " For the shouting for thy summer fruits and
for thy harvest is fallen ;" and again, ver. 10 : " And in
the vineyards there shall be no singing, their shouting
shall be no shouting." Hence, then, or from some of the
Phœnician colonies, is our traditionary " shouting the
churn." But it seems these Orientals shouted both for
joy of their harvest of grapes, and of corn. We have no
quantity of the first to occasion so much joy as does our
plenty of the last ; and I do not remember to have heard
whether their vintages abroad are attended with this custom. Bread or cakes compose part of the Hebrew offering (*Levit.* xxiii. 13), and a cake thrown upon the head
of the victim was also part of the Greek offering to
Apollo (see *Hom. Il. a*), whose worship was formerly celebrated in Britain, where the May-pole yet continues one
remain of it. This they adorned with garlands on May-
day, to welcome the approach of Apollo, or the sun,
towards the north, and to signify that those flowers were
the product of his presence and influence. But, upon the
progress of Christianity, as was observed above, Apollo
lost his divinity again, and the adoration of his deity
subsided by degrees. Yet so permanent is custom, that
this right of the harvest-supper, together with that of the
May-pole (of which last see *Voss. de Orig.* and *Prag Idolatr.*
1, 2), have been preserved in Britain ; and what had
been anciently offered to the god, the reapers as prudently
eat up themselves.

At last the use of the meal of the new corn was
neglected, and the supper, so far as meal was concerned,

was made indifferently of old or new corn, as was most agreeable to the founder.   And here the usage itself accounts for the name of *Melsupper* (where *mel* signifies meal, or else the instrument called with us a *Mell*, wherewith antiquity reduced their corn to meal in a mortar, which still amounts to the same thing), for provisions of meal, or of corn in furmity, &c., composed by far the greatest part in these elder and country entertainments, perfectly conformable to the simplicity of those times, places, and persons, however meanly they may now be looked upon. And as the harvest was last concluded with several preparations of meal, or brought to be ready for the mell, this term became, in a translated signification, to mean the last of other things ; as, when a horse comes last in the race, they often say in the north, " *he has got the mell.*"

All the other names of this country festivity sufficiently explain themselves, except *Churn-supper*, and this is entirely different from *Melsupper ;* but they generally happen so near together, that they are frequently confounded. The *Churn-supper* was always provided when all was shorn, but the *Melsupper* after all was got in.   And it was called the *Churn-supper*, because, from immemorial times, it was customary to produce in a churn a great quantity of cream, and to circulate it by dishfuls to each of the rustic company, to be eaten with bread.   And here sometimes very extraordinary execution has been done upon cream. And though this custom has been disused in many places, and agreeably commuted for by ale, yet it survives still, and that about Whitby and Scarborough in the east, and round about Gisburn, &c., in Craven, in the west. But, perhaps, a century or two more will put an end to it, and both the thing and the name shall die. Vicarious ale is now more approved, and the *tankard* almost everywhere politely preferred to the Churn.

This Churn (in our provincial pronunciation Kern) is the Hebrew Kern, קֶרֶן or Keren, from its being circular like most horns : and it is the Latin *corona*, named so either from *radii*, resembling horns, as on some very ancient coins, or from its encircling the head ; so a ring of people is called *corona*. Also the Celtic Koren, Keren, or corn, which continues according to its old pronunciation in Cornwall, &c., and our modern word horn, is no more than this ; the ancient hard sound of *k* in corn being softened into the aspirate *h*, as has been done in number-less instances.

The Irish Celtæ also called a round stone, *clogh crene*, where the variation is merely dialectic.   Hence, too, our crane-berries, *i. e.* round berries, from this Celtic adjec-tive, *crene*, round.

N.B.—The quotations from Scripture in Aram's ori-ginal MS. were both in the Hebrew character, and their value in English sounds.

EUGENE ARAM.

———◆———

BOOK I.—CHAPTER I.

The Village.—Its Inhabitants.—An old Manor-house and an English Family; their History, involving a mysterious event.

———

Protected by the divinity they adored, supported by the earth which they cultivated, and at peace with themselves, they enjoyed the sweets of life without dreading or desiring dissolution.—Numa Pompilius.

———

IN the county of —— there is a sequestered hamlet, which I have often sought occasion to pass, and which I have never left without a certain reluctance and regret. The place, indeed, is associated with the memory of events that still retain a singular and fearful interest—but the scene needs not the charm of legend to arrest the attention of the traveller. In no part of the world which it has been my lot to visit, have I seen a landscape of more pastoral beauty. The hamlet, to which I shall here give the name of Grassdale, is situated in a valley, which, for about the length of a mile, winds among gardens and orchards laden with fruit, between two chains of gentle and fertile hills.

Here, singly or in pairs, are scattered cottages, which bespeak a comfort and a rural luxury less often than our poets have described the characteristics of the English peasantry. It has been observed, that wherever you see a flower in a cottage garden, or a bird-cage at the cottage casement, you may feel sure that the inmates are better and wiser than their neighbours ; and such humble tokens of attention to something beyond the sterile labour of life, were (we must now revert to the past) to be remarked in almost every one of the lowly abodes at Grassdale. The jasmine here—there the rose or honeysuckle, clustered over the lattice and threshold, not so wildly as to testify negligence, but rather to sweeten the air than exclude the light. Each of the cottages possessed at its rear its plot of ground apportioned to the more useful and nutritious products of nature ; while the greater part of them fenced also from the unfrequented road a little spot for the lupin, the sweet-pea, the wallflower, or the stock. And it is not unworthy of remark, that the bees came in greater clusters to Grassdale than to any other part of that rich and cultivated district. A small piece of waste land, which was intersected by a brook, fringed with osier and dwarf and fantastic pollards, afforded pasture for a few cows and the only carrier's solitary horse. The stream itself was of no ignoble repute among the gentle craft of the Angle, the brotherhood whom our associations defend in the spite of our mercy ; and this repute drew welcome and periodical itinerants to the village, who furnished it with its scanty news of the great world without, and maintained in a decorous custom the little and single hostelry of the place. Not that Peter Dealtry, the proprietor of the "Spotted Dog," was altogether contented to subsist upon the gains of his hospitable profession; he joined thereto the light cares of a small farm, held under a wealthy and an easy landlord; and being moreover honoured with the dignity of clerk to the parish, he was deemed by his neighbours a person of no small accomplishment, and no insignificant distinction. He was a little, dry, thin man, of a turn rather sentimental than jocose. A memory well stored with fag-ends of psalms and hymns (which, being less familiar than the psalms to the ears of the villagers, were more than suspected to be his own composition), often gave a poetic and semi-religious colouring to his conversation, which accorded rather with his dignity in the church than his post at the "Spotted Dog." Yet he disliked not his joke, though it was subtle and delicate of nature; nor did he disdain to bear companionship over his own liquor with guests less gifted and refined.

In the centre of the village you chanced upon a cottage which had been lately whitewashed, where a certain preciseness in the owner might be detected in the clipped hedge, and the exact and newly-mended stile by which you approached the habitation. Herein dwelt the beau and bachelor of the village, somewhat antiquated it is true, but still an object of great attention and some hope to the elder damsels in the vicinity, and of a respectful popularity (that did not, however, prohibit a joke) among the younger.   Jacob Bunting —so was this gentleman called—had been for many years in the king's service, in which he had risen to the rank of corporal, and had saved and pinched to-gether a certain small independence, upon which he now rented his cottage and enjoyed his leisure.   He had seen a good deal of the world, and profited in shrewdness by his experience ; he had rubbed off, how-ever, all superfluous devotion as he rubbed off his pre-judices ; and though he drank more often than any one else with the landlord of the " Spotted Dog," there was not a wit in the place who showed so little indul-gence to the publican's segments of psalmody.   Jacob was a tall, comely, and perpendicular personage ; his threadbare coat was scrupulously brushed, and his hair punctiliously plastered at the sides into two stiff, ob-stinate-looking curls, and at the top into what he was pleased to call a feather, though it was much more like a tile.   His conversation had in it something peculiar ; generally it assumed a quick, short, abrupt turn, that, retrenching all superfluities of pronoun and conjunction, and marching at once upon the meaning of the sentence, had in it a military and Spartan significance, which be-trayed how difficult it often is for a man to forget that he has been a corporal.   Occasionally, indeed,—for where but in farces is the phraseology of the humorist always the same?—he escaped into a more enlarged and Christian-like method of dealing with the king's

English ; but that was chiefly noticeable when from conversation he launched himself into lecture,—a luxury the worthy soldier loved greatly to indulge, for much had he seen and somewhat had he reflected; and valuing himself, which was odd in a corporal, more on his knowledge of the world than his knowledge even of war, he rarely missed any occasion of edifying a patient listener with the result of his observations.

After you had sauntered by the veteran's door, beside which you generally, if the evening were fine, or he was not drinking with neighbour Dealtry, or taking his tea with gossip this or master that, or teaching some emulous urchins the broadsword exercise, or snaring trout in the stream, or, in short, otherwise engaged ; beside which, I say, you not unfrequently beheld him sitting on a rude bench, and enjoying with half-shut eyes, crossed legs, but still unindulgently-erect posture, the luxury of his pipe ; you ventured over a little wooden bridge, beneath which, clear and shallow, ran the rivulet we have before honourably mentioned, and a walk of a few minutes brought you to a moderately-sized and old-fashioned mansion—the manor-house of the parish. It stood at the very foot of the hill ; behind, a rich, ancient, and hanging wood, brought into relief the exceeding freshness and verdure of the patch of green meadow immediately in front. On one side, the garden was bounded by the village church-yard, with its simple mounds, and its few scattered and humble tombs. The church was of great antiquity ;

and it was only in one point of view that you caught
more than a glimpse of its grey tower and graceful
spire, so thickly and so darkly grouped the yew-tree
and the pine around the edifice.   Opposite the gate by
which you gained the house the view was not extended,
but rich with wood and pasture, backed by a hill which,
less verdant than its fellows, was covered with sheep ;
while you saw, hard by, the rivulet darkening and
stealing away till your sight, though not your ear, lost
it among the woodland.

Trained up the embrowned paling, on either side of
the gate, were bushes of rustic fruit ; and fruit and
flowers (through plots of which green and winding
alleys had been cut with no untasteful hand) testified,
by their thriving and healthful looks, the care bestowed
upon them.   The main boasts of the garden were, on
one side, a huge horse-chestnut tree—the largest in the
village ; and on the other, an arbour covered without
with honeysuckles, and tapestried within by moss.
The house, a grey and quaint building of the time of
James I., with stone copings and gable roof, could
scarcely in these days have been deemed a fitting residence for the lord of the manor.   Nearly the whole of
the centre was occupied by the hall, in which the meals
of the family were commonly held—only two other
sitting-rooms of very moderate dimensions had been
reserved by the architect for the convenience or ostentation of the proprietor.   An ample porch jutted from
the main building, and this was covered with ivy, as
the sides of the windows were with jasmine and

honeysuckle ; while seats were ranged inside the porch, carved with many a rude initial and long-past date.

The owner of this mansion bore the name of Rowland Lester. His forefathers, without pretending to high antiquity of family, had held the dignity of squires of Grassdale for some two centuries ; and Rowland Lester was perhaps the first of the race who had stirred above fifty miles from the house in which each successive lord had received his birth, or the green churchyard in which was yet chronicled his death. The present proprietor was a man of cultivated tastes ; and abilities, naturally not much above mediocrity, had been improved by travel as well as study. Himself and one younger brother had been early left masters of their fate and their several portions. The younger, Geoffrey, testified a roving and dissipated turn. Bold, licentious, extravagant, unprincipled—his career soon outstripped the slender fortunes of a cadet in the family of a country squire. He was early thrown into difficulties, but by some means or other they never seemed to overwhelm him ; an unexpected turn—a lucky adventure—presented itself at the very moment when Fortune appeared the most utterly to have deserted him.

Among these more propitious fluctuations in the tide of affairs, was, at about the age of forty, a sudden marriage with a young lady of what might be termed (for Geoffrey Lester's rank of life, and the rational expenses of that day) a very competent and respectable fortune.

Unhappily, however, the lady was neither handsome in feature, nor gentle in temper ; and, after a few years of quarrel and contest, the faithless husband, one bright morning, having collected in his proper person whatever remained of their fortune, absconded from the conjugal hearth without either warning or farewell. He left nothing to his wife but his house, his debts, and his only child, a son. From that time to the present little had been known, though much had been conjectured, concerning the deserter. For the first few years they traced, however, so far of his fate as to learn that he had been seen once in India ; and that previously he had been met in England by a relation, under the disguise of assumed names : a proof that, whatever his occupations, they could scarcely be very respectable. But of late nothing whatsoever relating to the wanderer had transpired. By some he was imagined dead, by most he was forgotten. Those more immediately connected with him—his brother in especial—cherished a secret belief, that wherever Geoffrey Lester should chance to alight, the manner of alighting would (to use the significant and homely metaphor) be always on his legs : and coupling the wonted luck of the scapegrace with the fact of his having been seen in India, Rowland in his heart not only hoped, but fully expected, that the lost one would, some day or other, return home laden with the spoils of the East, and eager to shower upon his relatives, in recompense of long desertion,

" With richest hand......barbaric pearl and gold."

But we must return to the forsaken spouse. Left in this abrupt destitution and distress, Mrs Lester had only the resource of applying to her brother-in-law, whom indeed the fugitive had before seized many opportunities of not leaving wholly unprepared for such an application. Rowland promptly and generously obeyed the summons : he took the child and the wife to his own home ; he freed the latter from the persecutions of all legal claimants ; and, after selling such effects as remained, he devoted the whole proceeds to the forsaken family, without regarding his own expenses on their behalf, ill as he was able to afford the luxury of that self-neglect. The wife did not long need the asylum of his hearth—she, poor lady, died of a slow fever produced by irritation and disappointment, a few months after Geoffrey's desertion. She had no need to recommend her child to his kind-hearted uncle's care. And now we must glance over the elder brother's domestic fortunes.

In Rowland, the wild dispositions of his brother were so far tamed, that they assumed only the character of a buoyant temper and a gay spirit. He had strong principles as well as warm feelings, and a fine and resolute sense of honour utterly impervious to attack. It was impossible to be in his company an hour and not see that he was a man to be respected. It was equally impossible to live with him a week and not see that he was a man to be beloved. He also had married, and about a year after that era in the life of his brother, but not for the same advantage of for-

tune. He had formed an attachment to the portion-
less daughter of a man in his own neighbourhood and
of his own rank. He wooed and won her, and for a
few years he enjoyed that greatest happiness which the
world is capable of bestowing—the society and the
love of one in whom we could wish for no change, and
beyond whom we have no desire. But what Evil cannot corrupt Fate seldom spares. A few months after
the birth of a second daughter, the young wife of Rowland Lester died. It was to a widowed hearth that
the wife and child of his brother came for shelter.
Rowland was a man of an affectionate and warm heart;
if the blow did not crush, at least it changed him.
Naturally of a cheerful and ardent disposition, his
mood now became more sober and sedate. He shrunk
from the rural gaieties and companionship he had before courted and enlivened, and, for the first time in
his life, the mourner felt the holiness of solitude. As
his nephew and his motherless daughters grew up,
they gave an object to his seclusion and a relief to his
reflections. He found a pure and unfailing delight in
watching the growth of their young minds, and guid-
ing their differing dispositions; and as time at length
enabled them to return his affection, and appreciate
his cares, he became once more sensible that he had a
HOME.

The elder of his daughters, Madeline, at the time
our story opens, had attained the age of eighteen. She
was the beauty and the boast of the whole country.
Above the ordinary height, her figure was richly and

exquisitely formed. So translucently pure and soft
was her complexion, that it might have seemed the
token of delicate health but for the dewy redness of
her lips, and the freshness of teeth whiter than pearls.
Her eyes, of a deep blue, wore a thoughtful and serene
expression; and her forehead, higher and broader than
it usually is in women, gave promise of a certain nobleness of intellect, and added dignity, but a feminine
dignity, to the more tender characteristics of her beauty.
And, indeed, the peculiar tone of Madeline's mind fulfilled the indication of her features, and was eminently
thoughtful and high-wrought. She had early testified
a remarkable love for study, and not only a desire for
knowledge, but a veneration for those who possessed it.
The remote corner of the country in which they lived,
and the rarely-broken seclusion which Lester habitually
preserved from the intercourse of their few and scattered neighbours, had naturally cast each member of
the little circle upon his or her own resources. An
accident, some five years ago, had confined Madeline
for several weeks, or rather months, to the house; and
as the old hall possessed a very respectable share of
books, she had then matured and confirmed that love
for reading and reflection which she had at a yet earlier
period prematurely evinced. The woman's tendency to
romance naturally tinctured her meditations, and thus,
while they dignified, they also softened her mind. Her
sister Ellinor, younger by two years, was of a character
equally gentle, but less elevated. She looked up to
her sister as a superior being. She felt pride, without

a shadow of envy, for Madeline's superior and surpassing beauty; and was unconsciously guided in her pursuits and predilections by a mind which she cheerfully acknowledged to be loftier than her own. And yet Ellinor had also her pretensions to personal loveliness, and pretensions perhaps that would be less reluctantly acknowledged by her own sex than those of her sister. The sunlight of a happy and innocent heart sparkled on her face, and gave a beam it gladdened you to behold to her quick hazel eye, and a smile that broke out from a thousand dimples. She did not possess the height of Madeline, and though not so slender as to be curtailed of the roundness and feminine luxuriance of beauty, her shape was slighter, feebler, and less rich in its symmetry than her sister's. And this the tendency of the physical frame to require elsewhere support, nor to feel secure of strength, perhaps influenced her mind, and made love and the dependence of love more necessary to her than to the thoughtful and lofty Madeline. The latter might pass through life, and never see the one to whom her heart could give itself away. But every village might possess a hero whom the imagination of Ellinor could clothe with unreal graces, and towards whom the lovingness of her disposition might bias her affections. Both, however, eminently possessed that earnestness and purity of heart which would have made them, perhaps in an equal degree, constant and devoted to the object of an attachment once formed, in defiance of change, and to the brink of death.

Their cousin Walter, Geoffrey Lester's son, was now in his twenty-first year; tall and strong of person, and with a face, if not regularly handsome, striking enough to be generally deemed so. High-spirited, bold, fiery, impatient; jealous of the affections of those he loved; cheerful to outward seeming, but restless, fond of change, and subject to the melancholy and pining mood common to young and ardent minds: such was the character of Walter Lester. The estates of Lester were settled in the male line, and devolved therefore upon him. Yet there were moments when he keenly felt his orphan and deserted situation, and sighed to think that, while his father perhaps yet lived, he was a dependent for affection, if not for maintenance, on the kindness of others. This reflection sometimes gave an air of sullenness or petulance to his character, that did not really belong to it. For what in the world makes a man of just pride appear so unamiable as the sense of dependence?

CHAPTER II.

A Publican, a Sinner, and a Stranger.

Ah, Don Alphonso, is it you ? Agreeable accident ! Chance presents you to my eyes where you were least expected.—*Gil Blas.*

IT was an evening in the beginning of summer, and Peter Dealtry and the *ci-devant* corporal sat beneath the sign of the "Spotted Dog" (as it hung motionless from the bough of a friendly elm), quaffing a cup of boon companionship. The reader will imagine the two men very different from each other in form and aspect; the one short, dry, fragile, and betraying a love of ease in his unbuttoned vest, and a certain lolling, see-sawing method of balancing his body, upon his chair; the other, erect and solemn, and as steady on his seat as if he were nailed to it. It was a fine, tranquil, balmy evening; the sun had just set, and the clouds still retained the rosy tints which they had caught from its parting ray. Here and there, at scattered intervals, you might see the cottages peeping from the trees around them; or mark the smoke that rose from their roofs—roofs green with mosses and house-leek—in graceful and spiral curls against the

clear soft air.   It was an English scene, and the two
men, the dog at their feet (for Peter Dealtry favoured
a wiry stone-coloured cur, which he called a terrier),
and just at the door of the little inn, two old gossips,
loitering on the threshold, in familiar chat with the
landlady in cap and kerchief—all together made a
group equally English, and somewhat picturesque,
though homely enough, in effect.

"Well, now," said Peter Dealtry, as he pushed the
brown jug towards the corporal, "this is what I call
pleasant; it puts me in mind——"

"Of what?" quoth the corporal.

"Of those nice lines in the hymn, Master Bunting:—

> 'How fair ye are, ye little hills:
>   Ye little fields also:
>   Ye murmuring streams that sweetly run;
>   Ye willows in a row!'

There is something very comfortable in sacred verses,
Master Bunting; but you're a scoffer."

"Psha, man!" said the corporal, throwing out his
right leg and leaning back, with his eyes half shut,
and his chin protruded, as he took an unusually long
inhalation from his pipe—"psha, man!—send verses
to the rightabout—fit for girls going to school of a
Sunday; full-grown men more up to snuff.   I've seen
the world, Master Dealtry;—the world, and be d——d
to you!—augh!"

"Fie, neighbour, fie!   What's the good of profane-
ness, evil-speaking, and slandering?—

> 'Oaths are the debts your spendthrift soul must pay;
>   All scores are chalked against the reckoning day.'

Just wait a bit, neighbour; wait till I light my pipe."

"Tell you what," said the corporal, after he had communicated from his own pipe the friendly flame to his comrades—"tell you what—talk nonsense; the commander-in-chief's no martinet—if we're all right in action, he'll wink at a slip word or two. Come, no humbug—hold jaw. D'ye think God would sooner have a snivelling fellow like you in his regiment, than a man like me, clean-limbed, straight as a dart, six feet one without his shoes?—Baugh!"

This notion of the corporal's, by which he would have likened the dominion of heaven to the King of Prussia's body-guard, and only admitted the elect on account of their inches, so tickled mine host's fancy, that he leaned back in his chair and indulged in a long, dry, obstreperous cachinnation. This irreverence mightily displeased the corporal. He looked at the little man very sourly, and said, in his least smooth accentuation—

"What—devil—cackling at?—Always grin, grin, grin—giggle, giggle, giggle—psha!"

"Why really, neighbour," said Peter, composing himself, "you must let a man laugh now and then."

"Man!" said the corporal; "*man's* a noble animal! Man's a musket, primed, loaded, ready to save a friend or kill a foe—charge not to be wasted on every tom-tit. But you! not a musket, but a cracker! noisy, harmless, can't touch you, but off you go, whizz, pop, bang in one's face! baugh!"

"Well!" said the good-humoured landlord, "I should think Master Aram, the great scholar who lives down the vale yonder, a man quite after your own heart. He is grave enough to suit you. He does not laugh very easily, I fancy."

"After *my* heart? Stoops like a bow!"

"Indeed he does look on the ground as he walks; when I think, I do the same. But what a marvellous man it is! I hear that he reads the Psalms in Hebrew. He's very affable and meek-like for such a scholard."

"Tell you what. Seen the world, Master Dealtry, and know a thing or two. Your shy dog is always a deep one. Give me a man who looks me in the face as he would a cannon!"

"Or a lass," said Peter, knowingly.

The grim corporal smiled.

"Talking of lasses," said the soldier, refilling his pipe, "what creature Miss Lester is! Such eyes!— such nose! Fit for a colonel, by Gad! ay, or a major-general!"

"For my part, I think Miss Ellinor almost as handsome; not so grand-like, but more lovesome."

"Nice little thing!" said the corporal, condescendingly. "But zooks! whom have we here?"

This last question was applied to a man who was slowly turning from the road towards the inn. The stranger, for such he was, was stout, thick-set, and of middle height. His dress was not without pretension to a rank higher than the lowest; but it was threadbare and worn, and soiled with dust and travel. His

appearance was by no means prepossessing : small
sunken eyes of a light hazel, and a restless and rather
fierce expression ; a thick flat nose, high cheek-bones,
a large bony jaw from which the flesh receded, and a
bull throat indicative of great strength, constituted his
claims to personal attraction.   The stately corporal,
without moving, kept a vigilant and suspicious eye
upon the new-comer, muttering to Peter,—" Customer
for you ; rum customer too—by Gad ! "

The stranger now reached the little table, and, halt-
ing short, took up the brown jug, without ceremony or
preface, and emptied it at a draught.

The corporal stared — the corporal frowned ; but
before—for he was somewhat slow of speech—he had
time to vent his displeasure, the stranger, wiping his
mouth with his sleeve, said, in rather a civil and
apologetic tone—

" I beg pardon, gentlemen.   I have had a long
march of it, and very tired I am."

" Humph ! march ! " said the corporal, a little
appeased ; "not in his majesty's service—eh ? "

" Not now," answered the traveller ; then, turning
round to Dealtry, he said—" Are you landlord here ? "

" At your service," said Peter, with the indifference
of a man well to do, and not ambitious of halfpence.

" Come, then, quick — budge," said the traveller,
tapping him on the back ; " bring more glasses —
another jug of the October ; and anything or everything your larder is able to produce—d'ye hear ? "

Peter, by no means pleased with the briskness of

this address, eyed the dusty and way-worn pedestrian'
from head to foot; then, looking over his shoulder
towards the door, he said, as he ensconced himself
yet more firmly on his seat :—

"There's my wife by the door, friend; go, tell her
what you want."

"Do you know," said the traveller, in a slow and
measured accent — "do you know, Master Shrivel-
face, that I have more than half a mind to break your
head for impertinence ? You a landlord !—you keep
an inn, indeed ! Come, sir, make off, or——"

"Corporal ! — corporal !" cried Peter, retreating
hastily from his seat as the brawny traveller approached menacingly towards him—"You won't see
the peace broken. Have a care, friend, have a care.
I'm clerk to the parish—clerk to the parish, sir—and
I'll indict you for sacrilege."

The wooden features of Bunting relaxed into a sort
of grin at the alarm of his friend. He puffed away,
without making any reply ; meanwhile the traveller,
taking advantage of Peter's hasty abandonment of his
cathedrarian accommodation, seized the vacant chair,
and, drawing it yet closer to the table, flung himself
upon it, and placing his hat on the table, wiped his
brows with the air of a man about to make himself
thoroughly at home.

Peter Dealtry was assuredly a personage of peaceable disposition ; but then he had the proper pride of
a host and a clerk. His feelings were exceedingly
wounded at this cavalier treatment—before the very

eyes of his wife, too!—what an example! He thrust
his hands deep into his breeches'-pockets, and strut-
ting with a ferocious swagger towards the traveller, he
said:—

"Harkye, sirrah! This is not the way folks are
treated in this country; and I'd have you to know,
that I'm a man what has a brother a constable."

"Well, sir!"

"Well, sir, indeed! Well!—Sir, it's not well, by
no manner of means; and if you don't pay for the ale
you drank, and go quietly about your business, I'll
have you put in the stocks for a vagrant."

This, the most menacing speech Peter Dealtry was
ever known to deliver, was uttered with so much
spirit, that the corporal, who had hitherto preserved
silence—for he was too strict a disciplinarian to thrust
himself unnecessarily into brawls—turned approvingly
round, and nodding, as well as his stock would suffer
him, at the indignant Peter, he said, "Well done!
'fegs—you've a soul, man!—a soul fit for the Forty-
second! augh!—A soul above the inches of five feet
two!"

There was something bitter and sneering in the
traveller's aspect as he now, regarding Dealtry, repeated:—

"Vagrant!—humph! And pray what is a vagrant?"

"What is a vagrant?" echoed Peter, a little puzzled.

"Yes! answer me that."

"Why, a vagrant is a man what wanders, and what
has no money."

" Truly," said the stranger, smiling ; but the smile
by no means improved his physiognomy—" an excellent definition ; but one which, I will convince you,
does not apply to me. So saying, he drew from his
pocket a handful of silver coins, and, throwing them
on the table, added,—" Come, let's have no more of
this. You see I can pay for what I order ; and now,
do recollect that I am a weary and hungry man."

No sooner did Peter behold the money, than a sudden placidity stole over his ruffled spirit—nay, a certain benevolent commiseration for the fatigue and
wants of the traveller replaced at once, and as by a
spell, the angry feelings that had previously roused
him.

" Weary and hungry," said he ; " why did you not
say that before ? That would have been quite enough
for Peter Dealtry. Thank Heaven ! I am a man what
can feel for my neighbours. I have bowels—yes, I
have bowels. Weary and hungry !—you shall be
served in an instant. I may be a little hasty or so, but
I'm a good Christian at bottom—ask the corporal.
And what says the Psalmist, Psalm 147 :—

> ' By Him the beasts that loosely range '
> With timely food are fed :
> He speaks the word—and what He wills
> Is done as soon as said.' "

Animating his kindly emotions by this apt quotation,
Peter turned to the house. The corporal now broke
silence : the sight of the money had not been without
an effect upon him, as well as the landlord.

"Warm day, sir : your health.   Oh ! forget you
emptied jug—baugh ! You said you were not *now*
in his majesty's service.   Beg pardon ;—were you
ever ? "

" Why, once I was, many years ago."

" Ah !—and what regiment ?   I was in the Forty-
second.   Heard of the Forty-second ?   Colonel's name,
Dysart ; captain's, Trotter ; corporal's, Bunting, at
your service."

" I am much obliged by your confidence," said the
traveller, dryly.   " I daresay you have seen much
service."

" Service !   Ah ! may well say that ;—twenty-three
years' hard work ; and not the better for it !   A man
that loves his country is 'titled to a pension, that's my
mind !   But the world don't smile upon corporals—
augh ! "

Here Peter reappeared with a fresh supply of the
October, and an assurance that the cold meat would
speedily follow.

" I hope yourself and this gentleman will bear me
company," said the traveller, passing the jug to the
corporal ; and in a few moments, so well pleased grew
the trio with each other, that the sound of their laugh-
ter came loud and frequent to the ears of the good
housewife within.

The traveller now seemed to the corporal and mine
host a right jolly, good-humoured fellow.   Not, however, that he bore a fair share in the conversation ; he
rather promoted the hilarity of his new acquaintances

than led it. He laughed heartily at Peter's jests, and
the corporal's repartees; and the latter, by degrees
assuming the usual sway he bore in the circles of the
village, contrived, before the viands were on the table,
to monopolise the whole conversation.

The traveller found in the repast a new excuse for
silence. He ate with a most prodigious and most con-
tagious appetite; and in a few seconds the knife and
fork of the corporal were as busily engaged as if
he had only three minutes to spare between a march
and a dinner.

"This is a pretty retired spot," quoth the traveller,
as at length he finished his repast, and threw himself
back on his chair—"a very pretty spot. Whose neat,
old-fashioned house was that I passed on the green,
with the gable-ends and the flower-pots in front?"

"Oh, the squire's," answered Peter. "Squire Lester's,
an excellent gentleman."

"A rich man, I should think, for these parts; the
best house I have seen for some miles," said the
stranger, carelessly.

"Rich!—yes, he's well to do; he does not live so
as not to have money to lay by."

"Any family?"

"Two daughters and a nephew."

"And the nephew does not ruin him?—Happy
uncle! Mine was not so lucky!" said the traveller.

"Sad fellows we soldiers, in our young days!" observed the corporal, with a wink. "No, Squire Walter's a good young man, a pride to his uncle!"

" So," said the pedestrian, " they are not forced to keep up a large establishment, and ruin themselves by a retinue of servants ?—Corporal, the jug."

" Nay !" said Peter, " Squire Lester's gate is always open to the poor ; but as for show, he leaves that to my lord at the castle."

" The castle ! where's that ? "

" About six miles off; you've heard of my Lord ———, I'll swear."

" Ay, to be sure—a courtier. But who else lives about here ? I mean, who are the principal persons, barring the corporal and yourself—Mr Eelpry, I think our friend here calls you."

" Dealtry, Peter Dealtry, sir, is my name. Why, the most noticeable man, you must know, is a great scholard, a wonderfully learned man ; there, yonder, you may just catch a glimpse of the tall what-d'ye-call-it he has built out on the top of his house, that he may get nearer to the stars. He has got glasses by which I've heard that you may see the people in the moon walking on their heads ; but I can't say as I believe all I hear."

" You are too sensible for that, I'm sure. But this scholar, I suppose, is not very rich : learning does not clothe men nowadays—eh, corporal ? "

" And why should it ? Zounds ! can it teach a man how to defend his country ? Old England wants soldiers, and be d—d to them ! But the man's well enough, I must own, civil, modest——"

" And not by no means a beggar," added Peter ; " he

gave as much to the poor last winter as the squire himself."

"Indeed !" said the stranger; "this scholar is rich then?"

"So, so; neither one nor t' other. But if he were as rich as my lord, he could not be more respected; the greatest folks in the country come in their carriages-and-four to see him. Lord bless you! there is not a name more talked on in the whole country than Eugene Aram."

"What!" cried the traveller, his countenance changing as he sprang from his seat—"what!—Aram!—did you say Aram? Great God! how strange !"

Peter, not a little startled by the abruptness and vehemence of his guest, stared at him with open mouth, and even the corporal involuntarily took his pipe from his lips.

"What!" said the former, "you know him, do you? You've heard of him, eh?"

The stranger did not reply; he seemed lost in a reverie; he muttered inaudible words between his teeth; now he strode two steps forward, clenching his hands; now smiled grimly; and then returning to his seat, threw himself on it, still in silence. The soldier and the clerk exchanged looks, and now outspake the corporal—

"Rum tantrums! What the devil! did the man eat your grandmother?"

Roused perhaps by so pertinent and sensible a question, the stranger lifted his head from his breast, and said, with a forced smile, "You have done me, without knowing it, a great kindness, my friend. Eugene Aram was an early and intimate acquaintance of mine; we have not met for many years. I never guessed that he lived in these parts; indeed I did not know where he resided. I am truly glad to think I have lighted upon him thus unexpectedly."

"What! you did not know where he lived? Well, I thought all the world knew that! Why, men from the universities have come all the way, merely to look at the spot."

"Very likely," returned the stranger; "but I am not a learned man myself, and what is celebrity in one set is obscurity in another. Besides, I have never been in this part of the world before!"

Peter was about to reply, when he heard the shrill voice of his wife behind.

"Why don't you rise, Mr Lazyboots? Where are your eyes? Don't you see the young ladies?"

Dealtry's hat was off in an instant—the stiff corporal rose like a musket; the stranger would have kept his seat, but Dealtry gave him an admonitory tug by the collar; accordingly he rose, muttering a hasty oath, which certainly died on his lips when he saw the cause which had thus constrained him into courtesy.

Through a little gate close by Peter's house, Madeline and her sister had just passed on their evening walk, and with the kind familiarity for which they were both noted, they had stopped to salute the landlady of the "Spotted Dog," as she now, her labour done, sat by the threshold, within hearing of the convivial group, and plaiting straw. The whole family of Lester were so beloved, that we question whether my lord himself, as the great nobleman of the place was always called (as if there were only one lord in the peerage), would have obtained the same degree of respect that was always lavished upon them.

"Don't let us disturb you, good people," said Ellinor, as they now moved towards the boon companions; when her eye suddenly falling on the stranger, she stopped short. There was something in his appearance, and especially in the expression of his countenance at that moment, which no one could have marked for the first time without apprehension and distrust; and it was so seldom that, in that retired spot, the young ladies encountered even one unfamiliar face, that the effect the stranger's appearance might have produced on any one, might well be increased for them to a startling and painful degree. The traveller saw at once the sensation he had created; his brow lowered; and the same unpleasant smile, or rather sneer, that we have noted before, distorted his lip, as with affected humility he made his obeisance.

"How!—a stranger!" said Madeline, sharing, though in a less degree, the feelings of her sister; and then, after a pause, she said, as she glanced over his garb, "not in distress, I hope?"

"No, madam!" said the stranger; "if by distress is meant beggary. I am in *all* respects, perhaps, better than I seem."

There was a general titter from the corporal, my host, and his wife, at the traveller's semi-jest at his own unprepossessing appearance: but Madeline, a little disconcerted, bowed hastily, and drew her sister away.

"A proud quean!" said the stranger, as he reseated himself and watched the sisters gliding across the green.

All mouths were opened against him immediately. He found it no easy matter to make his peace; and before he had quite done it, he called for his bill, and rose to depart.

"Well!" said he, as he tendered his hand to the corporal, "we may meet again, and enjoy together some more of your good stories. Meanwhile, which is my way to this—this—famous scholar's?—Ehem!"

"Why," quoth Peter, "you saw the direction in which the young ladies went: you must take the same. Cross the stile you will find at the right—wind along the foot of the hill for about three parts of a mile, and you will then see in the middle of a broad plain a lonely grey house, with a thingumbob at the top; a servatory they call it. That's Master Aram's."

"Thank you."

"And a very pretty walk it is too," said the dame, "the prettiest hereabouts to my liking, till you get to the house at least: and so the young ladies think, for it's their usual walk every evening!"

"Humph—then I may meet them."

"Well, and if you do, make yourself look as Christian-like as you can," retorted the hostess.

There was a second grin at the ill-favoured traveller's expense, amidst which he went his way.

"An odd chap!" said Peter, looking after the sturdy form of the traveller. "I wonder what he is—he seems well edicated—makes use of good words."

"What sinnifies," said the corporal, who felt a sort of fellow-feeling for his new acquaintance's bluffness of manner; "what sinnifies what he is? Served his country,—that's enough;—never told me, by the by, his regiment—set me a-talking, and let out nothing himself; old soldier every inch of him!"

"He can take care of number one," said Peter. "How he emptied the jug! and, my stars! what an appetite!"

"Tush" said the corporal, "hold jaw. Man of the world—man of the world—that's clear."

CHAPTER III.

A Dialogue and an Alarm.—A student's House.

A fellow by the hand of Nature marked,
Quoted, and signed, to do a deed of shame.
SHAKESPEARE; *King John.*

He is a scholar, if a man may trust
The liberal voice of Fame, in her report.
.   .   .   .   .
Myself was once a student, and indeed
Fed with the self-same humour he is now.
BEN JONSON: *Every Man in his Humour.*

THE two sisters pursued their walk along a scene
which might well be favoured by their selection. No
sooner had they crossed the stile than the village
seemed vanished into earth—so quiet, so lonely, so far
from the evidence of life was the landscape through
which they passed. On their right sloped a green and
silent hill, shutting out all view beyond itself, save the
deepening and twilight sky; to the left, and immediately
along their road, lay fragments of stone covered with
moss, or shadowed by wild shrubs, that here and there
gathered into copses, or breaking abruptly away from
the rich sod, left frequent spaces through which you
caught long vistas of forest land, or the brooklet
gliding in a noisy and rocky course, and breaking into
a thousand tiny waterfalls or mimic eddies. So secluded

was the scene, and so unwitnessing of cultivation, that you would not have believed that a human habitation could be at hand, and this air of perfect solitude and quiet gave an additional charm to the spot.

"But I assure you," said Ellinor, earnestly continuing a conversation they had begun, "I assure you I was not mistaken : I saw it as plainly as I see you."

"What ! in the breast-pocket ?"

"Yes; as he drew out his handkerchief I saw the barrel of the pistol quite distinctly."

"Indeed ! I think we had better tell my father as soon as we get home ; it may be as well to be on our guard, though robbery, I believe, has not been heard of in Grassdale for these twenty years."

"Yet for what purpose, save that of evil, could he, in these peaceable times and this peaceable country, carry firearms about him ? And what a countenance ! Did you note the shy and yet ferocious eye, like that of some animal that longs, yet fears to spring upon you ?"

"Upon my word, Ellinor," said Madeline, smiling, " you are not very merciful to strangers. After all, the man might have provided himself with the pistol which you saw as a natural precaution ; reflect that, as a stranger, he may well not know how safe this district usually is, and he may have come from London, in the neighbourhood of which they say robberies have been frequent of late. As to his looks, they are, I own, unpardonable ; for so much ugliness there can be no excuse. Had the man been as handsome as our cousin

Walter, you would not, perhaps, have been so un-
charitable in your fears at the pistol."

"Nonsense, Madeline," said Ellinor, blushing and
turning away her face : there was a moment's pause,
which the younger sister broke.

"We do not seem," said she, "to make much
progress in the friendship of our singular neighbour.
I never knew my father court any one so much as he
has courted Mr Aram, and yet you see how seldom he
calls upon us,—nay, I often think that he seeks to shun
us; no great compliment to our attractions, Madeline !"

"I regret his want of sociability for his own sake,"
said Madeline; "for he seems melancholy as well as
thoughtful; and he leads so secluded a life that I
cannot but think my father's conversation and society,
if he would but encourage it, might afford some relief
to his solitude."

"And he always seems," observed Ellinor, "to take
pleasure in my father's conversation—as who would
not? How his countenance lights up when he con-
verses ! it is a pleasure to watch it. I think him
positively handsome when he speaks."

"Oh, more than handsome !" said Madeline, with
enthusiasm; "with that high, pale brow, and those
deep, unfathomable eyes."

Ellinor smiled, and it was now Madeline's turn to
blush.

"Well," said the former, "there is something about
him that fills one with an indescribable interest; and
his manner, if cold at times, is yet always so gentle."·

"And to hear him converse," said Madeline, "it is like music. His thoughts, his very words, seem so different from the language and ideas of others. What a pity that he should ever be silent!"

"There is one peculiarity about his gloom, it never inspires one with distrust," said Ellinor; "if I had observed him in the same circumstances as that ill-omened traveller, I should have had no apprehension."

"Ah! that traveller still runs in your head. If we were to meet him on this spot!"

"Heaven forbid!" cried Ellinor, turning hastily round in alarm—and, lo! as if her sister had been a prophet, she saw the very person in question at some little distance behind them, and walking on with rapid strides.

She uttered a faint shriek of surprise and terror, and Madeline, looking back at the sound, immediately participated in her alarm. The spot looked so desolate and lonely, and the imagination of both had been already so worked upon by Ellinor's fears, and their conjectures respecting the ill-boding weapon she had witnessed, that a thousand apprehensions of outrage and murder crowded at once upon the minds of the two sisters. Without, however, giving vent in words to their alarm, they quickened their pace involuntarily, every moment stealing a glance behind, to watch the progress of the suspected robber. They thought that he also seemed to accelerate his movements; and this observation increased their terror, and would appear, indeed, to give it some more rational ground. At length, as by a sudden turn of the road, they lost sight of the dreaded stranger, their alarm suggested to them but one resolution, and they fairly fled on as fast as the fear which actuated would allow them. The nearest, and indeed the only house in that direction, was Aram's; but they both imagined if they could come within sight of that, they should be safe. They looked back at every interval; now they did not see their fancied pursuer—now he emerged again into view— now—yes—*he* also was running. "Faster — faster, Madeline, for God's sake! he is gaining upon us!" cried Ellinor. The path grew more wild, and the trees more thick and frequent; at every cluster that marked their progress, they saw the stranger closer and closer; at length a sudden break—a sudden turn in the land-scape—a broad plain burst upon them, and in the midst of it the student's solitary abode!

"Thank Heaven we are safe!" cried Madeline. She turned once more to look for the stranger; in so doing her foot struck against a fragment of stone, and she fell with great violence to the ground. She endeavoured to rise, but found herself, at first, unable to stir from the spot. In this state, however, she looked back, and saw the traveller at some little distance. But he also halted, and, after a moment's seeming delibera-tion, turned aside, and was lost among the bushes.

With great difficulty Ellinor now assisted Madeline to rise; her ankle was violently sprained, and she could not put her foot to the ground; but though she had evinced so much dread at the apparition of the stranger, she now testified an almost equal degree of fortitude in bearing pain. "I am not much hurt, Ellinor," she said, faintly smiling, to encourage her sister, who supported her in speechless alarm : "but what is to be done? I cannot use this foot. How shall we get home?"

"But are you sure you are not much hurt?" said poor Ellinor, almost crying; "lean on me—heavier—pray! Only try and reach the house, and we can then stay there till Mr Aram sends home for the carriage."

"But what will he think? how strange it will seem!" said Madeline, the colour once more visiting her cheek, which a moment since had been blanched as pale as death.

"Is this a time for scruples and ceremony!" said Ellinor. "Come! I entreat you, come; if you linger thus, the man may take courage and attack us yet. There! that's right! Is the pain very great?"

"I do not mind the pain," murmured Madeline; "but if he should think we intrude? His habits are so reserved—so secluded; indeed I fear——"

"Intrude!" interrupted Ellinor. "Do you think so ill of him?—Do you suppose that, hermit as he is, he has lost common humanity? But lean more on me, dearest; you do not know how strong I am!"

Thus, alternately chiding, caressing, and encouraging her sister, Ellinor led on the sufferer, till they had crossed the plain, though with slowness and labour, and stood before the porch of the recluse's house.

They had looked back from time to time, but the cause of so much alarm appeared no more. This they deemed a sufficient evidence of the justice of their apprehensions.

Madeline even now would fain have detained her sister's hand from the bell that hung without the porch half imbedded in ivy; but Ellinor, out of patience—as she well might be—with her sister's unseasonable prudery, refused any longer delay. So singularly still and solitary was the plain around the house, that the sound of the bell breaking the silence had in it something startling, and appeared, in its sudden and shrill voice, a profanation of the deep tranquillity of the spot. They did not wait long—a step was heard within—the door was slowly unbarred, and the student himself stood before them.

He was a man who might, perhaps, have numbered some five-and-thirty years; but, at a hasty glance, he would have seemed considerably younger. He was above the ordinary stature; though a gentle, and not ungraceful bend in the neck, rather than the shoulders, somewhat curtailed his proper advantages of height. His frame was thin and slender, but well knit and fair proportioned. Nature had originally cast his form in an athletic mould; but sedentary habits, and the wear of mind, seemed somewhat to have impaired her gifts. His cheek was pale and delicate; yet it was rather the delicacy of thought than of weak health. His hair, which was long, and of a rich and deep brown, was thrown back from his face and temples, and left a broad, high, majestic forehead, utterly unrelieved and bare; and on the brow there was not a single wrinkle; it was as smooth as it might have been some fifteen years ago. There was a singular calmness, and, so to speak, profundity of thought, eloquent upon its clear expanse, which suggested the idea of one who had passed his life rather in contemplation than emotion. It was a face that a physiognomist would have loved to look upon, so much did it speak both of the refinement and the dignity of intellect.

Such was the person—if pictures convey a faithful resemblance—of a man, certainly among the most eminent in his day for various and profound learning, and especially for a genius wholly self-taught, yet never contented to repose upon the wonderful stores it had laboriously accumulated.

He now stood before the two girls, silent, and evidently surprised; and it would have been no unworthy subject for a picture—that ivied porch—that still spot—Madeline's reclining and subdued form and downcast eyes—the eager face of Ellinor, about to narrate the nature and cause of their intrusion—and the pale student himself, thus suddenly aroused from his solitary meditations, and converted into the protector of beauty.

No sooner did Aram learn from Ellinor the outline of their story, and Madeline's accident, than his countenance and manner testified the liveliest and most eager interest. Madeline was inexpressibly touched and surprised at the kindly and respectful earnestness

with which this recluse scholar, usually so cold and
abstracted in mood, assisted and led her into the
house : the sympathy he expressed for her pain—the
sincerity of his tone—the compassion of his eyes—and
as those dark, and, to use her own thought, unfathomable orbs, bent admiringly and yet so gently upon her,
Madeline, even in spite of her pain, felt an indescribable, a delicious thrill at her heart, which in the presence of no one else had she ever experienced before.

Aram now summoned the only domestic his house
possessed, who appeared in the form of an old woman,
whom he seemed to have selected from the whole
neighbourhood as the person most in keeping with
the rigid seclusion he preserved. She was exceedingly deaf, and was a proverb in the village for her
extreme taciturnity. Poor old Margaret! she was a
widow, and had lost ten children by early deaths.
There was a time when her gaiety had been as noticeable as her reserve was now. In spite of her infirmity,
she was not slow in comprehending the accident Madeline had met with ; and she busied herself with a
promptness which showed that her misfortunes had
not deadened her natural kindness of disposition, in
preparing fomentations and bandages for the wounded
foot.

Meanwhile Aram undertook to seek the manor-
house, and bring back the old family coach, which had
dozed inactively in its shelter for the last six months, to
convey the sufferer home.

"No, Mr Aram," said Madeline, colouring ; "pray

do not go yourself; consider, the man may still be loitering on the road. He is armed : good heavens ! if he should meet you ! "

"Fear not, madam," said Aram, with a faint smile. "*I* also keep arms, even in this obscure and safe retreat; and to satisfy you, I will not neglect to carry them with me."

As he spoke, he took from the wainscot, where they hung, a brace of large horse-pistols, slung them round him by a leather belt; and flinging over his person, to conceal weapons so alarming to any less dangerous passenger he might encounter, the long cloak then usually worn in inclement seasons, as an outer garment, he turned to depart.

"But are they loaded ? " asked Ellinor.

Aram answered briefly in the affirmative. It was somewhat singular, but the sisters did not then remark it, that a man so peaceable in his pursuits, and seemingly possessed of no valuables that could tempt cupidity, should in that spot, where crime was never heard of, use such habitual precaution.

When the door closed upon him, and while the old woman relieved the anguish of the sprain with a light hand and soothing lotions, which she had shown some skill in preparing, Madeline cast glances of interest and curiosity around the apartment into which she had had the rare good fortune to obtain admittance.

The house had belonged to a family of some note, whose heirs had outstripped their fortunes. It had been long deserted and uninhabited ; and when Aram

settled in those parts, the proprietor was too glad to
get rid of the incumbrance of an empty house, at a
nominal rent. The solitude of the place had been the
main attraction to Aram; and as he possessed what
would be considered a very extensive assortment of
books, even for a library of these days, he required a
larger apartment than he would have been able to
obtain in an abode more compact and more suitable to
his fortunes and mode of living.

The room in which the sisters now found themselves
was the most spacious in the house, and was indeed of
considerable dimensions. It contained in front one
large window, jutting from the wall. Opposite was
an antique and high mantelpiece of black oak. The
rest of the room was walled from the floor to the roof
with books; volumes of all languages, and it might
even be said, without much exaggeration, upon all
sciences, were strewed around, on the chairs, the
tables, or the floor. By the window stood the student's desk, and a large old-fashioned oak chair. A
few papers, filled with astronomical calculations, lay
on the desk, and these were all the witnesses of the
result of study. Indeed, Aram does not appear to
have been a man much inclined to reproduce the
learning he acquired; what he wrote was in very
small proportion to what he had read.

So high and grave was the scholar's reputation, that
the retreat and sanctum of so many learned hours
would have been interesting, even to one who could
not appreciate learning; but to Madeline, with her

peculiar disposition and traits of mind, we may readily conceive that the room presented a powerful and pleasing charm. As the elder sister looked round in silence, Ellinor attempted to draw the old woman into conversation. She would fain have elicited some particulars of the habits and daily life of the recluse ; but the deafness of their attendant was so obstinate and hopeless, that she was forced to give up the attempt in despair. "I fear," said she at last, her good nature so far overcome by impatience as not to forbid a slight yawn—"I fear we shall have a dull time of it till my father arrives. Just consider, the fat black mares, never too fast, *can* only creep along that broken path, —for road there is none : it will be quite night before the coach arrives."

"I am sorry, dear Ellinor, my awkwardness should occasion you so stupid an evening," answered Madeline.

"Oh," cried Ellinor, throwing her arms around her sister's neck, "it is not for myself I spoke ; and, indeed, I am delighted to think we have got into this wizard's den, and seen the instruments of his art. But I do so trust Mr Aram will not meet that terrible man."

"Nay," said the prouder Madeline, "he is armed, and it is but one man. I feel too high a respect for him to allow myself much fear."

"But these bookmen are not often heroes," remarked Ellinor, laughing.

"For shame," said Madeline, the colour mounting to her forehead. "Do you not remember how, last summer, Eugene Aram rescued Dame Grenfield's child from the bull, though at the literal peril of his own life? And who but Eugene Aram, when the floods in the year before swept along the low lands by Fairleigh, went day after day to rescue the persons, or even to save the goods of those poor people; at a time, too, when the boldest villagers would not hazard themselves across the waters? But bless me, Ellinor, what is the matter? you turn pale—you tremble."

"Hush!" said Ellinor under her breath, and, putting her finger to her mouth, she rose and stole lightly to the window; she had observed the figure of a man pass by, and now, as she gained the window, she saw him halt by the porch, and recognised the formidable stranger. Presently the bell sounded, and the old woman, familiar with its shrill sound, rose from her kneeling position beside the sufferer to attend to the summons. Ellinor sprang forward and detained her: the poor old woman stared at her in amazement, wholly unable to comprehend her abrupt gestures and her rapid language. It was with considerable difficulty, and after repeated efforts, that she at length impressed the dulled sense of the crone with the nature of their alarm, and the expediency of refusing admittance to the stranger. Meanwhile the bell had rung again— again, and the third time, with a prolonged violence which testified the impatience of the applicant. As soon as the good dame had satisfied herself as to Ellinor's meaning, she could no longer be accused of unreasonable taciturnity; she wrung her hands, and poured forth a volley of lamentations and fears, which effectually relieved Ellinor from the dread of her unheeding the admonition. Satisfied at having done thus much, Ellinor now herself hastened to the door, and secured the ingress with an additional bolt, and then, as the thought flashed upon her, returned to the old woman, and made her, with an easier effort than before, now that her senses were sharpened by fear, comprehend the necessity of securing the back entrance also : both hastened away to effect this precaution, and Madeline, who herself desired Ellinor to accompany the old woman, was left alone. She kept her eyes fixed on the window with a strange sentiment of dread at being thus left in so helpless a situation; and though a door of no ordinary dimensions, and doubly locked, interposed between herself and the intruder, she expected, in breathless terror, every instant, to see the form of the ruffian burst into the apartment. As she thus sat and looked, she shudderingly saw the man, tired perhaps of repeating a summons so ineffectual, come to the window and look pryingly within : their eyes met; Madeline had not the power to shriek. Would he break through the window? that was her only idea, and it deprived her of words, almost of sense. He gazed upon her evident terror for a moment with a grim smile of contempt : he then knocked at the window, and his voice broke harshly on a silence yet more dreadful than the interruption.

"Ho, ho! so there is some life stirring? I beg pardon, madam, is Mr Aram—Eugene Aram, within?"

"No," said Madeline, faintly; and then, sensible that her voice did not reach him, she reiterated the answer in a louder tone. The man, as if satisfied, made a rude inclination of his head, and withdrew from the window. Ellinor now returned, and with difficulty Madeline found words to explain to her what had passed. It will be conceived that the two young ladies waited for the arrival of their father with no lukewarm expectation; the stranger, however, appeared no more; and in about an hour, to their inexpressible joy, they heard the rumbling sound of the old coach as it rolled towards the house. This time there was no delay in unbarring the door.

CHAPTER IV.

The Soliloquy, and the Character, of a Recluse. — The
Interruption.

Or let my lamp at midnight hour
Be seen in some high lonely tower,
Where I may oft outwatch the Bear,
Or thrice great Hermes, and unsphere
The spirit of Plato.—MILTON: *Il Penseroso.*

As Aram assisted the beautiful Madeline into the
carriage—as he listened to her sweet voice—as he
marked the grateful expression of her soft eyes—as he
felt the slight yet warm pressure of her fairy hand,
that vague sensation of delight which preludes love,
for the first time in his sterile and solitary life, agitated his breast. Lester held out his hand to him
with a frank cordiality which the scholar could not
resist.

"Do not let us be strangers, Mr Aram," said he,
warmly. "It is not often that I press for companionship out of my own circle; but in your company I
should find pleasure as well as instruction. Let us
break the ice boldly, and at once. Come and dine
with me to-morrow, and Ellinor shall sing to us in the
evening."

The excuse died upon Aram's lips.   Another glance
at Madeline conquered the remains of his reserve : he
accepted the invitation, and he could not but mark,
with an unfamiliar emotion of the heart, that the eyes
of Madeline sparkled as he did so.

With an abstracted air, and arms folded across his
breast, he gazed after the carriage till the winding of
the valley snatched it from his view.   He then, waking
from his reverie with a start, turned into the house,
and carefully closing and barring the door, mounted
with slow steps to the lofty chamber with which, the
better to indulge his astronomical researches, he had
crested his lonely abode.

It was now night.   The heavens broadened round
him in all the loving yet august tranquillity of the
season and the hour; the stars bathed the living
atmosphere with a solemn light; and above—about
—around—

> "The holy time was quiet as a nun,
> Breathless with adoration."

He looked forth upon the deep and ineffable stillness
of the night, and indulged the reflections that it suggested.

" Ye mystic lights," said he, soliloquising : " worlds
upon worlds—infinite—incalculable.   Bright defiers
of rest and change, rolling for ever above our petty
sea of mortality, as, wave after wave, we fret forth our
little life, and sink into the black abyss;—can we look
upon you, note your appointed order, and your unvarying courses, and not feel that we are, indeed, the

poorest puppets of an all-pervading and resistless destiny? Shall we see throughout creation each marvel fulfilling its pre-ordered fate—no wandering from its orbit—no variation in its seasons—and yet imagine that the Arch-ordainer will hold back the tides He has sent from their unseen source, at our miserable bidding? Shall we think that our prayers can avert a doom woven with the skein of events? To change a particle of our fate might change the destiny of millions! Shall the link forsake the chain and yet the chain be unbroken? Away, then, with our vague repinings and our blind demands. All must walk onward to their goal; be he the wisest who looks not one step behind. The colours of our existence were doomed before our birth—our sorrows and our crimes; millions of ages back, when this hoary earth was peopled by other kinds, yea, ere its atoms had formed one layer of its present soil, the eternal and all-seeing Ruler of the universe, Destiny or God, had here fixed the moment of our birth and the limits of our career. What, then, is crime?—Fate! What life?—Submission!"

Such were the strange and dark thoughts which, too familiar to his musings, now obtruded their mournful dogmas on his mind. He sought a fairer subject for meditation, and Madeline Lester rose before him.

Eugene Aram was a man whose whole life seemed to have been one sacrifice to knowledge. What is termed pleasure had no attraction for him. From the mature manhood at which he had arrived he looked back along his youth, and recognised no youthful folly. Love he had hitherto regarded with a cold though not an incurious eye: intemperance had never lured him to a momentary self-abandonment. Even the innocent relaxations with which the austerest minds relieve their accustomed toils, had had no power to draw him from his beloved researches. The delight *monstrari digito*, the gratification of triumphant wisdom, the whispers of an elevated vanity, existed not for his self-dependent and solitary heart. He was one of those earnest and high-wrought enthusiasts who now are almost extinct upon earth, and whom Romance has not hitherto attempted to portray; men not uncommon in the last century, who were devoted to knowledge, yet disdainful of its fame; who lived for nothing else than to learn. From store to store, from treasure to treasure, they proceeded in exulting labour, and having accumulated all, they bestowed naught; they were the arch-misers of the wealth of letters. Wrapped in obscurity, in some sheltered nook, remote from the great stir of men, they passed a life at once unprofitable and glorious; the least part of what they ransacked would appal the industry of a modern student, yet the most superficial of modern students might effect more for mankind. They lived among oracles, but they gave none forth. And yet, even in this very barrenness, there seems nothing high; it was a rare and great spectacle—men, living aloof from the roar and strife of the passions that raged below, devoting themselves to the know-

ledge which is our purification and our immortality
on earth, and yet deaf and blind to the allurements
of the vanity which generally accompanies research ;
refusing the ignorant homage of their kind, making
their sublime motive their only meed, adoring Wisdom for her sole sake, and set apart in the populous
universe, like those remoter stars which interchange
no light with earth—gild not our darkness, and colour
not our air.

From his youth to the present period, Aram had
dwelt little in cities, though he had visited many, yet
he could scarcely be called ignorant of mankind ; there
seems something intuitive in the science which teaches
us the knowledge of our race. Some men emerge
from their seclusion, and find, all at once, a power to
dart into the minds and drag forth the motives of
those they see ; it is a sort of second sight, born with
them, not acquired. And Aram, it may be, rendered
yet more acute by his profound and habitual investi-
gations of our metaphysical frame, never quitted his
solitude to mix with others without penetrating into
the broad traits or prevalent infirmities their characters possessed. In this, indeed, he differed from the
scholar tribe, and even in abstraction was mechanically
vigilant and observant. Much in his nature, had
early circumstances given it a different bias, would
have fitted him for worldly superiority and command.
A resistless energy, an unbroken perseverance, a profound, and scheming, and subtle thought, a genius
fertile in resources, a tongue clothed with eloquence

—all, had his ambition so chosen, might have given
him the same empire over the physical, that he had
now attained over the intellectual world. It could
not be said that Aram wanted benevolence, but it was
dashed and mixed with a certain scorn : the benevolence was the offspring of his nature ; the scorn seemed
the result of his pursuits. He would feed the birds
from his window, he would tread aside to avoid the
worm on his path ; were one of his own tribe in
danger he would save him at the hazard of his life ;
yet in his heart he despised men, and believed them
beyond amelioration. Unlike the present race of
schoolmen, who incline to the consoling hope of human perfectibility, he saw in the gloomy past but a
dark prophecy of the future. As Napoleon wept over
one wounded soldier in the field of battle, yet ordered,
without emotion, thousands to a certain death ; so
Aram would have sacrificed himself for an individual,
but would not have sacrificed a momentary gratification for his race. And this sentiment towards men,
at once of high disdain and profound despondency,
was perhaps the cause why he rioted in indolence
upon his extraordinary mental wealth, and could not
be persuaded either to dazzle the world or to serve it.
But by little and little his fame had broke forth from
the limits with which he would have walled it : a man
who had taught himself, under singular difficulties,
nearly all the languages of the civilised earth ; the
profound mathematician, the elaborate antiquarian,
the abstruse philologist, uniting with his graver lore
the more florid accomplishments of science, from the

scholastic trifling of heraldry to the gentle learning
of herbs and flowers, could scarcely hope for utter
obscurity in that day when all intellectual acquire-
ment was held in high honour, and its possessors were
drawn together into a sort of brotherhood by the fellowship of their pursuits. And though Aram gave little
or nothing to the world himself, he was ever willing
to communicate to others any benefit or honour deriv-
able from his researches. On the altar of science he
kindled no light, but the fragrant oil in the lamps of
his more pious brethren was largely borrowed from his
stores. From almost every college in Europe came to
his obscure abode letters of acknowledgment or inquiry ; and few foreign cultivators of learning visited
this country without seeking an interview with Aram.
He received them with all the modesty and the courtesy that characterised his demeanour ; but it was noticeable that he never allowed these interruptions to be
more than temporary. He proffered no hospitality,
and shrunk back from all offers of friendship ; the
interview lasted its hour, and was seldom renewed.
Patronage was not less distasteful to him than social-
ity. Some occasional visits and condescensions of the
great he had received with a stern haughtiness, rather
than his habitual subdued urbanity. The precise
amount of his fortune was not known ; his wants
were so few, that what would have been poverty to
others might easily have been competence to him ;
and the only evidence he manifested of the command
of money was in his extended and various library.

He had been now about two years settled in his

present retreat. Unsocial as he was, every one in the neighbourhood loved him ; even the reserve of a man so eminent, arising as it was supposed to do from a painful modesty, had in it something winning ; and he had been known to evince, on great occasions, a charity and a courage in the service of others, which removed from the seclusion of his habits the semblance of misanthropy and of avarice. The peasant threw kindly pity into his respectful greeting, as in his homeward walk he encountered the pale and thoughtful student, with the folded arms and downcast eyes which characterised the abstraction of his mood ; and the village maiden, as she curtsied by him, stole a glance at his handsome but melancholy countenance ; and told her sweetheart she was certain the poor scholar had been crossed in love !

And thus passed the student's life ; perhaps its monotony and dulness required less compassion than they received : no man can judge of the happiness of another. As the moon plays upon the waves, and seems to our eyes to favour with a peculiar beam one long tract amidst the waters, leaving the rest in comparative obscurity, yet all the while she is no niggard in her lustre—for though the rays that meet not our eyes seem to us as though they were not, yet *she*, with an equal and unfavouring loveliness, mirrors herself on every wave :—even so, perhaps, happiness falls with the same brightness and power over the whole expanse of life, though to our limited eyes it seems only to rest on those billows from which the ray is reflected on our sight.

From his contemplations, of whatsoever nature, Aram was now aroused by a loud summons at the door;—the clock had gone eleven. Who, at that late hour, when the whole village was buried in sleep, could demand admittance? He recollected that Madeline had said the stranger who had so alarmed them had inquired for him; at that recollection his cheek suddenly blanched, but again, that stranger was surely only some poor traveller who had heard of his wonted charity, and had called to solicit relief; for he had not met the stranger on the road to Lester's house, and he had naturally set down the apprehensions of his fair visitants to mere female timidity. Who could this be? No humble wayfarer would at that hour crave assistance;—some disaster, perhaps, in the village? From his lofty chamber he looked forth and saw the stars watch quietly over the scattered cottages and the dark foliage that slept breathlessly around. All was still as death, but it seemed the stillness of innocence and security: again! the bell again! He thought he heard his name shouted without; he strode once or twice irresolutely to and fro the chamber; and then his step grew firm, and his native courage returned. His pistols were still girded round him; he looked to the priming, and muttered some incoherent words; he then descended the stairs, and slowly unbarred the door. Without the porch, the moonlight full upon his harsh features and sturdy frame, stood the ill-omened traveller.

CHAPTER V.

A Dinner at the Squire's Hall.—A Conversation between two Retired Men with different objects in Retirement.—Disturbance
first introduced into a peaceful Family.

Can he not be sociable ?—*Troilus and Cressida.*

Subit quippe etiam ipsius inertiæ dulcedo; et invisa primò desidia postremò amatur.*—
TACITUS.

How use doth breed a habit in a man !
This shadowy desert, unfrequented woods,
I better brook than flourishing peopled towns.—*Winter's Tale.*

THE next day, faithful to his appointment, Aram arrived at Lester's. The good squire received him with
a warm cordiality, and Madeline with a blush and a
smile that ought to have been more grateful to him
than acknowledgments. She was still a prisoner to
the sofa, but, in compliment to Aram, the sofa was
wheeled into the hall where they dined, so that she
was not absent from the repast. It was a pleasant
room, that old hall! Though it was summer, more
for cheerfulness than warmth, the log burnt on the
spacious hearth; but at the same time the latticed

* Forasmuch as the very sweetness of idleness stealthily introduces itself into the mind, and the sloth, which was at first hateful, becomes at length beloved.

windows were thrown open, and the fresh yet sunny
air stole in, rich from the embrace of the woodbine
and clematis which clung around the casement.

A few old pictures were panelled in the open wainscot ; and here and there the horns of the mighty stag
adorned the walls, and united with the cheeriness of
comfort associations of that of enterprise. The good
old board was crowded with the luxuries meet for a
country squire. The speckled trout, fresh from the
stream, and the four-year-old mutton, modestly dis-
claiming its own excellent merits by affecting the
shape and assuming the adjuncts of venison. Then
for the confectionery—it was worthy of Ellinor, to
whom that department generally fell ; and we should
scarcely be surprised to find, though we venture not to
affirm, that its delicate fabrication owed more to her
than superintendence. Then the ale, and the cider
with rosemary in the bowl, were incomparable potations ; and to the gooseberry wine, which would have
filled Mrs Primrose with envy, was added the more
generous warmth of port, which, in the Squire's
younger days, had been the talk of the country, and
which had now lost none of its attributes, save "the
original brightness" of its colour.

But (the wine excepted) these various dainties met
with slight honour from their abstemious guest; and—
for, though habitually reserved, he was rarely gloomy
—they remarked that he seemed unusually fitful and
sombre in his mood. Something appeared to rest
upon his mind, from which, by the excitement of

wine and occasional bursts of eloquence more animated than ordinary, he seemed striving to escape;
and at length he apparently succeeded. Naturally
enough, the conversation turned upon the curiosities
and scenery of the country around; and here Aram
shone with a peculiar grace. Vividly alive to the influences of nature, and minutely acquainted with its
varieties, he invested every hill and glade to which
remark recurred with the poetry of his descriptions;
and from his research he gave even scenes the most
familiar a charm and interest which had been strange
to them till then. To this stream some romantic legend had once attached itself, long forgotten and now
revived; that moor, so barren to an ordinary eye,
was yet productive of some rare and curious herb,
whose properties afforded scope for lively description;
—that old mound was yet rife in attraction to one
versed in antiquities, and able to explain its origin,
and from such explanation deduce a thousand classic
or Celtic episodes.

No subject was so homely or so trite, but the knowledge that had neglected nothing was able to render it
luminous and new. And as he spoke, the scholar's
countenance brightened, and his voice, at first hesitating and low, compelled the attention to its earnest and
winning music. Lester himself, a man who, in his
long retirement, had not forgotten the attractions of
intellectual society, nor even neglected a certain cultivation of intellectual pursuits, enjoyed a pleasure that
he had not experienced for years. The gay Ellinor

was fascinated into admiration ; and Madeline, the most silent of the group, drank in every word, unconscious of the sweet poison she imbibed. Walter alone seemed not carried away by the eloquence of their guest. He preserved an unadmiring and sullen demeanour, and every now and then regarded Aram with looks of suspicion and dislike. This was more remarkable when the men were left alone; and Lester, in surprise and anger, darted significant and admonitory glances towards his nephew, which at length seemed to rouse him into a more hospitable bearing. As the cool of the evening now came on, Lester proposed to Aram to enjoy it without, previous to returning to the parlour, to which the ladies had retired. Walter excused himself from joining them. The host and the guest accordingly strolled forth alone.

" Your solitude," said Lester, smiling, " is far deeper and less broken than mine ; do you never find it irksome ?"

" Can humanity be at all times contented ?" said Aram. " No stream, howsoever secret or subterranean, glides on in eternal tranquillity."

" You allow, then, that you feel some occasional desire for a more active and animated life ?"

" Nay," answered Aram ; " that is scarcely a fair corollary from my remark. I may, at times, feel the weariness of existence—the *tedium vitæ ;* but I know well that the cause is not to be remedied by a change from tranquillity to agitation. The objects of the great world are to be pursued only by the excitement

of the passions. The passions are at once our masters
and our deceivers;—they urge us onward, yet present
no limit to our progress. The farther we proceed the
more dim and shadowy grows the goal. It is impossible for a man who leads the life of the world, the
life of the passions, ever to experience content. For
the life of the passions is that of a perpetual desire;
but a state of content is the absence of all desire.
Thus philosophy has become another name for mental
quietude; and all wisdom points to a life of intellectual indifference, as the happiest which earth can
bestow."

"This may be true enough," said Lester, reluctantly,
"but——"

"But what?"

"A something at our hearts—a secret voice—an involuntary impulse—rebels against it, and points to
action—action, as the true sphere of man."

A slight smile curved the lip of the student; he
avoided, however, the argument, and remarked—

"Yet, if you think so, the world lies before you;
why not return to it?"

"Because constant habit is stronger than occasional
impulse; and my seclusion, after all, has its sphere of
action—has its object."

"All seclusion has."

"All? Scarcely so; for me, I have my object of
interest in my children."

"And mine is in my books."

"And engaged in your object, does not the whisper

of Fame ever animate you with the desire to go forth
into the world, and receive the homage that would
await you ?"

"Listen to me," replied Aram. "When I was a
boy I went once to a theatre. The tragedy of *Hamlet*
was performed; a play full of the noblest thoughts,
the subtlest morality. The audience listened with
attention, with admiration, with applause. I said to
myself, when the curtain fell, 'It must be a glorious
thing to obtain this empire over men's intellects and
emotions.' But now an Italian mountebank appeared
on the stage—a man of extraordinary personal strength
and sleight of hand. He performed a variety of jug-
gling tricks, and distorted his body into a thousand
surprising and unnatural postures. The audience were
transported beyond themselves : if they had felt delight in *Hamlet*, they glowed with rapture at the
mountebank; they had listened with attention to the
lofty thought, but they were snatched from themselves
by the marvel of the strange posture. 'Enough' said
I ; 'I correct my former notion. Where is the glory
of ruling men's minds, and commanding their admiration, when a greater enthusiasm is excited by mere
bodily agility than was kindled by the most wonderful emanations of a genius little less than divine ?' I
have never forgotten the impression of that evening."

Lester attempted to combat the truth of the illustration ; and thus conversing, they passed on through
the village green, when the gaunt form of Corporal
Bunting arrested their progress.

"Beg pardon, squire," said he, with a military salute, "beg pardon, your honour," bowing to Aram; "but I wanted to speak to you, squire, 'bout the rent of the bit cot yonder: times very hard—pay scarce—and——"

"You desire a little delay, Bunting, eh?—Well, well, we'll see about it; look up at the hall to-morrow. Mr Walter, I know, wants to consult you about letting the water from the great pond, and you must give us your opinion of the new brewing."

"Thank your honour, thank you; much obliged, I'm sure. I hope your honour liked the trout I sent up. Beg pardon, Master Aram, mayhap you would condescend to accept a few fish now and then; they're very fine in these streams, as you probably know; if you please to let me, I'll send some up by the old 'oman to-morrow, that is, if the day's cloudy a bit."

The scholar thanked the good Bunting, and would have proceeded onward, but the corporal was in a familiar mood.

"Beg pardon, beg pardon, but strange-looking dog here last evening—asked after you—said you were old friend of his—trotted off in your direction—hope all was right, master?—augh!"

"All right!" repeated Aram, fixing his eyes on the corporal, who had concluded his speech with a significant wink, and pausing a full moment before he continued; then, as if satisfied with his survey, he added—

"Ay, ay, I know whom you mean; he had become

acquainted with me some years ago. So you saw him! What said he to you—of me?"

"Augh! little enough, Master Aram: he seemed to think only of satisfying his own appetite; said he'd been a soldier."

"A soldier!—true!"

"Never told me the regiment, though; shy!—did he ever desert, pray, your honour?"

"I don't know," answered Aram, turning away. "I know little, very little about him!" He was going away, but stopped to add—"The man called on me last night for assistance; the lateness of the hour a little alarmed me. I gave him what I could afford, and he has now proceeded on his journey."

"Oh, then, he won't take up his quarters hereabouts, your honour?" said the corporal, inquiringly.

"No, no; good evening."

"What! this singular stranger, who so frightened my poor girls, is really known to you!" said Lester, in surprise. "Pray, is he as formidable as he seemed to them?"

"Scarcely," said Aram, with great composure; "he has been a wild roving fellow all his life, but—but there is little real harm in him. He is certainly ill-favoured enough to——" here, interrupting himself, and breaking into a new sentence, Aram added, "but at all events he will frighten your nieces no more—he has proceeded on his journey northward. And now, yonder lies my way home. Good evening." The abruptness of this farewell did indeed take Lester by surprise.

"Why, you will not leave me yet? The young ladies expect your return to them for an hour or so! What will they think of such desertion! No, no, come back, my good friend, and suffer me by-and-by to walk some part of the way home with you."

"Pardon me," said Aram, "I must leave you now. As to the ladies," he added, with a faint smile, half in melancholy, half in scorn, "I am not one whom they could miss; forgive me if I seem unceremonious. Adieu."

Lester at first felt a little offended, but when he recalled the peculiar habits of the scholar, he saw that the only way to hope for a continuance of that society which had so pleased him was to indulge Aram at first in his unsocial inclinations, rather than annoy him by a troublesome hospitality; he therefore, without further discourse, shook hands with him, and they parted.

When Lester regained the little parlour, he found his nephew sitting, silent and discontented, by the window. Madeline had taken up a book, and Ellinor, in an opposite corner, was plying her needle with an air of earnestness and quiet, very unlike her usual playful and cheerful vivacity. There was evidently a cloud over the group, the good Lester regarded them with a searching, yet kindly eye.

"And what has happened?" said he: "something of mighty import, I am sure, or I should have heard my pretty Ellinor's merry laugh long before I crossed the threshold."

Ellinor coloured and sighed, and worked faster than ever. Walter threw open the window, and whistled

a favourite air quite out of tune. Lester smiled, and
seated himself by his nephew.

"Well, Walter," said he, "I feel, for the first time
these ten years, that I have a right to scold you.
What on earth could make you so inhospitable to
your uncle's guest? You eyed the poor student as
if you wished him among the books of Alexandria!"

"I would he were burnt with them!" answered
Walter, sharply. "He seems to have added the black
art to his other accomplishments, and bewitched my fair
cousins here into a forgetfulness of all but himself."

"Not me!" said Ellinor, eagerly, and looking up.

"No, not you, that's true enough; you are too just,
too kind;—it is a pity that Madeline is not more like
you."

"My dear Walter," said Madeline, "what is the
matter? You accuse me of what? being attentive to a
man whom it is impossible to hear without attention!"

"There!" cried Walter, passionately, "you confess
it. And so for a stranger — a cold, vain, pedantic
egotist, you can shut your ears and heart to those
who have known and loved you all your life; and—
and——"

"Vain!" interrupted Madeline, unheeding the latter
part of Walter's address.

"Pedantic!" repeated her father.

"Yes! I say vain, pedantic!" cried Walter, work-
ing himself into a passion. "What on earth but the
love of display could make him monopolise the whole
conversation?—What but pedantry could make him

bring out those anecdotes, and allusions, and descriptions, or whatever you call them, respecting every old wall or stupid plant in the country?"

"I never thought you guilty of meanness before," said Lester, gravely.

"Meanness!"

"Yes! for is it not mean to be jealous of superior acquirements, instead of admiring them?"

"What has been the use of those acquirements? Has he benefited mankind by them? Show me the poet—the historian—the orator, and I will yield to none of you; no, not to Madeline herself, in homage of their genius; but the mere creature of books—the dry and sterile collector of other men's learning—no —no. What should I admire in such a machine of literature except a waste of perseverance?—And Madeline calls him handsome, too!"

At this sudden turn from declamation to reproach, Lester laughed outright; and his nephew, in high anger, rose and left the room.

"Who could have thought Walter so foolish?" said Madeline.

"Nay," observed Ellinor, gently, "it is the folly of a kind heart, after all. He feels sore at our seeming to prefer another—I mean another's conversation—to his!"

Lester turned round in his chair, and regarded with a serious look the faces of both sisters.

"My dear Ellinor," said he, when he had finished his survey, "you are a kind girl—come and kiss me!"

CHAPTER VI.

> The soft season, the firmament serene.
> The loun illuminate air, and firth amene
> The silver scalit fishes on the grete
> O'er-thwart clear streams sprinkillond for the heat.
>   GAWIN DOUGLAS.
>
>   Illa subter
> Cæcum vulnus habes; sed lato balteus auro
> Prætegit.*—PERSIUS.

SEVERAL days elapsed before the family of the manor-house encountered Aram again. The old woman came once or twice to present the inquiries of her master as to Miss Lester's accident; but Aram himself did not appear. This want of interest certainly offended Madeline, although she still drew upon herself Walter's displeasure, by disputing and resenting the unfavourable strictures on the scholar, in which that young gentleman delighted to indulge. By degrees, however, as the days passed without maturing the acquaintance which Walter had disapproved, the youth relaxed in his attacks, and seemed to yield to the remonstrances of his uncle. Lester had, indeed, conceived an espe-

---

* You have a wound deep hidden in your heart; but the broad belt of gold conceals it.

cial inclination towards the recluse. Any man of reflection, who has lived for some time alone, and who
suddenly meets with one who calls forth in him, and
without labour or contradiction, the thoughts which
have sprung up in his solitude, scarcely felt in their
growth, will comprehend the new zest, the awakening, as it were, in the mind, which Lester found in
the conversation of Eugene Aram. His solitary walk
(for his nephew had the separate pursuits of youth)
appeared to him more dull than before; and he longed
to renew an intercourse which had given to the monotony of his life both variety and relief. He called
twice upon Aram, but the student was, or affected to
be, from home; and an invitation that Lester sent
him, though couched in friendly terms, was, but with
great semblance of kindness, refused.

"See, Walter," said Lester, disconcerted, as he
finished reading the refusal—"see what your rudeness has effected. I am quite convinced that Aram
(evidently a man of susceptible as well as retired
mind) observed the coldness of your manner towards
him, and that thus *you* have deprived me of the only
society which, in this wilderness of boors and savages,
gave me any gratification."

Walter replied apologetically, but his uncle turned
away with a greater appearance of anger than his
placid features were wont to exhibit; and Walter,
cursing the innocent cause of his uncle's displeasure
towards him, took up his fishing-rod, and went out
alone, in no happy or exhilarated mood.

It was waxing towards eve — an hour especially lovely in the month of June, and, not without reason, favoured by the angler. Walter sauntered across the rich and fragrant fields, and came soon into a sheltered valley, through which the brooklet wound its shadowy way. Along the margin the grass sprang up long and matted, and profuse with a thousand weeds and flowers —the children of the teeming June. Here the ivy-leafed bell-flower, and not far from it the common enchanter's nightshade, the silver weed, and the water-aven; and by the hedges that now and then neared the water, the guelder-rose, and the white briony, overrunning the thicket with its emerald leaves and luxuriant flowers. And here and there, silvering the bushes, the elder offered its snowy tribute to the summer. All the insect youth were abroad, with their bright wings and glancing motion; and from the lower depths of the bushes the blackbird darted across, or higher and unseen the first cuckoo of the eve began its continuous and mellow note. All this cheeriness and gloss of life, which enamour us with the few bright days of the English summer, make the poetry in an angler's life, and convert every idler at heart into a moralist, and not a gloomy one, for the time.

Softened by the quiet beauty and voluptuousness around him, Walter's thoughts assumed a more gentle dye, and he broke out into the old lines—

> " Sweet day, so soft, so calm, so bright;
> The bridal of the earth and sky,'

as he dipped his line into the current and drew it across the shadowy hollows beneath the bank. The river gods were not, however, in a favourable mood, and after waiting in vain for some time, in a spot in which he was usually successful, he proceeded slowly along the margin of the brooklet, crushing the reeds at every step into that fresh and delicious odour which furnished Bacon with one of his most beautiful comparisons.

He thought, as he proceeded, that beneath a tree that overhung the waters in the narrowest part of their channel, he heard a voice, and as he approached, he recognised it as Aram's. A curve in the stream brought him close by the spot, and he saw the student half-reclined beneath the tree, and muttering, but at broken intervals, to himself.

The words were so scattered that Walter did not trace their clue; but involuntarily he stopped short within a few feet of the soliloquist; and Aram, suddenly turning round, beheld him. A fierce and abrupt change broke over the scholar's countenance; his cheek grew now pale, now flushed, and his brows knit over his flashing and dark eyes with an intent anger that was the more withering from its contrast to the usual calmness of his features. Walter drew back, but Aram, stalking directly up to him, gazed into his face as if he would read his very soul.

"What! eavesdropping?" said he, with a ghastly smile. "You overheard me, did you? Well, well, what said I?—what said I?" Then pausing, and noting that Walter did not reply, he stamped his foot violently, and grinding his teeth, repeated in a smothered tone,—" Boy ! what said I ? "

" Mr Aram," said Walter, " you forget yourself. I am not one to play the listener, more especially to the learned ravings of a man who can conceal nothing I care to know. Accident brought me hither."

" What ! surely—surely I spoke aloud, did I not ? —did I not ? "

" You did, but so incoherently and indistinctly, that I did not profit by your indiscretion. I cannot plagiarise, I assure you, from any scholastic designs you might have been giving vent to."

Aram looked on him for a moment, and then, breathing heavily, turned away.

" Pardon me," he said ; " I am a poor, half-crazed man ; much study has unnerved me ; I should never live but with my own thoughts ; forgive me, sir, I pray you."

Touched by the sudden contrition of Aram's manner, Walter forgot, not only his present displeasure, but his general dislike ; he stretched forth his hand to the student, and hastened to assure him of his ready forgiveness. Aram sighed deeply as he pressed the young man's hand, and Walter saw, with surprise and emotion, that his eyes were filled with tears.

" Ah ! " said Aram, gently shaking his head, " it is a hard life we bookmen lead ! Not for us is the bright face of noonday or the smile of woman, the gay unbending of the heart, the neighing steed, and the shrill trump; the pride, pomp, and circumstance of life. Our enjoyments are few and calm; our labour constant; but that is not the evil, sir!—the body avenges its own neglect. We grow old before our time; we wither up; the sap of youth shrinks from our veins; there is no bound in our step. We look about us with dimmed eyes, and our breath grows short and thick, and pains, and coughs, and shooting aches, come upon us at night: it is a bitter life—a bitter life—a joyless life. I would I had never commenced it. And yet the harsh world scowls upon us: our nerves are broken, and they wonder why we are querulous; our blood curdles, and they ask why we are not gay; our brain grows dizzy and indistinct (as with me just now), and, shrugging their shoulders, they whisper their neighbours that we are mad. I wish I had worked at the plough, and known sleep, and loved mirth—and—and not been what I am."

As the student uttered the last sentence, he bowed his head, and a few tears stole silently down his cheek. Walter was greatly affected—it took him by surprise: nothing in Aram's ordinary demeanour betrayed any facility to emotion; and he conveyed to all the idea of a man, if not proud, at least cold.

"You do not suffer bodily pain, I trust?" asked Walter, soothingly.

"Pain does not conquer me," said Aram, slowly recovering himself. "I am not melted by that which I would fain despise. Young man, I wronged you—you have forgiven me. Well, well, we will say no

more on that head; it is past and pardoned. Your
uncle has been kind to me, and I have not returned
his advances; you shall tell him why. I have lived
thirteen years by myself, and I have contracted strange
ways and many humours not common to the world—
you have seen an example of this. Judge for yourself
if I be fit for the smoothness, and confidence, and ease
of social intercourse; I am not fit, I feel it! I am
doomed to be alone; tell your uncle this—tell him to
suffer me to live so! I am grateful for his goodness—
I know his motives—but I have a certain pride of
mind; I cannot bear sufferance—I loathe indulgence.
Nay, interrupt me not, I beseech you. Look round on
Nature—behold the only company that humbles me
not—except the dead whose souls speak to us from the
immortality of books. These herbs at your feet, I
know their secrets—I watch the mechanism of their
life; the winds—they have taught me their language;
the stars—I have unravelled their mysteries; and
these, the creatures and ministers of God—these I
offend not by my mood—to them I utter my thoughts,
and break forth into my dreams, without reserve and
without fear. But men disturb me—I have nothing
to learn from them—I have no wish to confide in
them; they cripple the wild liberty which has become
to me a second nature. What its shell is to the
tortoise, solitude has become to me—my protection;
nay, my life!"

"But," said Walter, "with us, at least, you would
not have to dread restraint; you might come when

you would; be silent or converse, according to your will."

Aram smiled faintly, but made no immediate reply.

"So, you have been angling!" he said, after a short pause, and as if willing to change the thread of conversation. "Fie! it is a treacherous pursuit, it encourages man's worst propensities—cruelty and deceit."

"I should have thought a lover of Nature would have been more indulgent to a pastime which introduces us to her most quiet retreats."

"And cannot Nature alone tempt you without need of such allurements? What! that crisped and winding stream, with flowers on its very tide—the water-violet and the water-lily—these silent brakes—the cool of the gathering evening—the still and luxuriance of the universal life around you; are not these enough of themselves to tempt you forth? If not, go to!—your excuse is hypocrisy."

"I am used to these scenes," replied Walter; "I am weary of the thoughts they produce in me, and long for any diversion or excitement."

"Ay, ay, young man! The mind is restless at your age: have a care. Perhaps you long to visit the world, to quit these obscure haunts which you are fatigued in admiring?"

"It may be so," said Walter, with a slight sigh. "I should at least like to visit our great capital, and note the contrast; I should come back, I imagine, with a greater zest to these scenes."

Aram laughed. "My friend," said he, "when men

have once plunged into the great sea of human toil and passion, they soon wash away all love and zest for innocent enjoyments. What once was a soft retirement, will become the most intolerable monotony; the gaming of social existence—the feverish and desperate chances of honour and wealth, upon which the men of cities set their hearts, render all pursuits less exciting, utterly insipid and dull. The brook and the angle—ha! ha!—these are not occupations for men who have once battled with the world."

"I can forego them, then, without regret," said Walter, with the sanguineness of his years. Aram looked upon him wistfully; the bright eye, the healthy cheek, and vigorous frame of the youth, suited with his desire to seek the conflict of his kind, and gave a natural grace to his ambition, which was not without interest, even to the recluse.

"Poor boy!" said he, mournfully, "how gallantly the ship leaves the port; how worn and battered it will return!"

When they parted, Walter returned slowly homewards, filled with pity for the singular man whom he had seen so strangely overpowered, and wondering how suddenly his mind had lost its former rancour to the student. Yet there mingled even with these kindly feelings a little displeasure at the superior tone which Aram had unconsciously adopted towards him; and to which, from any one, the high spirit of the young man was not readily willing to submit.

Meanwhile, the student continued his path along

the water-side, and as, with his gliding step and musing air, he roamed onward, it was impossible to imagine a form more suited to the deep tranquillity of the scene. Even the wild birds seemed to feel, by a sort of instinct, that in him there was no cause for fear, and did not stir from the turf that neighboured, or the spray that overhung, his path.

"So," said he, soliloquising, but not without casting frequent and jealous glances round him, and in a murmur so indistinct as would have been inaudible even to a listener—"so, I was not overheard. Well, I must cure myself of this habit; our thoughts, like nuns, ought not to go abroad without a veil. Ay, this tone will not betray me; I will preserve its tenor, for I can scarcely altogether renounce my sole confidant—SELF: and thought seems more clear when uttered even thus. 'Tis a fine youth! full of the impulse and daring of his years; *I* was never so young at heart. I was—nay, what matters it? Who is answerable for his nature? Who can say,—'I controlled all the circumstances which made me what I am?' Madeline,—heavens! did I bring on myself this temptation? Have I not fenced it from me throughout all my youth, when my brain did at moments forsake me, and the veins did bound? And now, when the yellow hastens on the green of life; now, for the first time, this emotion—this weakness—and for whom? One I have lived with—known—beneath whose eyes I have passed through all the fine gradations, from liking to love, from love to passion! No;—one, whom I have seen

but little; who, it is true, arrested my eye at the first
glance it caught of her two years since, but to whom,
till within the last few weeks, I have scarcely spoken!
Her voice rings in my ear, her look dwells on my heart;
when I sleep she is with me; when I wake I am
haunted by her image. Strange, strange! Is love,
then, after all, the sudden passion which in every age
poetry has termed it, though till now my reason has
disbelieved the notion. . . . And now, what is
the question? To resist, or to yield. Her father
invites me, courts me; and I stand aloof! Will this
strength, this forbearance, last? Shall I *encourage* my
mind to this decision?" Here Aram paused abruptly,
and then renewed: "It is true! I ought to weave
my lot with none. Memory sets me apart and alone
in the world; it seems unnatural to me—a thought of
dread—to bring another being to my solitude, to set
an everlasting watch on my uprisings and my down-
sittings; to invite eyes to my face when I sleep at
nights, and ears to every word that may start unbidden
from my lips. But if the watch be the watch of love
—away! does love endure for ever? He who trusts
to woman, trusts to the type of change. Affection
may turn to hatred, fondness to loathing, anxiety to
dread; and, at the best, woman is weak—she is the
minion to her impulses. Enough; I will steel my
soul—shut up the avenues of sense, brand with the
scathing-iron these yet green and soft emotions of
lingering youth—and freeze, and chain, and curdle up
feeling, and heart, and manhood, into ice and age!"

CHAPTER VII.

The Power of Love over the Resolution of the Student.—Aram
becomes a Frequent Guest at the Manor-House.—A Walk.—
Conversation with Dame Darkmans.—Her History.—Poverty
and its Effects.

Mad. Then, as Time won thee frequent to our hearth,
Didst thou not breathe, like dreams, into my soul
Nature's more gentle secrets, the sweet lore
Of the green herb and the bee-worshipped flower?
And when deep Night did o'er the nether Earth
Diffuse meek quiet, and the Heart of Heaven
With love grew breathless—didst thou not unroll
The volume of the weird Chaldean stars,
And of the winds, the clouds, the invisible air,
Make eloquent discourse, until, methought,
No human lip, but some diviner spirit
Alone, could preach such truths of things divine?
And so—and so——
  Aram.   From Heaven we turned to Earth,
And Wisdom fathered Passion.

.   .   .   .   .

Aram. Wise men have praised the Peasant's thoughtless lot,
And learned Pride hath envied humble Toil;
If they were right, why let us burn our books,
And sit us down, and play the fool with Time,
Mocking the prophet Wisdom's high decrees,
And walling this trite Present with dark clouds,
Till Night becomes our Nature; and the ray
Even of the stars, but meteors that withdraw
The wandering spirit from the sluggish rest
Which makes its proper bliss. I will accost
This denizen of toil.—*From "Eugene Aram," a MS. Tragedy.*

A wicked hag, and envy's self excelling
In mischiefs, for herself she only vext,
But this same, both herself and others eke perplext.

.   .   .   .   .

Who then can strive with strong necessity,
That holds the world in his still changing state, &c. &c.
Then do no further go, no further stray,
But here lie down, and to thy rest betake.—Spenser.

Few men, perhaps, could boast of so masculine and
firm a mind as, despite his eccentricities, Aram assuredly possessed. His habits of solitude had strength-

ened its natural hardihood ; for, accustomed to make all the sources of happiness flow solely from himself, his thoughts the only companions—his genius the only vivifier—of his retreat, the tone and faculty of his spirit could not but assume that austere and vigorous energy which the habit of self-dependence almost invariably produces ; and yet the reader, if he be young, will scarcely feel surprised that the resolution of the student, to battle against incipient love, from whatever reasons it might be formed, gradually and reluctantly melted away. It may be noted, that the enthusiasts of learning and reverie have, at one time or another in their lives, been, of all the tribes of men, the most keenly susceptible to love; their solitude feeds their passion ; and deprived, as they usually are, of the more hurried and vehement occupations of life, when love is once admitted to their hearts, there is no counter-check to its emotions, and no escape from its excitement. Aram, too, had just arrived at that age when a man usually feels a sort of revulsion in the current of his desires. At that age, those who have hitherto pursued love, begin to grow alive to ambition ; those who have been slaves to the pleasures of life, awaken from the dream, and direct their desire to its interests. And in the same proportion, they who till then have wasted the prodigal fervours of youth upon a sterile soil—who have served Ambition, or, like Aram, devoted their hearts to Wisdom, relax from their ardour, look back on the departed years with regret, and commence, in their manhood, the fiery pleasures and delirious follies

which are only pardonable in youth. In short, as in
every human pursuit there is a certain vanity, and as
every acquisition contains within itself the seed of disappointment, so there is a period of life when we pause
from the pursuit, and are discontented with the acquisition. We then look around us for something new—
again follow — and are again deceived. Few men
throughout life are the servants to one desire. When
we gain the middle of the bridge of our mortality, different objects from those which attracted us upward
almost invariably lure us down the descent. Happy
they who exhaust in the former part of the journey all
the foibles of existence! But how different is the
crude and evanescent love of that age when thought
has not given intensity and power to the passions, from
the love which is felt *for the first time*, in maturer but
still youthful years! As the flame burns the brighter
in proportion to the resistance which it conquers, this
later love is the more glowing in proportion to the
length of time in which it has overcome temptation;
all the solid and concentred faculties, ripened to their
full height, are no longer capable of the infinite dis-
tractions, the numberless caprices of youth; the rays
of the heart, not rendered weak by diversion, collect
into one burning focus; * the same earnestness and
unity of purpose which render what we undertake in
manhood so far more successful than what we would

---

* Love is of the nature of a burning-glass, which, kept still in one
place, fireth; changed often, it doth nothing!—*Letters by Sir John
Suckling.*

effect in youth, are equally visible and equally triumphant, whether directed to interest or to love. But then,
as in Aram, the feelings must be fresh as well as matured ; they must not have been fritted away by previous indulgence ; the love must be the first produce
of the soil, not the languid after-growth.

The reader will remark, that the first time in which
our narrative has brought Madeline and Aram together
was not the first time they had met : Aram had long
noted with admiration a beauty which he had never
seen paralleled, and certain vague and unsettled feelings had preluded the deep emotion that her image now
excited within him. But the main cause of his present
and growing attachment had been in the evident sentiment of kindness which he could not but feel Madeline
bore towards him. So retiring a nature as his might
never have harboured love, if the love bore the character of presumption ; but that one so beautiful beyond
his dreams as Madeline Lester should deign to cherish
for him a tenderness that might suffer him to hope, was
a thought that, when he caught her eye unconsciously
fixed upon him, and noted that her voice grew softer
and more tremulous when she addressed him, forced
itself upon his heart, and woke there a strange and
irresistible emotion, which solitude and the brooding
reflection that solitude produces—a reflection so much
more intense in proportion to the paucity of living
images it dwells upon—soon ripened into love. Perhaps, even, he would not have resisted the impulse as
he now did, had not at this time certain thoughts con-

nected with past events been more forcibly than of late years obtruded upon him, and thus in some measure divided his heart. By degrees, however, those thoughts receded from their vividness, into the habitual deep, but not oblivious shade, beneath which his commanding mind had formerly driven them to repose ; and as they thus receded, Madeline's image grew more undisturbedly present, and his resolution to avoid its power more fluctuating and feeble. Fate seemed bent upon bringing together these two persons, already so attracted towards each other. After the conversation recorded in our last chapter, between Walter and the student, the former, touched and softened as we have seen in spite of himself, had cheerfully forborne (what before he had done reluctantly) the expressions of dislike which he had once lavished so profusely upon Aram ; and Lester, who, forward as he had seemed, had nevertheless been hitherto a little checked in his advances to his neighbour by the hostility of his nephew, felt no scruple to deter him from urging them with a pertinacity that almost forbade refusal. It was Aram's constant habit, in all seasons, to wander abroad at certain times of the day, especially towards the evening ; and if Lester failed to win entrance to his house, he was thus enabled to meet the student in his frequent rambles, and with a seeming freedom from design. Actuated by his great benevolence of character, Lester earnestly desired to win his solitary and unfriended neighbour from a mood and habit which he naturally imagined must engender a growing melancholy of mind ; and since

Walter had detailed to him the particulars of his meeting with Aram, this desire had been considerably increased. There is not, perhaps, a stronger feeling in the world than pity, when united with admiration. When one man is resolved to know another it is almost impossible to prevent it : we see daily the most remarkable instances of perseverance on one side conquering distaste on the other. By degrees, then, Aram relaxed from his insociability ; he seemed to surrender himself to a kindness, the sincerity of which he was compelled to acknowledge; if he for a long time refused to accept the hospitality of his neighbour, he did not reject his society when they met ; and this intercourse increased by little and little, until ultimately the recluse yielded to solicitation, and became the guest as well as companion. This, at first, accident, grew, though not without many interruptions, into habit ; and at length few evenings were passed by the inmates of the manor-house without the society of the student.

As his reserve wore off, his conversation mingled with its attractions a tender and affectionate tone. He seemed grateful for the pains which had been taken to allure him to a scene in which, at last, he acknowledged he found a happiness that he had never experienced before : and those who had hitherto admired him for his genius, admired him now yet more for his susceptibility to the affections.

There was not in Aram anything that savoured of the harshness of pedantry, or the petty vanities of dog-

matism ; his voice was soft and low, and his manner
always remarkable for its singular gentleness, and a
certain dignified humility.   His language did, indeed,
at times, assume a tone of calm and patriarchal command ; but it was only the command arising from an
intimate persuasion of the truth of what he uttered.
Moralising upon our nature, or mourning over the
delusions of the world, a grave and solemn strain
breathed throughout his lofty words and the profound
melancholy of his wisdom :· but it touched, not offended
—elevated, not humbled—the lesser intellect of his
listeners ; and even this air of unconscious superiority
vanished when he was invited to teach or explain.

That task which so few do gracefully, that an accurate
and shrewd thinker has said—"It is always safe to learn,
even from our enemies ; seldom safe to instruct even
our friends,"*—Aram performed with a meekness and
simplicity that charmed the vanity, even while it corrected the ignorance of the applicant ; and so various
and minute was the information of this accomplished
man, that there scarcely existed any branch even of that
knowledge usually called practical, to which he could
not impart from his stores something valuable and new.
The agriculturist was astonished at the success of his
suggestions ; and the mechanic was indebted to him
for the device which abridged his labour in improving
its result.

It happened that the study of botany was not, at
that day, so favourite and common a diversion with

* LACON.

young ladies as it is now; and Ellinor, captivated by the notion of a science that gave a life and a history to the loveliest of earth's offspring, besought Aram to teach her its principles.

As Madeline, though she did not second the request, could scarcely absent herself from sharing the lesson, this pursuit brought the pair—already lovers—closer and closer together. It associated them not only at home, but in their rambles throughout that enchanting country; and there is a mysterious influence in nature which renders us, in her loveliest scenes, the most susceptible to love! Then, too, how often in their occupation their hands and eyes met: how often, by the shady wood or the soft water-side, they found themselves alone. In all times, how dangerous the connection, when of different sexes, between the scholar and the teacher! Under how many pretences, in that connection, the heart finds the opportunity to speak out.

Yet it was not with ease and complacency that Aram delivered himself to the intoxication of his deepening attachment. Sometimes he was studiously cold, or evidently wrestling with the powerful passion that mastered his reason. It was not without many throes and desperate resistance, that love at length overwhelmed and subdued him; and these alternations of his mood, if they sometimes offended Madeline and sometimes wounded, still rather increased than lessened the spell which bound her to him. The doubt and the fear, the caprice and the change, which agitate the surface, swell also the tides of passion. Woman, too, whose love is so much the creature of her imagination, always asks something of mystery and conjecture in the object of her affection. It is a luxury to her to perplex herself with a thousand apprehensions ; and the more restlessly her lover occupies her mind, the more deeply he enthrals it.

Mingling with her pure and tender attachment to Aram a high and unswerving veneration, she saw in his fitfulness, and occasional abstraction and contradiction of manner, a confirmation of the modest sentiment that most weighed upon her fears ; and imagined that, at those times, he thought her, as she deemed herself, unworthy of his love. And this was the only struggle which she conceived to pass between the affection he evidently bore her, and the feelings which had as yet restrained him from its open avowal.

One evening Lester and the two sisters were walking with the student along the valley that led to the house of the latter, when they saw an old woman engaged in collecting firewood among the bushes, and a little girl holding out her apron to receive the sticks with which the crone's skinny arms unsparingly filled it. The child trembled and seemed half-crying ; while the old woman, in a harsh, grating croak, was muttering forth mingled objurgation and complaint.

There was something in the appearance of the latter at once impressive and displeasing ; a dark, withered, furrowed skin was drawn like parchment over harsh and aquiline features : the eyes, through the rheum of

age, glittered forth black and malignant ; and even her
stooping posture did not conceal a height greatly above
the common stature, though gaunt and shrivelled with
years and poverty. It was a form and face that might
have recalled at once the celebrated description of
Otway, on a part of which we have already unconsciously
encroached, and the remaining part of which we shall
wholly borrow :—

> " On her crooked shoulders had she wrapped
> The tattered remnants of an old striped hanging,
> That served to keep her carcass from the cold,
> So there was nothing of a piece about her.
> Her lower weeds were all o'er coarsely patched
> With different-coloured rags, black, red, white, yellow,
> And seemed to speak variety of wretchedness."

" See," said Lester, " one of the eyesores of our
village (I might say), the only discontented person."

" What ! Dame Darkmans !" said Ellinor, quickly.
" Ah ! let us turn back. I hate to encounter that old
woman ; there is something so evil and savage in her
manner of talk—and look, how she rates that poor girl,
whom she has dragged or decoyed to assist her !"

Aram looked curiously on the old hag. " Poverty,"
said he, " makes some humble, but more malignant ;
is it not want that grafts the devil on this poor woman's
nature ? Come, let us accost her—I like conferring
with distress."

" It is hard labour this ?" said the student, gently.

The old woman looked up askant—the music of the
voice that addressed her sounded harsh on her ear.

" Ay, ay !" she answered. " You fine gentlefolks

can know what the poor suffer; ye talk and ye talk, but ye never assist."

"Say not so, dame," said Lester; "did I not send you but yesterday bread and money? And when did you ever look up at the hall without obtaining relief?"

"But the bread was as dry as a stick," growled the hag; "and the money, what was it? will it last a week? Oh, yes! Ye think as much of your doits and mites, as if ye stripped yourselves of a comfort to give it to us. Did ye have a dish less—a 'tato less, the day ye sent me—your charity I 'spose ye calls it? Och! fie! But the Bible's the poor cretur's comfort."

"I am glad to hear you say that, dame," said the good-natured Lester; "and I forgive everything else you have said, on account of that one sentence."

The old woman dropped the sticks she had just gathered, and glowered at the speaker's benevolent countenance with a malicious meaning in her dark eyes.

"An' ye do? Well, I'm glad I please ye there. Och! yes! the Bible's a mighty comfort; for it says as much that the rich man shall not *inter* the kingdom of Heaven! There's a truth for you, that makes the *poor* folks' heart chirp like a cricket—ho! ho! *I* sits by the *imbers* of a night, and I thinks and thinks as how I shall see you all burning; and ye'll ask me for a drop o' water, and I shall laugh thin from my pleasant seat with the angels. Och! it's a book for the poor, that!"

The sisters shuddered. "And you think, then, that

with envy, malice, and all uncharitableness at your heart, you are certain of Heaven ? For shame ! Pluck the mote from your own eye ! "

" What sinnifies praching ? Did not the Blessed Saviour come for the poor ? Them as has rags and dry bread here will be ixalted in the nixt world ; an' if we poor folk have malice, as ye calls it, whose fault's that ? What do ye tache us ? Eh ?—Answer me that. Ye keeps all the larning an' all the other fine things to yoursel', and then ye scould, and thritten, and haug us, 'cause we are not as wise as you. Och ! there's no jistice in the Lamb, if Heaven is not made for us ; and tho iverlasting Hell, with its brimstone and fire, and its gnawing an' gnashing of teeth, an' its theirst, an' its torture, an' its worm that niver dies, for the like o' you ! "

" Come ! come away," said Ellinor, pulling her father's arm.

" And if," said Aram, pausing, " if I were to say to you, Name your want and it shall be fulfilled, would you have no charity for me also ? "

" Umph ! " returned the hag, " ye are the great scolard ; and they say ye knows what no one else do. Till me now," and she approached, and familiarly laid her bony finger on the student's arm ; till me,—have ye iver, among other fine things, known poverty ? "

" I have, woman ! " said Aram, sternly.

" Och, ye have thin ! And did ye not sit, and gloom, and eat up your own heart, an' curse the sun that looked so gay, an' the winged things that played so blithe-like,

an' scowl at the rich folk that niver wasted a thought
on ye? Till me now, your honour, till me!"

And the crone curtsied with a mock air of beseech-
ing humility.

. "I never forgot, even in want, the love due to my
fellow-sufferers; for, woman, we all suffer—the rich
and the poor: there are worse pangs than those of
want!"

"Ye think there be, do ye? That's a comfort,—
umph! Well, I'll till ye now, I feel a rispict for you
that I don't for the rest on 'em; for your face does not
insult me with being cheary like theirs yonder; an' I
have noted ye walk in the dust with your eyes down
and your arms crossed; an' I have said, That man I
do not hate, somehow, for he has something dark at his
heart like me!"

"The lot of earth is woe," answered Aram, calmly,
yet shrinking back from the crone's touch; "judge we
charitably, and act we kindly to each other. There—
this money is not much, but it will light your hearth
and heap your table without toil, for some days at
least!"

"Thank your honour: an' what think you I'll do
with the money?"

"What?"

"Drink, drink, drink!" cried the hag, fiercely.
"There's nothing like drink for the poor, for thin we
fancy ourselves what we wish; and," sinking her voice
into a whisper, "I thinks thin that I have my foot on
the billies of the rich folks, and my hands twisted about

their intrails, and I hear them shriek, and—thin I'm happy."

"Go home!" said Aram, turning away, "and open the Book of Life with other thoughts."

The little party proceeded; and, looking back, Lester saw the old woman gaze after them, till a turn in the winding valley hid her from his sight.

"That is a strange person, Aram; scarcely a favourable specimen of the happy English peasant," said Lester, smiling.

"Yet they say," added Madeline, "that she was not always the same perverse and hateful creature she is now."

"Ay," said Aram; "and what, then, is her history?"

"Why," replied Madeline, slightly blushing to find herself made the narrator of a story, "some forty years ago this woman, so gaunt and hideous now, was the beauty of the village. She married an Irish soldier, whose regiment passed through Grassdale, and was heard of no more till about ten years back, when she returned to her native place, the discontented, envious, altered being you now see her."

"She is not reserved in regard to her past life," said Lester. "She is too happy to seize the attention of any one to whom she can pour forth her dark and angry confidence. She saw her husband, who was afterwards dismissed the service—a strong, powerful man, a giant of his tribe — pine and waste, inch by inch, from mere physical want, and at last literally die

from hunger. It happened that they had settled in
the county in which her husband was born, and in
that county, those frequent famines which are the
scourge of Ireland were for two years especially
severe. You may note that the old woman has a
strong vein of coarse eloquence at her command, perhaps acquired in (for it partakes of the natural character of) the country in which she lived so long ; and
it would literally thrill you with horror to hear her
descriptions of the misery and destitution that she
witnessed, and amidst which her husband breathed
his last. Out of four children, not one survives. One,
an infant, died within a week of the father ; two sons
were executed, one at the age of sixteen, one a year
older, for robbery committed under aggravated circumstances ; and a fourth, a daughter, died in the hos-
pitals of London. The old woman became a wanderer
and a vagrant, and was at length passed to her native
parish, where she has since dwelt. These are the misfortunes which have turned her blood to gall ; and
these are the causes which fill her with so bitter a
hatred against those whom wealth has preserved from
sharing or witnessing a fate similar to hers."

"Oh !" said Aram, in a low, but deep tone, "when
—when will these hideous disparities be banished from
the world ? How many noble natures—how many
glorious hopes—how much of the seraph's intellect,
have been crushed into the mire, or blasted into guilt,
by the mere force of physical want ! What are the
temptations of the rich to those of the poor ! Yet, see

how lenient we are to the crimes of the one—how relentless to those of the other ! It is a bad world : it makes a man's heart sick to look around him. The consciousness of how little individual genius can do to relieve the mass, grinds out, as with a stone, all that is generous in ambition ; and to aspire from the level of life is but to be more graspingly selfish."

" Can legislators, or the moralists that instruct legislators, do so little, then, towards universal good ? " said Lester, doubtingly.

" Why, what can they do but forward civilisation ? And what is civilisation but an increase of human disparities ? The more the luxury of the few, the more startling the wants, and the more galling the sense, of poverty. Even the dreams of the philanthropist only tend towards equality ; and where is equality to be found but in the state of the savage ? No : I thought otherwise once ; but I now regard the vast lazar-house around us without hope of relief ;—death is the sole physician !"

" Ah, no," said the high-souled Madeline, eagerly ; "do not take away from us the best feeling and the highest desire we can cherish. How poor, even in this beautiful world, with the warm sun and fresh air about us, would be life, if we could not make the happiness of others ! "

Aram looked at the beautiful speaker with a soft and half-mournful smile. There is one very peculiar pleasure that we feel as we grow older ;—it is to see embodied, in another and a more lovely shape, the

thoughts and sentiments we once nursed ourselves; it
is as if we viewed before us the incarnation of our own
youth; and it is no wonder that we are warmed towards the object, that thus seems the living apparition
of all that was brightest in ourselves! It was with
this sentiment that Aram now gazed on Madeline.
She felt the gaze, and her heart beat delightedly; but
she sunk at once into a silence, which she did not
break during the rest of their walk.

"I do not say," said Aram, after a pause, "that we
are not able to make the happiness of those immediately around us. I speak only of what we can effect
for the mass. And it is a deadening thought to mental
ambition, that the circle of happiness we can create is
formed more by our moral than our mental qualities.
A warm heart, though accompanied but by a mediocre
understanding, is even more likely to promote the happiness of those around, than are the absorbed and abstract, though kindly powers of a more elevated genius:
but" (observing Lester about to interrupt him) "let us
turn from this topic—let us turn from man's weakness to the glories of the Mother-Nature from which
he sprung."

And kindling, as he ever did, the moment he approached a subject so dear to his studies, Aram now
spoke of the stars, which began to sparkle forth—of
the vast illimitable career which recent science had
opened to the imagination—and of the old, bewilder-
ing, yet eloquent theories, which from age to age had
at once misled and elevated the conjecture of past

sages.   All this was a theme to which his listeners
loved to listen, and Madeline not the least.   Youth,
beauty, pomp, what are these, in point of attraction,
to a woman's heart, when compared to eloquence?
The magic of the tongue is the most dangerous of all
spells!

CHAPTER VIII.

The Privilege of Genius.—Lester's Satisfaction at the Aspect of Events.—His Conversation with Walter.—A Discovery.

Alc. I am for Lidian :
This accident, no doubt, will draw him from his hermit's life !

Lis. Spare my grief, and apprehend
What I should speak.

BEAUMONT AND FLETCHER : *The Lover's Progress.*

IN the course of the various conversations our family of Grassdale enjoyed with their singular neighbour, it appeared that his knowledge had not been confined to the closet. At times he dropped remarks which showed that he had been much among cities, and travelled with the design, or at least with the vigilance, of the observer ; but he did not love to be drawn into any detailed accounts of what he had seen, or whither he had been ; an habitual, though a gentle reserve, kept watch over the past—not, indeed, that character of reserve which excites the doubt, but which inspires the interest. His most gloomy moods were rather abrupt and fitful than morose, and his usual bearing was calm, soft, and even tender.

There is a certain charm about great superiority of intellect that winds into deep affections, which a much more constant and even amiability of manners in lesser men often fails to reach. Genius makes many enemies, but it makes sure friends—friends who forgive much, who endure long, who exact little; they partake of the character of disciples as well as friends. There lingers about the human heart a strong inclination to look up-ward—to revere : in this inclination lies the source of religion, of loyalty, and also of the worship and immor-tality which are rendered so cheerfully to the great of old. And, in truth, it is a divine pleasure! admiration seems in some measure to appropriate to ourselves the qualities it honours in others. We wed—we root our-selves to the natures we so love to contemplate, and their life grows a part of our own. Thus when a great man, who has engrossed our thoughts, our conjectures, our homage, dies, a gap seems suddenly left in the world; a wheel in the mechanism of our own being appears abruptly stilled; a portion of ourselves, and not our worst portion—for how many pure, high, generous sentiments it contains—dies with him! Yes! it is this love, so rare, so exalted, and so denied to all ordinary men, which is the especial privilege of great-ness, whether that greatness be shown in wisdom, in enterprise, in virtue, or even, till the world learns better, in the more daring and lofty order of crime. A Socrates may claim it to-day—a Napoleon to-mor-row; nay, a brigand chief, illustrious in the circle in which he lives, may call it forth no less powerfully than the generous failings of a Byron, or the sublime excellence of the greater Milton.

Lester saw with evident complacency the passion
growing up between his friend and his daughter : he
looked upon it as a tie that would permanently reconcile Aram to the hearth of social and domestic life ; a
tie that would constitute the happiness of his daughter,
and secure to himself a relation in the man he felt
most inclined, of all he knew, to honour and esteem.
He remarked in the gentleness and calm temper of
Aram much that was calculated to insure domestic
peace ; and, knowing the peculiar disposition of Madeline, he felt that she was exactly the person, not only
to bear with the peculiarities of the student, but to
venerate their source.   In short, the more he contem-
plated the idea of this alliance, the more he was charmed with its probability.

Musing on this subject, the good squire was one day
walking in his garden, when he perceived his nephew
at some distance, and remarked that Walter, on seeing
him, instead of coming forward to meet him, was about
to turn down an alley in an opposite direction.

A little pained at this, and remembering that Walter
had of late seemed estranged from himself, and greatly
altered from the high and cheerful spirits natural to
his temper, Lester called to his nephew ; and Walter,
reluctantly and slowly changing his purpose of avoid-
ance, advanced and met him.

"Why, Walter!" said the uncle, taking his arm,
"this is somewhat unkind to shun me ; are you engaged in any pursuit that requires secrecy or haste ?"

"No, indeed, sir!" said Walter, with some embarrassment; "but I thought you seemed wrapped in reflection, and would naturally dislike being disturbed."

"Hem! As to that, I have no reflections I wish concealed from you, Walter, or which might not be benefited by your advice." The youth pressed his uncle's hand, but made no reply; and Lester, after a pause, continued :—

"I am delighted to think, Walter, that you seem entirely to have overcome the unfavourable prepossession which at first you testified towards our excellent neighbour. And, for my part, I think he appears to be especially attracted towards yourself: he seeks your company; and to me he always speaks of you in terms which, coming from such a quarter, give me the most lively gratification."

Walter bowed his head, but not in the delighted vanity with which a young man generally receives the assurance of another's praise.

"I own," renewed Lester, "that I consider our friendship with Aram one of the most fortunate occurrences in my life; at least," added he, with a sigh, "of late years. I doubt not but you must have observed the partiality with which our dear Madeline evidently regards him; and yet more, the attachment to her which breaks forth from Aram, in spite of his habitual reserve and self-control. You have surely noted this, Walter?"

"I have," said Walter, in a low tone, and turning away his head.

"And doubtless you share my satisfaction. It happens fortunately now, that Madeline early contracted that studious and thoughtful turn, which, I must own, at one time gave me some uneasiness and vexation. It has taught her to appreciate the value of a mind like Aram's. Formerly, my dear boy, I hoped that at one time or another she and yourself might form a dearer connection than that of cousins. But I was disappointed, and I am now consoled. And indeed I think there is that in Ellinor which might be yet more calculated to render you happy; that is, if the bias of your mind should ever lean that way."

"You are very good," said Walter, bitterly. "I own I am not flattered by your selection; nor do I see why the plainer and less brilliant of the two sisters must necessarily be the fitter for me."

"Nay," replied Lester, piqued, and justly angry; "I do not think, even if Madeline have the advantage of her sister, that you can find any fault with the personal or mental attractions of Ellinor. But, indeed, this is not a matter in which relations should interfere. I am far from any wish to prevent you from choosing throughout the world any one whom you may prefer. All I hope is, that your future wife will be like Ellinor in kindness of heart and sweetness of temper."

"From choosing throughout the world!" repeated Walter: "and how in this nook am I to see the world?"

"Walter, your voice is reproachful!—Do I deserve it?"

Walter was silent.

"I have of late observed," continued Lester, "and with wounded feelings, that you do not give me the same confidence, or meet me with the same affection, that you once delighted me by manifesting towards me. I know of no cause for this change. Do not let us, my son, for I may so call you—do not let us, as we grow older, grow also more apart. Time divides with a sufficient demarcation the young from the old ; why deepen the necessary line ? You know well, that I have never from your childhood insisted heavily on a guardian's authority. I have always loved to contribute to your enjoyments, and shown you how devoted I am to your interests, by the very frankness with which I have consulted you on my own. If there be now on your mind any secret grievance, or any secret wish, speak it, Walter,—you are alone with the friend on earth who loves you best ! "

Walter was wholly overcome by this address ; he pressed his good uncle's hand to his lips, and it was some moments before he mustered self-composure sufficient to reply.

"You have ever, ever been to me all that the kindest parent, the tenderest friend, could have been :—believe me, I am not ungrateful. If of late I have been altered, the cause is not in you. Let me speak freely : you encourage me to do so. I am young, my temper is restless : I have a love of enterprise and adventure : is it not natural that I should long to see the world ? This is the cause of my late abstraction of mind. I have now told you all : it is for you to decide."

Lester looked wistfully on his nephew's countenance before he replied—

"It is as I gathered," said he, "from various remarks which you have lately let fall. I cannot blame your wish to leave us ; it is certainly natural : nor can I oppose it. Go, Walter, when you will."

The young man turned round with a lighted eye and flushed cheek.

"And why, Walter," said Lester, interrupting his thanks, "why this surprise ; why this long doubt of my affection ? Could you believe I should refuse a wish that, at your age, I should have expressed myself ? You have wronged me ; you might have saved a world of pain to us both by acquainting me with your desire when it was first formed : but, enough. I see Madeline and Aram approach,—let us join them now, and to-morrow we will arrange the time and method of your departure."

"Forgive me, sir," said Walter, stopping abruptly as the glow faded from his cheek, " I have not yet recovered myself; I am not fit for other society than yours. Excuse my joining my cousin, and——"

"Walter !" said Lester, also stopping short, and looking full on his nephew ; "a painful thought flashes upon me ! Would to Heaven I may be wrong !—Have you ever felt for Madeline more tenderly than for her sister ?"

Walter literally trembled as he stood. The tears rushed into Lester's eyes :—he grasped his nephew's hand warmly—

"God comfort thee, my poor boy!" said he, with great emotion; "I never dreamed of this."

Walter felt now that he was understood. He gratefully returned the pressure of his uncle's hand, and then, withdrawing his own, darted down one of the intersecting walks, and was almost instantly out of sight.

CHAPTER IX.

The state of Walter's mind.—An Angler and a Man of the World.—
A Companion found for Walter.

This great disease for love I dre,*
  There is no tongue can tell the woe;
I love the love that loves not me,
  I may not mend, but mourning mo.
                    The Mourning Maiden.

I in these flowery meads would be,
These crystal streams should solace me,
To whose harmonious bubbling voice,
I with my angle would rejoice.—IZAAK WALTON.

WHEN Walter left his uncle, he hurried, scarcely conscious of his steps, towards his favourite haunt by the
water-side. From a child he had singled out that scene
as the witness of his early sorrows or boyish schemes ;
and still the solitude of the place cherished the habits
of his boyhood.

Long had he, unknown to himself, nourished an
attachment to his beautiful cousin; nor did he awaken
to the secret of his heart, until, with an agonising jealousy, he penetrated the secret at her own. The reader
has, doubtless, already perceived that it was this jealousy which at the first occasioned Walter's dislike to
Aram : the consolation of that dislike was forbid him

* Bear.

now. The gentleness and forbearance of the student's deportment had taken away all ground of offence ; and Walter had sufficient generosity to acknowledge his merits, while tortured by their effect. Silently, till this day, he had gnawed his heart, and found for its despair no confidant and no comfort. The only wish that he cherished was a feverish and gloomy desire to leave the scene which witnessed the triumph of his rival. Everything around had become hateful to his eyes, and a curse had lighted upon the face of home. He thought now, with a bitter satisfaction, that his escape was at hand ; in a few days he might be rid of the gall and the pang which every moment of his stay at Grassdale inflicted upon him. The sweet voice of Madeline he should hear no more, subduing its silver sound for his rival's ear :—no more he should watch apart, and himself unheeded, how timidly her glance roved in search of another, or how vividly her cheek flushed when the step of that happier one approached. Many miles would at least shut out this picture from his view ; and in absence, was it not possible that he might teach himself to forget? Thus meditating, he arrived at the banks of the little brooklet, and was awakened from his reverie by the sound of his own name. He started, and saw the old corporal seated on the stump of a tree, and busily employed in fixing to his line the mimic likeness of what anglers, and, for aught we know, the rest of the world, call the "violet-fly."

"Ha ! master,—at my day's work, you see ;—fit for

nothing else now. When a musket's half worn out,
schoolboys buy it—pop it at sparrows. I be like the
musket ! but never mind—have not seen the world for
nothing. We get reconciled to all things : that's my
way—augh ! Now, sir, you shall watch me catch the
finest trout you have seen this summer : know where
he lies — under the bush yonder.   Whi—sh ! sir,
whi—sh ! "

The corporal now gave his warrior soul up to the
due guidance of the violet-fly : now he whipped it
lightly on the wave ; now he slid it coquettishly
along the surface ; now it floated, like an unconscious
beauty, carelessly with the tide ; and now, like an
artful prude, it affected to loiter by the way, or to
steal into designing obscurity under the shade of some
overhanging bank. But none of these manœuvres captivated the wary old trout, on whose acquisition the
corporal had set his heart ; and, what was especially
provoking, the angler could see distinctly the dark outline of the intended victim, as it lay at the bottom—
like some well-regulated bachelor, who eyes from afar
the charms he has discreetly resolved to neglect.

The corporal waited till he could no longer blind
himself to the displeasing fact that the violet-fly was
wholly inefficacious ; he then drew up his line, and
replaced the contemned beauty of the violet-fly with
the novel attractions of the yellow-dun.

" Now, sir," whispered he, lifting up his finger, and
nodding sagaciously to Walter. Softly dropped the
yellow-dun on the water, and swiftly did it glide be-

fore the gaze of the latent trout : and now the trout
seemed aroused from his apathy, behold he moved forward, balancing himself upon his fins ; now he slowly
ascended towards the surface : you might see all the
speckles of his coat :—the corporal's heart stood still
—he is now at a convenient distance from the yellow-
dun ; lo, he surveys it steadfastly; he ponders, he see-
saws himself to and fro. The yellow-dun sails away in
affected indifference ; that indifference whets the appetite of the hesitating gazer ; he darts forwards ; he is
opposite the yellow-dun—he pushes his nose against
it with an eager rudeness—he—no, he does *not* bite,
he recoils, he gazes again with surprise and suspicion
on the little charmer ; he fades back slowly into the
deeper water, and then, suddenly turning his tail towards the disappointed bait, he makes off as fast as he
can—yonder—yonder, and disappears ! No, that's he
leaping yonder from the wave : Jupiter ! what a noble
fellow ! what leaps he at ?—A real fly ! "D—n his
eyes !" growled the corporal.

"You might have caught him with a minnow," said
Walter, speaking for the first time.

"Minnow !" repeated the corporal, gruffly ; "ask
your honour's pardon. Minnow !—I have fished with
the yellow-dun these twenty years, and never knew it
fail before. Minnow ! — baugh ! But ask pardon :
your honour is very welcome to fish with a minnow,
if you please it."

"Thank you, Bunting. And pray what sport have
you had to-day."

"Oh,—good, good," quoth the corporal, snatching up his basket and closing the cover, lest the young squire should pry into it. No man is more tenacious of his secrets than your true angler. "Sent the best home two hours ago; one weighed three pounds, on the faith of a man; indeed, I'm satisfied now; time to give up:" and the corporal began to disjoint his rod.

"Ah, sir!" said he, with a half-sigh, "a pretty river this—don't mean to say it is not; but the river Lea for my money. You know the Lea?—not a morning's walk from Lunnun. Mary Gibson, my first sweetheart, lived by the bridge—caught such a trout there, by-the-by!—had beautiful eyes — black, round as a cherry—five feet eight without shoes — might have 'listed in the forty-second."

"Who, Bunting?" said Walter, smiling; "the lady or the trout?"

"Augh!—baugh!—what? Oh, laughing at me, your honour; you're welcome, sir. Love's a silly thing—know the world now—have not fallen in love these ten years. I doubt—no offence, sir, no offence —I doubt whether your honour and Miss Ellinor can say as much."

"I and Miss Ellinor!—you forget yourself strangely, Bunting," said Walter, colouring with anger.

"Beg pardon, sir, beg pardon—rough soldier—lived away from the world so long, words slipped out of my mouth—absent without leave."

"But why," said Walter, smothering or conquering

his vexation — "why couple me with Miss Ellinor? Did you imagine that we—we were in love with each other?"

"Indeed, sir, and if I did, 'tis no more than my neighbours imagine too."

"Humph! your neighbours are very silly, then, and very wrong."

"Beg pardon, sir, again — always getting askew. Indeed some did say it was Miss Madeline; but I says, says I,—'No! I'm a man of the world — see through a millstone; Miss Madeline's too easy like; Miss Nelly blushes when he speaks:' scarlet is Love's regimentals—it was ours in the forty-second, edged with yellow — pepper-and-salt pantaloons! For my part I think—but I've no business to think, howsomever—baugh!"

"Pray, what do you think, Mr Bunting? Why do you hesitate?"

"'Fraid of offence—but I do think that Master Aram — your honour understands — howsomever, squire's daughter too great a match for such as he!"

Walter did not answer; and the garrulous old soldier, who had been the young man's playmate and companion since Walter was a boy, and was therefore accustomed to the familiarity with which he now spoke, continued mingling with his abrupt prolixity an occasional shrewdness of observation, which showed that he was no inattentive commentator on the little and quiet world around him.

"Free to confess, Squire Walter, that I don't quite

like this larned man as much as the rest of 'em—something queer about him—can't see to the bottom of him—don't think he's quite so meek and lamblike as he seems :—once saw a calm, dead pool in foren parts—peered down into it—by little and little, my eye got used to it—saw something dark at the bottom—stared and stared—by Jupiter—a great big alligator !—walked off immediately—never liked quiet pools since—augh, no !"

"An argument against quiet pools, perhaps, Bunting ; but scarcely against quiet people."

"Don't know as to that, your honour—much of a muchness. I have seen Master Aram, demure as he looks, start, and bite his lip, and change colour, and frown—he has an ugly frown, I can tell ye—when he thought no one nigh. A man who gets in a passion with himself may be soon out of temper with others. Free to confess, I should not like to see him married to that stately, beautiful, young lady—but they do gossip about it in the village. If it is not true, better put the squire on his guard—false rumours often beget truths—beg pardon, your honour—no business of mine—baugh ! But I'm a lone man, who have seen the world, and I thinks on the things around me, and I turns over the quid—now on this side, now on the other—'tis my way, sir—and—but I offend your honour."

"Not at all ; I know you are an honest man, Bunting, and well affected to our family : at the same time, it is neither prudent nor charitable to speak harshly of our neighbours without sufficient cause. And really you seem to me to be a little hasty in your judgment of a man so inoffensive in his habits, and so justly and generally esteemed, as Mr Aram."

"May be, sir—may be—very right what you say. But I thinks what I thinks all the same ; and, indeed, it is a thing that puzzles me, how that strange-looking vagabond, as frighted the ladies so, and who Miss Nelly told me—for she saw them in his pocket—carried pistols about him, as if he had been among cannibals and Hottentots, instead of the peaceablest county that man ever set foot in, should boast of his friendship with this larned schollard, and pass I dare swear a whole night in his house ! Birds of a feather flock together—augh !—sir ! "

"A man cannot surely be answerable for the re-spectability of all his acquaintances, even though he feel obliged to offer them the accommodation of a night's shelter ? "

"Baugh !" grunted the corporal. "Seen the world, sir—seen the world—young gentlemen are always so good-natured ; 'tis a pity, that the more one sees the more suspicious one grows. One does not have gump-tion till one has been properly cheated—one must be made a fool very often in order not to be fooled at last !"

"Well, corporal, I shall now have opportunities enough of profiting by experience. I am going to leave Grassdale in a few days, and learn suspicion and wisdom in the great world."

"Augh ! baugh !—what ? " cried the corporal, start-ing from the contemplative air which he had hitherto assumed, "The great world?—how?—when?—going away?—who goes with your honour?"

"My honour's self; I have no companion, unless you like to attend me," said Walter, jestingly; but the corporal affected, with his natural shrewdness, to take the proposition in earnest.

"I! your honour's too good; and, indeed, though I say it, sir, you might do worse: not but what I should be sorry to leave nice snug home here, and this stream, though the trout have been shy lately—ah! that was a mistake of yours, sir, recommending the minnow; and neighbour Dealtry, though his ale's not so good as 'twas last year; and—and—but, in short, I always loved your honour—dandled you on my knees; —you recollect the broadsword exercise!—one, two, three—augh! baugh!—and if your honour really is going, why, rather than you should want a proper person, who knows the world, to brush your coat, polish your shoes, give you good advice—on the faith of a man, I'll go with you myself!"

This alacrity on the part of the corporal was far from displeasing to Walter. The proposal he had at first made unthinkingly, he now seriously thought advisable; and at length it was settled that the corporal should call the next morning at the manor-house, and receive instructions to conclude arrangements for the journey. Not forgetting, as the sagacious Bunting delicately insinuated, "the wee settlements as to wages, and board-wages, more a matter of form, like, than anything else—augh!"

CHAPTER X.

The Lovers.—The Encounter and Quarrel of the Rivals.

Two such I saw, what time the laboured ox,
In his loose traces from the furrow came.—*Comus.*

Pedro. Now do me noble right,
Rod. I'll satisfy you;
But not by the sword.
BEAUMONT AND FLETCHER : *The Pilgrim.*

WHILE Walter and the corporal enjoyed the above conversation, Madeline and Aram, whom Lester left to themselves, were pursuing their walk along the solitary fields. *Their* love had passed from the eye to the lip, and now found expression in words.

"Observe," said he, as the light touch of one, who he felt loved him entirely, rested on his arm—"observe, as the later summer now begins to breathe a more various and mellow glory into the landscape, how singularly pure and lucid the atmosphere becomes. When, two months ago in the full flush of June, I walked through these fields, a grey mist hid yon distant hills and the far forest from my view. Now, with what a transparent stillness the whole expanse of scenery spreads itself before us. And such, Madeline, is the change that has come over myself since that time.

Then, if I looked beyond the limited present, all was
dim and indistinct. Now, the mist has faded away—
the broad future extends before me, calm and bright
with the hope which is borrowed from your love !"

We will not tax the patience of the reader, who
seldom enters with keen interest into the mere dialogue of love, with the blushing Madeline's reply, or
with all the soft vows and tender confessions which
the rich poetry of Aram's mind made yet more delicious to the ear of his dreaming and devoted mistress.

"There is one circumstance," said Aram, "which
casts a momentary shade on the happiness I enjoy—
my Madeline probably guesses its nature. I regret to
see that the blessing of your love must be purchased
by the misery of another, and that other, the nephew
of my kind friend. You have doubtless observed the
melancholy of Walter Lester, and have long since
known its origin ?"

"Indeed, Eugene," answered Madeline, "it has given
me great pain to note what you refer to, for it would
be a false delicacy in me to deny that I have observed
it. But Walter is young and high-spirited ; nor do I
think he is of a nature to love long where there is no
return !"

"And what," said Aram, sorrowfully—"what deduction from reason can ever apply to love ? Love is
a very contradiction of all the elements of our ordinary
nature : it makes the proud man meek—the cheerful,
sad—the high-spirited, tame ; our strongest resolutions,
our hardiest energy, fail before it. Believe me, you

cannot prophesy of its future effect in a man from any
knowledge of his past character. I grieve to think
that the blow falls upon one in early youth, ere the
world's disappointments have blunted the heart, or the
world's numerous interests have multiplied its resources.
Men's minds have been turned when they have not
well sifted the cause themselves, and their fortunes
marred, by one stroke on the affections of their youth.
So at least have I read, Madeline, and so marked in
others. For myself, I knew nothing of love in its
reality till I knew you. But who can know you, and
not sympathise with him who has lost you?"

"Ah, Eugene! you at least overrate the influence
which love produces on men. A little resentment and
a little absence will soon cure my cousin of an ill-placed
and ill-requited attachment. You do not think how
easy it is to forget."

"Forget!" said Aram, stopping abruptly; "ay, forget—it is a strange truth! we *do* forget! The summer
passes over the furrow, and the corn springs up; the
sod forgets the flower of the past year; the battle-field
forgets the blood that has been spilt upon its turf;
the sky forgets the storm; and the water the noonday
sun that slept upon its bosom. All Nature preaches
forgetfulness. Its very order is the progress of oblivion.
And I—I—give me your hand, Madeline—I, ha! ha!
I forget too!"

As Aram spoke thus wildly, his countenance worked;
but his voice was slow and scarcely audible; he seemed

rather conferring with himself than addressing Madeline. But when his words ceased, and he felt the soft hand of his betrothed, and, turning, saw her anxious and wistful eyes fixed in alarm, yet in all unsuspecting confidence, on his face, his features relaxed into their usual serenity ; and kissing the hand he clasped, he continued, in a collected and steady tone—

" Forgive me, my sweetest Madeline. These fitful and strange moods sometimes come upon me yet. I have been so long in the habit of pursuing any train of thought, however wild, that presents itself to my mind, that I cannot easily break it, even in your presence. All studious men—the twilight eremites of books and closets—contract this ungraceful custom of soliloquy. You know our abstraction is a common jest and proverb ; you must laugh me out of it. But stay, dearest !—there is a rare herb at your feet, let me gather it. So, do you note its leaves—this bending and silver flower? Let us rest on this bank, and I will tell you of its qualities. Beautiful as it is, it has a poison."

The place in which the lovers rested is one which the villagers to this day call " The Lady's Seat;" for Madeline, whose history is fondly preserved in that district, was afterwards wont constantly to repair to that bank (during a short absence of her lover, hereafter to be noted), and subsequent events stamped with interest every spot she was known to have favoured with resort. And when the flower had been duly conned, and the study dismissed, Aram, to whom

all the signs of the seasons were familiar, pointed to
her the thousand symptoms of the month which are
unheeded by less observant eyes; not forgetting, as
they thus reclined, their hands clasped together, to
couple each remark with some allusion to his love, or
some deduction which heightened compliment into
poetry. He bade her mark the light gossamer as it
floated on the air; now soaring high—high into the
translucent atmosphere; now suddenly stooping, and
sailing away beneath the boughs, which ever and anon
it hung with a silken web, that by the next morn
would glitter with a thousand dewdrops. "And so,"
said he, fancifully, "does Love lead forth its number-
less creations, making the air its path and empire;
ascending aloof at its wild will, hanging its meshes on
every bough, and bidding the common grass break into
a fairy lustre at the beam of the daily sun!"

He pointed to her the spot, where, in the silent
brake, the harebells, now waxing rare and few, yet
lingered—or where the mystic ring on the soft turf
conjured up the associations of Oberon and his train.
That superstition gave licence and play to his full
memory and glowing fancy; and Shakespeare—Spenser — Ariosto — the magic of each mighty master of
Fairy Realm—he evoked, and poured into her transported ear. It was precisely such arts, which to a
gayer and more worldly nature than Madeline's might
have seemed but wearisome, that arrested and won her
imaginative and high-wrought mind. And thus he,
who to another might have proved but the retired and

moody student, became to her the very being of whom her "maiden meditation" had dreamed—the master and magician of her fate.

Aram did not return to the house with Madeline ; he accompanied her to the garden gate, and then, taking leave of her, bent his way homeward. He had gained the entrance of the little valley that led to his abode, when he saw Walter cross his path at a short distance. His heart, naturally susceptible to kindly emotions, smote him as he remarked the moody listlessness of the young man's step, and recalled the buoyant lightness it was once wont habitually to wear. He quickened his pace, and joined Walter before the latter was aware of his presence.

" Good evening," said he, mildly ; " if you are going my way, give me the benefit of your company."

" My path lies yonder," replied Walter, somewhat sullenly ; " I regret that it is different from yours."

" In that case," said Aram, " I can delay my return home, and will, with your leave, intrude my society upon you for some few minutes."

Walter bowed his head in reluctant assent. They walked on for some moments without speaking, the one unwilling, the other seeking an occasion, to break the silence.

" This, to my mind," said Aram, at length, " is the most pleasing landscape in the whole country; observe the bashful water stealing away among the woodlands Methinks the wave is endowed with an instinctive wisdom, that it thus shuns the world."

" Rather," said Walter, " with the love for change which exists everywhere in nature, it does not seek the shade until it has passed by ' towered cities,' and ' the busy hum of men.' "

" I admire the shrewdness of your reply," rejoined Aram ; " but note how far more pure and lovely are its waters in these retreats, than when washing the walls of the reeking town, receiving into its breast the taint of a thousand pollutions, vexed by the sound, and stench, and unholy perturbation of men's dwelling-place. Now it glasses only what is high or beautiful in nature—the stars or the leafy banks. The wind that ruffles it is clothed with perfumes ; the rivulet that swells it descends from the everlasting mountains, or is formed by the rains of heaven. Believe me, it is the type of a life that glides into solitude, from the weariness and fretful turmoil of the world.

> ' No flattery, hate, or envy lodgeth there.
>   There no suspicion walled in proved steel,
> Yet fearful of the arms herself doth wear ;
>   Pride is not there; no tyrant there we feel.' " *

" I will not cope with you in simile, or in poetry," said Walter, as his lip curved ; " it is enough for me to think that life should be spent in action. I hasten to prove if my judgment be erroneous."

" Are you, then, about to leave us ?" inquired Aram.

" Yes, within a few days."

" Indeed ! I regret to hear it."

* Phineas Fletcher.

The answer sounded jarringly on the irritated nerves of the disappointed rival.

"You do me more honour than I desire," said he, "in interesting yourself, however lightly, in my schemes or fortune."

"Young man," replied Aram, coldly, "I never see the impetuous and yearning spirit of youth without a certain and, it may be, a painful interest. How feeble is the chance that its hopes will be fulfilled! Enough if it lose not all its loftier aspirings as well as its brighter expectations."

Nothing more aroused the proud and fiery temper of Walter Lester than the tone of superior wisdom and superior age which his rival sometimes assumed towards him. More and more displeased with his present companion, he answered, in no conciliatory tone, "I cannot but consider the warning and the fears of one, neither my relation nor my friend, in the light of a gratuitous affront."

Aram smiled as he answered—

"There is no occasion for resentment. Preserve this hot spirit and this high self-confidence, till you return again to these scenes, and I shall be at once satisfied and corrected."

"Sir," said Walter, colouring, and irritated more by the smile than the words of his rival, "I am not aware by what right or on what ground you assume towards me the superiority, not only of admonition but reproof! My uncle's preference towards you gives you no authority over me. That preference I do not

pretend to share."—He paused for a moment, thinking Aram might hasten to reply; but as the student
walked on with his usual calmness of demeanour, he
added, stung by the indifference which he attributed,
not altogether without truth, to disdain,—" and since
you have taken upon yourself to caution me, and to
forebode my inability to resist the contamination, as
you would term it, of the world, I tell you that it may
be happy for you to bear so clear a conscience, so untouched a spirit, as that which I now boast, and with
which I trust in God and my own soul I shall return
to my birthplace. It is not the holy only that love
solitude; and men may shun the world from another
motive than that of philosophy."

It was now Aram's turn to feel resentment; and
this was indeed an insinuation not only unwarrantable
in itself, but one which a man of so peaceable and
guileless a life, affecting even an extreme and rigid
austerity of morals, might well be tempted to repel
with scorn and indignation; and Aram, however meek
and forbearing in general, testified in this instance
that his wonted gentleness arose from no lack of
man's natural spirit. He laid his hand command-
ingly on young Lester's shoulder, and surveyed his
countenance with a dark and menacing frown.

"Boy," said he, " were there meaning in your words,
I should (mark me!) avenge the insult;—as it is, I
despise it. Go!"

So high and lofty was Aram's manner—so majestic
was the sternness of his rebuke and the dignity of his

bearing, as, waving his hand, he now turned away, that Walter lost his self-possession and stood fixed to the spot, abashed, and humbled from his late anger. It was not till Aram had moved with a slow step several paces backward towards his home, that the bold and haughty temper of the young man returned to his aid. Ashamed of himself for the momentary weakness he had betrayed, and burning to redeem it, he hastened after the stately form of his rival, and, planting himself full in his path, said, in a voice half-choked with contending emotions—

"Hold!—you have given me the opportunity I have long desired; you yourself have now broken that peace which existed between us, and which to me was more bitter than wormwood. You have dared—yes, dared to use threatening language towards me! I call on you to fulfil your threat. I tell you that I meant, I desired, I thirsted to affront you. Now resent my purposed, premeditated affront, as you will and can!"

There was something remarkable in the contrasted figures of the rivals, as they now stood fronting each other. The elastic and vigorous form of Walter Lester, his sparkling eyes, his sunburnt and glowing cheek, his clenched hands, and his whole frame alive and eloquent with the energy, the heat, the hasty courage, and fiery spirit of youth : on the other hand, the bending frame of the student, gradually rising into the dignity of its full height—his pale cheek, in which the wan hues neither deepened nor waned, his large eye raised to meet Walter's, bright, steady, and yet how calm! Nothing weak, nothing irresolute, could be traced in that form or that lofty countenance; yet all resentment had vanished from his aspect. He seemed at once tranquil and prepared.

"You design to affront me!" said he; "it is well— it is a noble confession;—and wherefore? What do you propose to gain by it? A man whose whole life is peace, you would provoke to outrage? Would there be triumph in this, or disgrace? A man, whom your uncle honours and loves, you would insult without cause—you would waylay—you would, after watching and creating your opportunity, entrap into defending himself. Is this worthy of that high spirit of which you boasted!—is this worthy a generous anger, or a noble hatred? Away! you malign yourself. I shrink from no quarrel—why should I? I have nothing to fear: my nerves are firm—my heart is faithful to my will; my habits may have diminished my strength, but it is yet equal to that of most men. As to the weapons of the world, they fall not to my use. I might be excused, by the most punctilious, for reject- ing what becomes neither my station nor my habits of life; but I learned thus much from books long since, ' Hold thyself prepared for all things ;'—I am so pre- pared. And as I command the spirit, I lack not the skill to defend myself, or return the hostility of an- other." As Aram thus said, he drew a pistol from his bosom : and pointed it leisurely towards a tree, at the distance of some paces.

"Look," said he, "you note that small discoloured

and white stain in the bark—you can but just observe
it ;—he who can send a bullet through that spot, need
not fear to meet the quarrel which he seeks to avoid."

Walter turned mechanically, and indignant, though
silent, towards the tree. Aram fired, and the ball
penetrated the centre of the stain. He then replaced
the pistol in his bosom, and said—

" Early in life I had many enemies, and I taught
myself these arts. From habit, I still bear about me
the weapons I trust and pray I may never have occasion
to use. But to return. I have offended you—I have
incurred your hatred—why? What are my sins?"

" Do you ask the cause?" said Walter, speaking between his ground teeth. "Have you not traversed my
views—blighted my hopes—charmed away from me
the affections which were more to me than the world,
and driven me to wander from my home with a crushed
spirit and a cheerless heart? Are these no causes for
hate?"

" Have I done this?" said Aram, recoiling, and evidently and powerfully affected. " Have I so injured
you?—It is true! I know it—I perceive it—I read
it in your heart ; and—bear witness Heaven !—I feel
for the wound that I, but with no guilty hand, inflict
upon you. Yet be just :—ask yourself, have I done
aught that you, in my case, would have left undone?
Have I been insolent in triumph, or haughty in success? If so, hate me, nay, spurn me, now."

Walter turned his head irresolutely away.

" If it please you, that I accuse myself, in that I, a

man seared and lone at heart, presumed to come with-in the pale of human affections :—that I exposed my-self to cross another's better and brighter hopes, or dared to soften my fate with the tender and endearing ties that are meet alone for a more genial and youthful nature ;—if it please you that I accuse and curse my-self for this—that I yielded to it with pain and self-re-proach—that I shall think hereafter of what I uncon-sciously cost you, with remorse—then be consoled."

"It is enough," said Walter; "let us part. I leave you with more soreness at my late haste than I will acknowledge ; let that content you : for myself, I ask for no apology or——"

"But you shall have it amply," interrupted Aram, advancing with a cordial openness of mien not usual to him. "I was all to blame; I should have remembered you were an injured man, and suffered you to have said all you would. Words at best are but a poor vent for a wronged and burning heart. It shall be so in future : speak your will, attack, upbraid, taunt me, I will bear it all. And, indeed, even to myself there appears some witchcraft, some glamoury, in what has chanced. What! I favoured where you love? Is it possible? It might teach the vainest to forswear vanity. You, the young, the buoyant, the fresh, the beautiful!—And I, who have passed the glory and zest of life between dusty walls ; I who—well, well, Fate laughs at probabilities."

Aram now seemed relapsing into one of his more abstracted moods; he ceased to speak aloud, but his lips moved, and his eyes grew fixed in reverie on the ground. Walter gazed at him for some moments with fixed and contending sensations. Once more resentment and the bitter wrath of jealousy had faded back into the remoter depths of his mind, and a certain interest for his singular rival, despite of himself, crept into his breast. But this mysterious and fitful nature, —was it one in which the devoted Madeline would certainly find happiness and repose?—would she never regret her choice? This question obtruded itself upon him, and, while he sought to answer it, Aram, regaining his composure, turned abruptly and offered him his hand. Walter did not accept it; he bowed with a cold aspect. "I cannot give my hand without my heart," said he; "we were foes just now; we are not friends yet. I am unreasonable in this, I know, but——"

"Be it so," interrupted Aram; "I understand you. I press my goodwill on you no more. When this pang is forgotten, when this wound is healed, and when you will have learned more of him who is now your rival, we may meet again, with other feelings on your side."

Thus they parted, and the solitary lamp which for weeks past had been quenched at the wholesome hour in the student's home, streamed from the casement throughout the whole of that night: was it a witness of the calm and learned vigil, or of the unresting heart?

CHAPTER XI.

The Family Supper.—The two Sisters in their Chamber.—A Mis-
understanding followed by a Confession.—Walter's approaching
Departure, and the Corporal's behaviour thereon.—The Corporal's Favourite introduced to the Reader.—The Corporal proves
himself a subtle Diplomatist.

———

So we grew together,
Like to a double cherry, seeming parted,
But yet an union in partition.—*Midsummer Night's Dream.*

The corporal had not taken his measures so badly in this stroke of artillery-
ship.—*Tristram Shandy.*

———

IT was late that evening when Walter returned home :
the little family were assembled at the last and lightest
meal of the day ; Ellinor silently made room for her
cousin beside herself, and that little kindness touched
Walter. " Why did I not love *her?* " thought he ; and
he spoke to her in a tone so affectionate, that it made
her heart thrill with delight. Lester was, on the
whole, the most pensive of the group ; but the old
and young man exchanged looks of restored confidence,
which, on the part of the former, were softened by a
pitying tenderness.

When the cloth was removed, and the servants gone,
Lester took it on himself to break to the sisters the
intended departure of their cousin. Madeline received

the news with painful blushes, and a certain self-re-
proach; for even where a woman has no cause to blame
herself, she in these cases feels a sort of remorse at the
unhappiness she occasions. But Ellinor rose suddenly
and left the room.

"And now," said Lester, "London will, I suppose,
be your first destination. I can furnish you with
letters to some of my old friends there : merry fellows
they were once : you must take care of the prodigality
of their wine. There's John Courtland—ah! a seduc-
tive dog to drink with. Be sure and let me know how
honest John looks, and what he says of me. I recollect
him as if it were yesterday; a roguish eye, with a
moisture in it; full cheeks; a straight nose; black
curled hair; and teeth as even as dies :—honest John
showed his teeth pretty often, too : ha, ha! how the
dog loved a laugh! Well, and Peter Hales—*Sir* Peter
now, has his uncle's baronetcy—a generous, open-
hearted fellow as ever lived—will ask you very often
to dinner—nay, offer you money if you want it : but
take care he does not lead you into extravagances : out
of debt out of danger, Walter. It would have been
well for poor Peter Hales, had he remembered that
maxim. Often and often have I been to see him in
the Marshalsea! but he was the heir to good fortunes,
though his relations kept him close; so I suppose he
is well off now. His estates lie in ——shire, on your
road to London! so, if he is at his country-seat, you
can beat up his quarters, and spend a month or so with
him : a most hospitable fellow."

With these little sketches of his contemporaries the good squire endeavoured to while the time, taking, it is true, some pleasure in the youthful reminiscences they excited, but chiefly designing to enliven the melancholy of his nephew. When, however, Madeline had retired, and they were alone, he drew his chair closer to Walter's, and changed the conversation into a more serious and anxious strain. The guardian and the ward sat up late that night; and when Walter retired to rest, it was with a heart more touched by his uncle's kindness than his own sorrows.

But we are not about to close the day without a glance at the chamber which the two sisters held in common. The night was serene and starlit, and Madeline sat by the open window, leaning her face upon her hand, and gazing on the lone house of her lover, which might be seen afar across the landscape, the trees sleeping around it, and one pale and steady light gleaming from its lofty casement like a star.

"He has broken faith," said Madeline; "I shall chide him for this to-morrow. He promised me the light should be ever quenched before this hour."

"Nay," said Ellinor, in a tone somewhat sharpened from its native sweetness, and who now sat up in the bed, the curtain of which was half drawn aside, and the soft light of the skies rested full upon her rounded neck and youthful countenance—"nay, Madeline, do not loiter there any longer; the air grows sharp and cold, and the clock struck one several minutes since. Come, sister, come!"

"I cannot sleep," replied Madeline, sighing, "and think that yon light streams upon those studies which steal the healthful hues from his cheek, and the very life from his heart."

"You are infatuated—you are bewitched by that man," said Ellinor, peevishly.

"And have I not cause—ample cause?" returned Madeline, with all a girl's beautiful enthusiasm, as the colour mantled her cheek, and gave it the only additional loveliness it could receive. "When he speaks, is it not like music?—or rather, what music so arrests and touches the heart? Methinks it is heaven only to gaze upon him, to note the changes of that majestic countenance, to set down as food for memory every look and every movement. But when the look turns to me—when the voice utters my name, ah! Ellinor, *then* it is not a wonder that I love him thus much: but that any others should think they have known love, and yet not loved *him!* And, indeed, I feel assured that what the world calls love is not my love. Are there more Eugenes in the world than one? Who but Eugene *could* be loved as I love?"

"What! are there none as worthy?" said Ellinor, half-smiling.

"Can you ask it?" answered Madeline, with a simple wonder in her voice: "whom would you compare—compare! nay, place within a hundred grades of the height which Eugene Aram holds in this little world?"

"This is folly—dotage," said Ellinor, indignantly;

"surely there are others as brave, as gentle, as kind, and, if not so wise, yet more fitted for the world?"

"You mock me," replied Madeline, incredulously; "whom could you select?"

Ellinor blushed deeply—blushed from her snowy temples to her yet whiter bosom as she answered,—

"If I said Walter Leslie, could you deny it?"

"Walter!" repeated Madeline; "he equal to Eugene Aram!"

"Ay, and more than equal," said Ellinor, with spirit, and a warm and angry tone. "And, indeed, Madeline," she continued, after a pause, "I lose something of that respect which, passing a sister's love, I have always borne towards you, when I see the unthinking and lavish idolatry you manifest to one who, but for a silver tongue and florid words, would rather want attractions than be the wonder you esteem him. Fie, Madeline! I blush for you when you speak; it is unmaidenly so to love any one!"

Madeline rose from the window; but the angry word died on her lips when she saw that Ellinor, who had worked her mind beyond her self-control, had thrown herself back on the pillow, and now sobbed aloud.

The natural temper of the elder sister had always been much more calm and even than that of the younger, who united with her vivacity something of the passionate caprice and fitfulness of her sex. And Madeline's affection for her had been tinged by that character of

forbearance and soothing, which a superior nature often
manifests to one more imperfect, and which in this
instance did not desert her.   She gently closed the
window, and, gliding to the bed, threw her arms
around her sister's neck, and kissed away her tears
with a caressing fondness, that if Ellinor resisted for
one moment, she returned with equal tenderness the
next.

"Indeed, dearest," said Madeline, gently, "I cannot
guess how I hurt you, and still less how Eugene
has offended you?"

"He has offended me in nothing," replied Ellinor,
still weeping, "if he has not stolen away *all* your affection from me.   But I was a foolish girl; forgive me, as
you always do ; and at this time I need your kindness,
for I am very, very unhappy."

"Unhappy, dearest Nell, and why?"

Ellinor wept on without answering.

Madeline persisted in pressing for a reply ; and at
length her sister sobbed out :—

"I know that—that—Walter only has eyes for you,
and a heart for you, who neglect, who despise his love ;
and I—I—but no matter, he is going to leave us, and
of me—poor me, he will think no more !"

Ellinor's attachment to their cousin, Madeline had
long half suspected, and she had often rallied her sister
upon it; indeed, it might have been this suspicion
which made her at the first steel her breast against
Walter's evident preference to herself.   But Ellinor
had never till now seriously confessed how much her

heart was affected; and Madeline, in the natural en-
grossment of her own ardent and devoted love, had
not of late spared much observation to the tokens of
her sister's. She was therefore dismayed, if not surprised, as she now perceived the cause of the peevish-
ness Ellinor had just manifested, and by the nature of
the love she felt herself, she judged, and perhaps somewhat overrated the anguish that Ellinor endured.

She strove to comfort her by all the arguments which
the fertile ingenuity of kindness could invent; she
prophesied Walter's speedy return, with his boyish
disappointment forgotten, and with eyes no longer
blinded to the attractions of one sister by a bootless
fancy for another. And though Ellinor interrupted
her from time to time with assertions,—now of Walter's eternal constancy to his present idol,—now, with
yet more vehement declarations of the certainty of his
finding new objects for his affections in new scenes, she
yet admitted, by little and little, the persuasive power
of Madeline to creep into her heart, and brighten away
its griefs with hope, till at last, with the tears yet wet
on her cheek, she fell asleep in her sister's arms.

And Madeline, though she would not stir from her
post lest the movement should awaken her sister, was
yet prevented from closing her eyes in a similar repose.
Ever and anon she breathlessly and gently raised herself to steal a glimpse of that solitary light afar, and
ever, as she looked, the ray greeted her eyes with an
unswerving and melancholy stillness, till the dawn
crept greyly over the heavens, and that speck of light,

holier to her than the stars, faded also with them beneath the broader lustre of the day.

The next week was passed in preparations for Walter's departure. At that time, and in that distant part of the country, it was greatly the fashion among the younger travellers to perform their excursions on horseback, and it was this method of conveyance that Walter preferred. The best steed in the squire's stables was therefore appropriated to his service, and a strong black horse with a Roman nose and a long tail was consigned to the mastery of Corporal Bunting. The squire was delighted that his nephew had secured such an attendant, for the soldier, though odd and selfish, was a man of some sense and experience, and Lester thought such qualities might not be without their use to a young master, new to the common frauds and daily usages of the world he was about to enter.

As for Bunting himself, he covered his secret exultation at the prospect of change and board-wages with the cool semblance of a man sacrificing his wishes to his affections. He made it his peculiar study to impress upon the squire's mind the extent of the sacrifice he was about to make. The bit cot had been just white-washed, the pet cat just lain in; then, too, who would dig and gather seeds in the garden, defend the plants (plants! the corporal could scarce count a dozen, and nine out of them were cabbages!) from the impending frosts? It was exactly, too, the time of year when the rheumatism paid flying visits to the bones and loins of the worthy corporal; and to think of his "galavanting about the country" when he ought to be guarding against that sly foe, the lumbago, in the fortress of his chimney-corner!

To all these murmurs and insinuations the good Lester seriously inclined,—not with the less sympathy in that they invariably ended in the corporal's slapping his manly thigh, and swearing that he loved Master Walter like gunpowder, and that were it twenty times as much, he would cheerfully do it for the sake of his handsome young honour. Ever at this peroration the eyes of the squire began to twinkle, and new thanks were given to the veteran for his disinterested affection, and new promises pledged him in inadequate return. The pious Dealtry felt a little jealousy at the trust imparted to his friend. He halted, on his return from his farm, by the spruce stile which led to the demesne of the corporal, and eyed the warrior somewhat sourly, as he now, in the cool of the evening, sat without his door arranging his fishing-tackle and flies in various little papers, which he carefully labelled by the help of a stunted pen, that had seen at least as much service as himself.

"Well, neighbour Bunting," said the little landlord, leaning over the stile, but not passing its boundary, "and when do you go? You will have wet weather of it [looking up to the skies]; you must take care of the rumatiz. At your age it's no trifle, eh—hem."

"My age! should like to know—what mean by that! my age indeed!—augh!—bother!" grunted Bunting, looking up from his occupation. Peter

chuckled inly at the corporal's displeasure, and continued, as in an apologetic tone,—

"Oh, I ax your pardon, neighbour.　I don't mean
to say you are too old to travel.　Why there was Hal
Whitol, eighty-two come next Michaelmas, took a trip
to Lunnun last year,—

> 'For young and old, the stout, the poorly,
> The eye of God be on them surely.'"

"Bother!" said the corporal, turning round on his
seat.

"And what do you intend doing with the brindled
cat? put 'un up in the saddle-bags?　You wont surely
have the heart to leave 'un."

"As to that," quoth the corporal, sighing, "the poor
dumb animal makes me sad to think on't."　And, putting down his fish-hooks, he stroked the sides of an
enormous cat, who now, with tail on end, and back
bowed up, and uttering her *lenes susurrus*—*Anglicé*,
purr! rubbed herself to and fro athwart the corporal's
legs.

"What staring there for? won't ye step in, man?
Can climb the stile, I suppose?—augh!"

"No, thank ye, neighbour.　I do very well here,
that is, if you can hear me; your deafness is not so
troublesome as it was last win——"

"Bother!" interrupted the corporal, in a voice that
made the little landlord start bolt upright from the
easy confidence of his position.　Nothing on earth so
offended the perpendicular Jacob Bunting as any insinuation of increasing years or growing infirmities;

but at this moment, as he meditated putting Dealtry to some use, he prudently conquered the gathering anger, and added, like the man of the world he justly plumed himself on being, in a voice gentle as a dying howl,—

"What 'fraid on? come in, there's a good fellow: want to speak to ye. Come do—a-u-g-h!" the last sound being prolonged into one of unutterable coaxingness, and accompanied with a beck of the hand, and a wheedling wink.

These allurements the good Peter could not resist; he clambered the stile, and seated himself on the bench beside the corporal.

"There now, fine fellow, fit for the forty-second," said Bunting, clapping him on the back. "Well, and —a—nd—a beautiful cat, isn't her?"

"Ah!" said Peter, very shortly—for though a remarkably mild man, Peter did not love cats: moreover, we must now inform the reader that the cat of Jacob Bunting was one more feared than respected throughout the village. The corporal was a cunning instructor of all animals: he could teach goldfinches the use of the musket; dogs, the art of the broadsword; horses, to dance hornpipes and pick pockets; and he had relieved the *ennui* of his solitary moments by imparting sundry accomplishments to the ductile genius of his cat. Under his tuition puss had learned to fetch and carry; to turn over head and tail like a tumbler; to run up your shoulder when you least expected it; to fly as if she were mad at any one upon whom the corporal thought fit to set her; and, above all, to rob

larders, shelves, and tables, and bring the produce to
the corporal, who never failed to consider such stray
waifs lawful manorial acquisitions.   These little feline
cultivations of talent, however delightful to the corporal, and creditable to his powers of teaching the young
idea how to shoot, had, nevertheless, since the truth
must be told, rendered the corporal's cat a proverb and
byword throughout the neighbourhood.   Never was
cat in such bad odour ; and the dislike in which it was
held was wonderfully increased by terror ; for the
creature was singularly large and robust, and withal of
so courageous a temper, that if you attempted to resist
its invasion of your property it forthwith set up its
back, put down its ears, opened its mouth, and bade
you fully comprehend that what it feloniously seized it
could gallantly defend.   More than one gossip in the
village had this notable cat hurried into premature
parturition as, on descending at daybreak into her
kitchen, the dame would descry the animal perched on
the dresser, having entered Heaven knows how, and
glaring upon her with its great green eyes, and a malignant *brownie* expression of countenance.

Various deputations had, indeed, from time to time
arrived at the corporal's cottage requesting the death,
expulsion, or perpetual imprisonment of the favourite.
But the stout corporal received them grimly, and dismissed them gruffly, and the cat went on waxing in size
and wickedness, and baffling, as if inspired by the devil,
the various gins and traps set for its destruction.   But
never, perhaps, was there a greater disturbance and

perturbation in the little hamlet, than when, some three weeks since, the corporal's cat was known to be brought to bed, and safely delivered of a numerous offspring. The village saw itself overrun with a race and a perpetuity of corporal's cats ! Perhaps, too, their teacher growing more expert by practice, the descendants might attain to even greater accomplishments than their nefarious progenitor. No longer did the faint hope of being delivered from their tormentor by an untimely or even natural death occur to the harassed Grassdalians. Death was an incident natural to one cat, however vivacious, but here was a dynasty of cats ! *Principes mortales, respublica æterna!*

Now the corporal loved this creature better, yes, better than anything in the world except travelling and board-wages ; and he was sorely perplexed in his mind how he should be able to dispose of her safely in his absence. He was aware of the general enmity she had inspired, and trembled to anticipate its probable result when he was no longer by to afford her shelter and protection. The squire had indeed offered her an asylum at the manor-house ; but the squire's cook was the cat's most embittered enemy ; and what man can answer for the peaceable behaviour of his cook? The corporal, therefore, with a reluctant sigh, renounced the friendly offer; and after lying awake three nights, and turning over in his mind the characters, consciences, and capabilities of all his neighbours, he came at last to the conviction that there was no one with whom he could so safely intrust his cat as Peter Dealtry. It is true, as we said

before, that Peter was no lover of cats ; and the task of
persuading him to afford board and lodging to a cat, of
all cats the most odious and malignant, was therefore
no easy matter. But to a man of the world what
intrigue is impossible ?

The finest diplomatist in Europe might have taken
a lesson from the corporal, as he now proceeded earnestly
towards the accomplishment of his project.

He took the cat, which, by the by, we forgot to say
that he had thought fit to christen after himself, and
to honour with a name, somewhat lengthy for a cat
(but, indeed, this was no ordinary cat !)—viz. Jacobina :
he took Jacobina, then, we say, upon his lap, and,
stroking her brindled sides with great tenderness, he
bade Dealtry remark how singularly quiet the animal
was in its manners. Nay, he was not contented until
Peter himself had patted her with a timorous hand,
and had reluctantly submitted the said hand to the
honour of being licked by the cat in return. Jacobina,
who, to do her justice, was always meek enough in the
presence, and at the will of her master, was, fortunately,
this day on her very best behaviour.

"Them dumb animals be mighty grateful," quoth
the corporal.

"Ah !" rejoined Peter, wiping his hand with his
pocket-handkerchief.

"But, Lord ! what scandal there be in the world !

> 'Though slander's breath may raise a storm,
> It quickly does decay !' "

muttered Peter.

"Very well, very true; sensible verses those," said the corporal, approvingly: "and yet mischief's often done before the amends come. Body o' me, it makes a man sick of his kind, ashamed to belong to the race of men, to see the envy that abounds in this here sublunary wale of tears!" said the corporal, lifting up his eyes.

Peter stared at him with open mouth; the hypocritical rascal continued, after a pause,—

"Now there's Jacobina, 'cause she's a good cat, a faithful servant, the whole village is against her: such lies as they tell on her, such wappers, you'd think she was the devil in garnet! I grant, I grant," added the corporal, in a tone of apologetic candour, "that she's wild, saucy, knows her friends from her foes, steals Goody Solomon's butter; but what then? Goody Solomon's d—d b—h! Goody Solomon sold beer in opposition to you—set up a public; you do not like Goody Solomon, Peter Dealtry?"

"If that were all Jacobina had done!" said the landlord, grinning.

"All! what else did she do? Why, she eat up John Tomkins's canary-bird; and did not John Tomkins, saucy rascal! say you could not sing better nor a raven?"

"I have nothing to say against the poor creature for that," said Peter, stroking the cat of his own accord. "Cats *will* eat birds, 'tis the 'spensation of Providence. But what, corporal!" and Peter, hastily withdrawing his hand, hurried it into his breeches pocket—"but what! did not she scratch Joe Webster's little boy's hand into ribands, because the boy tried to prevent her running off with a ball of string ? "

" And well," grunted the corporal, " that was not Jacobina's doing ; that was my doing. I wanted the string—offered to pay a penny for it—think of that ! "

" It was priced twopence ha'penny," said Peter.

" Augh—baugh ! you would not pay Joe Webster all he asks ! What's the use of being a man of the world, unless one makes one's tradesmen bate a bit ? Bargaining is not cheating, I hope ? "

" Heaven forbid ! " said Peter.

" But as to the bit string, Jacobina took it solely for your sake. Ah, she did not think *you* were to turn against her ! "

So saying, the corporal got up, walked into his house, and presently came back with a little net in his hand.

" There, Peter, net for you, to hold lemons. Thank Jacobina for that ; she got the string. Says I to her one day, as I was sitting, as I might be now, without the door, ' Jacobina, Peter Dealtry's a good fellow, and he keeps his lemons in a bag : bad habit,—get mouldy,—we'll make him a net:' and Jacobina purred (stroke the poor creature, Peter !)—so Jacobina and I took a walk, and when we came to Joe Webster's, I pointed out the ball o' twine to her. So, for your sake, Peter, she got into this here scrape—augh."

" Ah ! " quoth Peter, laughing, " poor puss ! poor pussy ! poor little pussy ! "

" And now, Peter," said the corporal, taking his

friend's hand, "I am going to prove friendship to you
—going to do you great favour."

"Aha!" said Peter, "my good friend, I'm very
much obliged to you.   I know your kind heart, but I
really don't want any——"

"Bother!" cried the corporal; "I'm not the man
as makes much of doing a friend a kindness. Hold jaw!
tell you what,—tell you what: am going away on Wednesday at daybreak, and in my absence you shall——"

"What? my good corporal."

"Take charge of Jacobina!"

"Take charge of the devil!" cried Peter.

"Augh!—baugh!—what words are those?   Listen
to me."

"I won't!"

"You shall!"

"I'll be d—d if I do!" quoth Peter, sturdily.   It
was the first time he had been known to swear since
he was parish clerk!

"Very well, very well!" said the corporal, chucking
up his chin, "Jacobina can take care of herself! Jacobina knows her friends and her foes as well as her
master! Jacobina never injures her friends, never for-
gives foes. Look to yourself! look to yourself! insult
my cat, insult me!   Swear at Jacobina, indeed!"

"If she steals my cream!" cried Peter.

"Did she ever steal your cream?"

"No! but, if——"

"Did she ever steal your cream?"

"I can't say she ever did."

" Or anything else of yours ? "

" Not that I know of ; but——"

" Never too late to mend."

" If——"

" Will you listen to me, or not ? "

" Well."

" You'll listen ? "

" Yes."

" Know, then, that I wanted to do you kindness."

" Humph ! "

" Hold jaw ?   I taught Jacobina all she knows."

" More's the pity ! "

" Hold jaw ! I taught her to respect her friends,—
never to commit herself indoors—never to steal at home
—never to fly at home—never to scratch at home—to
kill mice and rats—to bring all she catches to her master
—to do what he tells her—and to defend his house as
well as a mastiff : and this invaluable creature I was
going to lend you :—won't now, d—d if I do ! "

" Humph ! "

" Hold jaw !   When I'm gone, Jacobina will have
no one to feed her.   She'll feed herself—will go to
every larder, every house in the place—your's best
larder, best house ;—will come to you oftenest.   If
your wife attempts to drive her away, scratch her
eyes out ; if you disturb her, serve you worse than Joe
Webster's little boy :—wanted to prevent this—won't
now, d—d if I do ! "

" But, corporal, how would it mend the matter to
take the devil indoors ? "

"Devil! don't call names. Did not I tell you, only one Jacobina does not hurt is her master?—make you her master; now d'ye see?"

"It is very hard," said Peter, grumblingly, "that the only way I can defend myself from this villanous creature is to take her into my house."

"Villanous! You ought to be proud of her affection. *She* returns good for evil—she always loved you; see how she rubs herself against you—and that's the reason why I selected you from the whole village, to take care of her; but you at once injure yourself and refuse to do your friend a service. Howsomever, you know I shall be with young squire, and he'll be master here one of these days, and I shall have an influence over him—you'll see—you'll see. Look that there's not another 'Spotted Dog' set up—augh!—bother!"

"But what would my wife say, if I took the cat? she can't abide it's name."

"Let me alone to talk to your wife. What would she say if I bring her from Lunnun town a fine silk-gown, or a neat shawl with a blue border—blue becomes her—or a tay-chest, that will do for you both, and would set off the little back parlour? Mahogany tay-chest, inlaid at top—initials in silver, J. B. to D. and P. D.; two boxes for tay, and a bowl for sugar in the middle. Ah! ah! Love me, love my cat! When was Jacob Bunting ungrateful?—augh!"

"Well, well! will you talk to Dorothy about it?"

"I shall have your consent, then? Thanks, my

dear, dear Peter; 'pon my soul you're a fine fellow! you see, you're great man of the parish. If you protect her, none dare injure; if you scout her, all set upon her. For, as you said, or rather sung, t'other Sunday —capital voice you were in, too,—

> ' The mighty tyrants without cause,
> Conspire her blood to shed.' "

"I did not think you had so good a memory, corporal," said Peter, smiling;—the cat was now curling itself up in his lap: "after all, Jacobina—what a deuce of a name!—seems gentle enough."

"Gentle as a lamb, soft as butter, kind as cream, and such a mouser!"

"But I don't think Dorothy——"

"I'll settle Dorothy."

"Well, when will you look up?"

"Come and take a dish of tay with you in half an hour;—you want a new tay-chest; something new and genteel."

"I think we do," said Peter, rising and gently depositing the cat on the ground.

"Aha! we'll see to it!—we'll see? Good-by for the present—in half an hour be with you!"

The corporal, left alone with Jacobina, eyed her intently, and burst into the following pathetic address :—

"Well, Jacobina! you little know the pains I take to serve you—the lies I tells for you—endangered my precious soul for your sake, you jade! Ah! may well rub your sides against me! Jacobina! Jacobina! you be the only thing in the world that cares a button for me. I have neither kith nor kin. You are daughter —friend—wife to me : if anything happened to you, I should not have the heart to love anything else. And body o' me, but you be as kind as any mistress, and much more tractable than any wife ; but the world gives you a bad name, Jacobina. Why? Is it that you do worse than the world do? You has no morality in you, Jacobina; well, but has the world? No ! But it has humbug—you have no humbug, Jacobina. On the faith of a man, Jacobina, you be better than the world !—baugh ! You takes care of your own interest, but you takes care of your master's too. You loves me as well as yourself. Few cats can say the same, Jacobina ! and no gossip that flings a stone at your pretty brindled skin can say half as much. We must not forget your kittens, Jacobina ; you have four left—they must be provided for. Why not a cat's children as well as a courtier's? I have got you a comfortable home, Jacobina ; take care of yourself, and don't fall in love with every tom-cat in the place. Be sober, and lead a single life till my return. Come, Jacobina, we will lock up the house, and go and see the quarters I have provided for you. Heigho !"

As he finished his harangue, the corporal locked the door of his cottage, and, Jacobina trotting by his side, he stalked with his usual stateliness to the "Spotted Dog."

Dame Dorothy Dealtry received him with a clouded

brow; but the man of the world knew whom he had to deal with. On Wednesday morning Jacobina was inducted into the comforts of the hearth of mine host; and her four little kittens mewed hard by, from the sinecure of a basket lined with flannel.

Reader! Here is wisdom in this chapter: it is not every man who knows how to dispose of his cat!

CHAPTER XII.

Fall. Out, out, unworthy to speak where he breatheth,
&c.
Punt. Well, now, my whole venture is forth, I will resolve to depart.
BEN JONSON; *Every Man out of his Humour.*

IT was now the eve before Walter's departure, and on
returning home from a farewell walk among his favourite haunts, he found Aram, whose visit had been
made during Walter's absence, now standing on the
threshold of the door, and taking leave of Madeline
and her father. Aram and Walter had only met twice
before since the interview we recorded, and each time
Walter had taken care that the meeting should be but
of short duration. In these brief encounters Aram's
manner had been even more gentle than heretofore;
that of Walter's more cold and distant. And now, as
they thus unexpectedly met at the door, Aram, looking at him earnestly, said—

"Farewell, sir! You are to leave us for some
time, I hear. Heaven speed you!" Then he added,

in a lower tone, " Will you take my hand, now, in parting ? "

As he said, he put forth his hand—it was the left.

" Let it be the right hand," observed the elder Lester, smiling : " it is a luckier omen."

" I think not," said Aram, drily. And Walter noted that he had never remembered him to give his right hand to any one, even to Madeline ; the peculiarity of this habit might, however, arise from an awkward early habit : it was certainly scarce worth observing, and Walter had already coldly touched the hand extended to him when Lester said, carelessly—

" Is there any superstition that makes you think, as some of the ancients did, the left hand luckier than the right ? "

" Yes," replied Aram ; " a superstition. Adieu."

The student departed ; Madeline slowly walked up one of the garden alleys, and thither Walter, after whispering to his uncle, followed her.

There is something in those bitter feelings which are the offspring of disappointed love ; something in the intolerable anguish of well-founded jealousy, that, when the first shock is over, often hardens, and perhaps elevates the character. The sterner powers that we arouse within us to combat a passion that can no longer be worthily indulged, are never afterwards wholly allayed. Like the allies which a nation summons to its bosom to defend it from its foes, they expel the enemy only to find a settlement for themselves. The mind of every man who *conquers* an un-

fortunate attachment becomes stronger than before ; it
may be for evil, it may be for good, but the capacities
for either are more vigorous and collected.

The last few weeks had done more for Walter's
character than years of ordinary, even of happy emotion, might have effected. He had passed from youth
to manhood, and, with the sadness, had acquired also
something of the dignity of experience. Not that we
would say that he had subdued his love, but he had
made the first step towards it ; he had resolved that
at all hazards it should *be* subdued.

As he now joined Madeline, and she perceived him
by her side, her embarrassment was more evident than
his. She feared some avowal, and from his temper,
perhaps some violence, on his part. However, she
was the first to speak : women, in such cases, always
are.

" It is a beautiful evening," said she, " and the sun
set in promise of a fine day for your journey to-
morrow."

Walter walked on silently ; his heart was full.
" Madeline," he said, at length, " dear Madeline, give
me your hand. Nay, do not fear me ; I know what
you think, and you are right. I loved—I still love
you! but I know well that I can have no hope in
making this confession ; and when I ask you for
your hand, Madeline, it is only to convince you that
I have no suit to press : had I, I would not dare to
touch that hand."

Madeline, wondering and embarrassed, gave him

her hand. He held it for a moment with a trembling clasp, pressed it to his lips, and then resigned it.

"Yes, Madeline, my cousin, my sweet cousin; I have loved you deeply, but silently, long before my heart could unravel the mystery of the feelings with which it glowed. But this—all this—it were now idle to repeat. I know that the heart whose possession would have made my whole life a dream, a transport, is given to another. I have not sought you now, Madeline, to repine at this, or to vex you by the tale of any suffering I may endure: I am come only to give you the parting wishes, the parting blessing, of one who, wherever he goes, or whatever befall him, will always think of you as the brightest and loveliest of human beings. May you be happy, yes, even with another!"

"Oh, Walter!" said Madeline, affected to tears, "if I ever encouraged—if I ever led you to hope for more than the warm, the sisterly affection I bear you, how bitterly I should reproach myself!"

"You never did, dear Madeline; I asked for no inducement to love you—I never dreamed of seeking a motive, or inquiring if I had cause to hope. But as I am now about to quit you, and as you confess you feel for me a sister's affection, will you give me leave to speak to you as a brother might?"

Madeline held out her hand to him with frank cordiality. "Yes!" said she, "speak!"

"Then," said Walter, turning away his head in a spirit of delicacy that did him honour, "is it yet all too late for me to say one word of caution that relates to—Eugene Aram?"

"Of caution! you alarm me, Walter; speak, has aught happened to him? I saw him as lately as yourself. Does aught threaten him? Speak, I implore you—quick!"

"I know of no danger to *him!*" replied Walter, stung to perceive the breathless anxiety with which Madeline spoke; "but pause, my cousin; may there be no danger to you from this man?"

"Walter!"

"I grant him wise, learned, gentle—nay, more than all, bearing about him a spell, a fascination, by which he softens or awes at will, and which even I cannot resist. But yet his abstracted mood, his gloomy life, certain words that have broken from him unawares—certain tell-tale emotions which words of mine, heedlessly said, have fiercely aroused, all united, inspire me—shall I say it?—with fear and distrust. I cannot think him altogether the calm and pure being he appears. Madeline, I have asked myself again and again, is this suspicion the effect of jealousy? do I scan his bearing with the jaundiced eye of disappointed rivalship? And I have satisfied my conscience that my judgment is not thus biased. Stay! listen yet a little while! You have a high, a thoughtful mind. Exert it now. Consider, your whole happiness rests on one step! Pause, examine, compare! Remember, you have not of Aram, as of those whom you have hitherto mixed with, the eyewitness of a

life ! You *can* know but little of his real temper, his
secret qualities ; still less of the tenor of his former
existence. I only ask of you, for your own sake, for
my sake, your sister's sake, and your good father's, not
to judge too rashly. Love him, if you will ; but observe him !"

" Have you done?" said Madeline, who had hitherto
with difficulty contained herself ; " then hear me.
Was it I—was it Madeline Lester whom you asked to
play the watch, to enact the spy upon the man whom
she exults in loving? Was it not enough that *you*
should descend to · mark down each incautious look—
to chronicle every heedless word—to draw dark deduc-
tions from the unsuspecting confidence of my father's
friend—to lie in wait—to hang with a foe's malignity
upon the unbendings of familiar intercourse—to extort
anger from gentleness itself, that you might wrest the
anger into crime? Shame, shame upon you for the
meanness ! And must you also suppose that I, to
whose trust he has given his noble heart, will receive it only to play the eavesdropper to its secrets?
Away !"

The generous blood crimsoned the cheek and brow
of this high-spirited girl, as she uttered her galling
reproof : her eyes sparkled, her lip quivered, her whole
frame seemed to have grown larger with the majesty
of indignant love.

" Cruel, unjust, ungrateful !" ejaculated Walter,
pale with rage, and trembling under the conflict of his
roused and wounded feelings. " Is it thus you answer

the warning of too disinterested and self-forgetful a love?"

"Love!" exclaimed Madeline. "Grant me patience! —Love! It was but now I thought myself honoured by the affection you said you bore me. At this instant, I blush to have called forth a single sentiment in one who knows so little what love is! Love!—methought that word denoted all that was high and noble in human nature—confidence, hope, devotion, sacrifice of all thought of self! but you would make it the type and concentration of all that lowers and debases!—suspicion—cavil—fear—selfishness in all its shapes! Out on you!—*love!*"

"Enough, enough! Say no more, Madeline; say no more. We part not as I had hoped: but be it so. You are changed indeed, if your conscience smite you not hereafter for this injustice. Farewell, and may you never regret, not only the heart you have rejected, but the friendship you have belied." With these words, and choked by his emotions, Walter hastily strode away.

He hurried into the house, and into a little room adjoining the chamber in which he slept, and which had been also appropriated solely to his use. It was now spread with boxes and trunks, some half-packed, some corded, and inscribed with the address to which they were to be sent in London. All these mute tokens of his approaching departure struck upon his excited feelings with a suddenness that overpowered him.

"And it is thus—thus," said he, aloud, "that I am to leave, for the first time, my childhood's home!"

He threw himself on his chair, and covering his face with his hands, burst, fairly subdued and unmanned, into a paroxysm of tears.

When this emotion was over, he felt as if his love for Madeline had also disappeared; a sore and insulted feeling was all that her image now recalled to him. This idea gave him some consolation.

"Thank Heaven!" he muttered, "thank Heaven, I am cured at last!"

The thanksgiving was scarcely over before the door opened softly, and Ellinor, not perceiving him where he sat, entered the room, and laid on the table a purse which she had long promised to knit him, and which seemed now designed as a parting gift.

She sighed heavily as she laid it down, and he observed that her eyes seemed red as with weeping.

He did not move, and Ellinor left the room without discovering him; but he remained there till dark, musing on her apparition; and before he went down stairs he took up the little purse, kissed it, and put it carefully into his bosom.

He sat next to Ellinor at supper that evening, and, though he did not say much, his last words were more to her than words had ever been before. When he took leave of her for the night, he whispered, as he kissed her cheek, "God bless you, dearest Ellinor! and till I return take care of yourself, for the sake of one who loves you *now*, better than anything on earth."

Lester had just left the room to write some letters for Walter; and Madeline, who had hitherto sat absorbed and silent by the window, approached Walter, and offered him her hand.

"Forgive me, my dear cousin," she said, in her softest voice, "I feel that I was hasty, and to blame. Believe me, I am now at least grateful, warmly grateful, for the kindness of your motives."

"Not so," said Walter, bitterly; "the advice of a friend is only meanness."

"Come, come, forgive me; pray do not let us part unkindly. When did we ever quarrel before? I was wrong, grievously wrong—I will perform any penance you may enjoin."

"Agreed, then: follow my admonitions."

"Ah! anything else," said Madeline, gravely, and colouring deeply.

Walter said no more: he pressed her hand lightly, and turned away.

"Is all forgiven?" said she, in so bewitching a tone, and with so bright a smile, that Walter, against his conscience, answered "Yes."

The sisters left the room; I know not which of the two received his last glance.

Lester now returned with the letters. "There is one charge, my dear boy," said he, in concluding the moral injunctions and experienced suggestions with which the young generally leave the ancestral home— "there is one charge which I need not commend to your ingenuity and zeal. You know my strong con-

viction, that your father, my poor brother, still lives.
Is it necessary for me to tell you to exert yourself by
all ways, and in all means, to discover some clue to his
fate? Who knows," added Lester, with a smile, "but
that you may find him a rich nabob? I confess that
I should feel but little surprise if it were so; but, at
all events, you will make every possible inquiry. I
have written down in this paper the few particulars
concerning him which I have been enabled to glean
since he left his home; the places where he was last
seen, the false names he assumed, &c. I shall wait
with great anxiety for any fuller success to your
researches."

"You needed not, my dear uncle," said Walter,
seriously, "to have spoken to me on this subject. No
one, not even yourself, can have felt what I have—can
have cherished the same anxiety, nursed the same hope,
indulged the same conjecture. I have not, it is true,
often of late years spoken to you on a matter so near
to us both; but I have spent whole hours in guesses
at my father's fate, and in dreams that for me was
reserved the proud task to discover it. I will not say,
indeed, that it makes at this moment the chief motive
for my desire to travel, but in travel it will become my
chief object. Perhaps I may find him not only rich—
that, for my part, is but a minor wish—but sobered,
and reformed from the errors and wildness of his earlier
manhood. Oh, what should be his gratitude to you
for all the care with which you have supplied to the
forsaken child the father's place; and not the least,

that you have, in softening the colours of his conduct, taught me still to prize and seek for a father's love!"

"You have a kind heart, Walter," said the good old man, pressing his nephew's hand, "and that has more than repaid me for the little I have done for you : it is better to sow a good heart with kindness than a field with corn, for the heart's harvest is perpetual."

Many and earnest, that night, were the meditations of Walter Lester. He was about to quit the home in which youth had been passed—in which first love had been formed and blighted : the world was before him ; but there was something more grave than pleasure— more steady than enterprise—that beckoned him to its paths. The deep mystery that for so many years had hung over the fate of his parent, it might indeed be his lot to pierce ; and with a common waywardness in our nature, the restless son felt his interest in that parent the livelier, from the very circumstance of remembering nothing of his person. Affection had been nursed by curiosity and imagination ; and the bad father was thus more fortunate in winning the heart of the son, than had he, perhaps by the tenderness of years, deserved that affection.

Oppressed and feverish, Walter opened the lattice of his room, and looked forth on the night. The broad harvest-moon was in the heavens, and filled the air as with a softer and holier day. At a distance its light just gave the dark outline of Aram's house, and beneath the window it lay, bright and steady, on the green still churchyard that adjoined the house. The·

air and the light allayed the fitfulness at the young man's heart, but served to solemnise the project and desire with which it beat. Still leaning from the casement, with his eyes fixed upon the tranquil scene below, he poured forth the prayer, that to his hands might the discovery of his lost sire be granted. The prayer seemed to lift the oppression from his breast; he felt cheerful and relieved, and, flinging himself on his bed, soon fell into the sound and healthful sleep of youth. And oh! let Youth cherish that happiest of earthly boons while yet it is at its command;—for there cometh the day to all, when "neither the voice of the lute nor the birds"* shall bring back the sweet slumbers that fell on their young eyes as unbidden as the dews. It is a dark epoch in a man's life when sleep forsakes him; when he tosses to and fro, and thought will not be silenced; when the drug and draught are the courtiers of stupefaction, not sleep; when the down pillow is as a knotted log; when the eyelids close but with an effort, and there is a drag, and a weight, and a dizziness in the eyes at morn. Desire, and grief, and love, these are the young man's torments; but they are the creatures of time : time removes them as it brings, and the vigils we keep, "while the evil days come not," if weary, are brief and few. But memory, and care, and ambition, and avarice, *these* are demon-gods that defy the Time that fathered them. The worldlier passions are the growth of mature years, and their grave is dug but in our own.

* Non avium citharæque, &c.—*Horat.*

As the dark spirits in the northern tale, that watch against the coming of one of a brighter and holier race, lest, if he seize them unawares, he bind them prisoners in his chain, they keep ward at night over the entrance of that deep cave—the human heart—and scare away the angel Sleep.

BOOK II.

CHAPTER I.

The Marriage settled.—Lester's Hopes and Schemes.—Gaiety of Temper a good Speculation.—The Truth and Fervour of Aram's Love.

Love is better than a pair of spectacles, to make everything seem greater which is seen through it.—Sir Philip Sidney: Arcadia.

ARAM's affection to Madeline having now been formally announced to Lester, and Madeline's consent having been somewhat less formally obtained, it only remained to fix the time for their wedding. Though Lester forbore to question Aram as to his circumstances, the student frankly confessed that, if not affording what the generality of persons would consider even a competence, they enabled one of his moderate wants and retired life (especially in the remote and cheap district in which they lived) to dispense with all fortune in a wife, who, like Madeline, was equally with himself enamoured of obscurity. The good Lester, however, proposed to bestow upon his daughter such a portion as might allow for the wants of an increased family, or the probable contingencies of Fate. For though Fortune may often slacken her wheel, there is no spot in which she suffers it to be wholly still.

It was now the middle of September, and by the end of the ensuing month it was agreed that the espousals of the lovers should be held. It is certain that Lester felt one pang for his nephew as he subscribed to this proposal; but he consoled himself with recurring to a hope he had long cherished—viz., that Walter would return home not only cured of his vain attachment to Madeline, but with the disposition to admit the attractions of her sister. A marriage between these two cousins had for years been his favourite project. The lively and ready temper of Ellinor, her household turn, her merry laugh, a winning playfulness that characterised even her defects, were all more after Lester's secret heart than the graver and higher nature of his elder daughter. This might mainly be that they were traits of disposition that more reminded him of his lost wife, and were, therefore, more accordant with his ideal standard of perfection; but I incline also to believe that the more persons advance in years, the more even, if of staid and sober temper themselves, they love gaiety and elasticity in youth. I have often pleased myself by observing, in some happy family circle embracing all ages, that it is the liveliest and wildest child that charms the grandsire the most.

And after all it is, perhaps, with characters as with books—the grave and thoughtful may be more admired than the light and cheerful, but they are less liked; it is not only that the former, being of a more abstruse and recondite nature, find fewer persons capable of judging of their merits, but also that the great object of the majority of human beings is to be amused, and that they naturally incline to love those the best who amuse them most. And to so great a practical extent is this preference pushed, that I think, were a nice observer to make a census of all those who have received legacies or dropped unexpectedly into fortunes, he would find that where one grave disposition had so benefited, there would be at least twenty gay. Perhaps, however, it may be said that I am here taking the cause for the effect.

But to return from our speculative disquisitions. Lester, then, who, though he had so slowly discovered his nephew's passion for Madeline, had long since guessed the secret of Ellinor's affection for him, looked forward with a hope rather sanguine than anxious to the ultimate realisation of his cherished domestic scheme. And he pleased himself with thinking that when all soreness would, by this double wedding, be banished from Walter's mind, it would be impossible to conceive a family group more united or more happy.

And Ellinor herself, ever since the parting words of her cousin, had seemed, so far from being inconsolable for his absence, more bright of cheek and elastic of step than she had been for months before. What a world of all feelings which forbid despondence, lies hoarded in the hearts of the young! As one fountain is filled by the channels that exhaust another, we cherish wisdom at the expense of hope. It thus happened, from one cause or another, that Walter's absence created a less cheerless blank in the family circle than might have been expected; and the approaching bridals of Madeline and her lover naturally diverted, in a great measure, the thoughts of each, and engrossed their conversation.

Whatever might be Madeline's infatuation as to the merits of Aram, one merit, the greatest of all in the eyes of a woman who loves, he at least possessed. Never was mistress more burningly and deeply loved than she, who, for the first time, awoke the long-slumbering passions in the heart of Eugene Aram. Every day the ardour of his affections seemed to increase. With what anxiety he watched her footsteps! with what idolatry he hung upon her words! with what unspeakable and yearning emotion he gazed upon the changeful eloquence of her cheek! Now that Walter was gone, he almost took up his abode at the manor-house. He came thither in the early morning, and rarely returned home before the family retired for the night; and even then, when all was hushed, and they believed him in his solitary home, he lingered for hours around the house, to look up to Madeline's window, charmed to the spot which held the intoxication of her presence. Madeline discovered this habit, and chid it; but so tenderly, that it was not cured. And still at times, by the autumnal moon, she marked from her window his dark figure gliding among the shadows of the trees, or pausing by the lowly tombs in the still churchyard—the resting-place of hearts that once, perhaps, beat as wildly as his own.

It was impossible that a love of this order, and from one so richly gifted as Aram—a love, which in substance was truth, and yet in language poetry—could fail wholly to subdue and enthral a girl so young, so romantic, so enthusiastic as Madeline Lester. How intense and delicious must have been her sense of happiness! In the pure heart of a girl loving for the first time, love is far more ecstatic than in man, inasmuch as it is unfevered by desire; love, then and there, makes the only state of human existence which is at once capable of calmness and transport!

CHAPTER II.

A favourable specimen of a Nobleman and a Courtier.—A Man of
some Faults and many Accomplishments.

***

*Titinius Capito is to rehearse. He is a man of an excellent disposition,
and to be numbered among the chief ornaments of his age. He cultivates
literature—he loves men of learning, &c.—LORD ORRERY's Pliny.*

***

ABOUT this time, the Earl of ——, the great nobleman of the district, and whose residence was within a
few miles of Grassdale, came down to pay his wonted
yearly visit to his country domains. He was a man
well known in the history of the times; though, for
various reasons, I conceal his name. He was a courtier
—deep, wily, accomplished; but capable of generous
sentiments and enlarged views. Though, from regard
to his interests, he seized and lived as it were upon the
fleeting spirit of the day, the penetration of his intellect went far beyond its reach. He claims the merit of
having been the one, of all his contemporaries (Lord
Chesterfield alone excepted), who most clearly saw and
most distinctly prophesied the dark and fearful storm
that, at the close of the century, burst over France—
visiting indeed the sins of the fathers upon the sons.

From the small circle of pompous trifles in which the

dwellers of a court are condemned to live, and which
he brightened by his abilities and graced by his accomplishments, the sagacious and far-sighted mind of Lord
—— comprehended the vast field without, usually invisible to those of his habits and profession. Men
who the best know the little nucleus which is called the
world, are often the most ignorant of mankind; but it
was the peculiar attribute of this nobleman, that he
could not only analyse the external customs of his
species, but also penetrate into their deeper and more
hidden interests.

The works and correspondence he has left behind
him, though far from voluminous, testify a consum-
mate knowledge of the varieties of human nature.
The refinement of his taste appears less remarkable
than the vigour of his understanding. It might be
that he knew the vices of men better than their
virtues; yet he was no shallow disbeliever in the
latter: he read the heart too accurately not to know
that it is guided as often by its affections as its interests. In his early life he had incurred, not without
truth, the charge of licentiousness; but, even in pursuit of pleasure, he had been neither weak on the
one hand, nor gross on the other—neither the head-
long dupe nor the callous sensualist; but his graces,
his rank, his wealth, had made his conquests a matter
of too easy purchase; and hence, like all voluptuaries,
the part of his worldly knowledge which was the most
fallible, was that which related to the sex. He judged
of women by a standard too distinct from that by which

he judged of men, and considered those foibles peculiar
to the sex, which in reality are incident to human
nature.

His natural disposition was grave and reflective; and
though he was not without wit, it was rarely used. He
lived, necessarily, with the frivolous and the ostenta-
tious; yet ostentation and frivolity were charges never
brought against himself. As a diplomatist and a states-
man, he was of the old and erroneous school of intriguers;
but his favourite policy was the science of conciliation.
He was one who would so far have suited the present
age, that no man could better have steered a nation from
the chances of war : James I. could not have been inspired with a greater affection for peace; but the peer's
dexterity would have made that peace as honourable as
the king's weakness made it degraded. Ambitious to
a certain extent, but neither grasping nor mean, he
never obtained for his genius the 'full and extensive
field it probably deserved. He loved a happy life
above all things; and he knew that, while activity is
the spirit, fatigue is the bane, of happiness.

In his day he enjoyed a large share of that public
attention which generally bequeaths fame; yet, from
several causes (of which his own moderation is not the
least), his present reputation is infinitely less great than
the opinions of his most distinguished contemporaries
foreboded.

It is a more difficult matter for men of high rank to
become illustrious to posterity, than for persons in a
sterner and more wholesome walk of life. Even the

greatest among the distinguished men of the patrician
order, suffer in the eyes of the after-age for the very
qualities, chiefly dazzling defects or brilliant eccentricities, which made them most popularly remarkable in
their day.   Men forgive Burns his amours and his
revellings, with greater ease than they will forgive
Bolingbroke and Byron for the same offences.

Our earl was fond of the society of literary men ; he
himself was well, perhaps even deeply, read.   Certainly
his intellectual acquisitions were more profound than
they have been generally esteemed, though, with the
common subtlety of a ready genius, he could make the
quick adaptation of a timely fact, acquired for the
occasion, appear the rich overflowing of a copious
erudition.   He was a man who instantly perceived, and
liberally acknowledged, the merits of others.   No con-
noisseur had a more felicitous knowledge of the arts, or
was more just in the general objects of his patronage.
In short, what with all his advantages, he was one whom
an aristocracy may boast of, though a people may forget ; and, if not a great man, was at least a most remarkable lord.

The Earl of ——, in his last visit to his estates, had
not forgotten to seek out the eminent scholar who shed
an honour upon his neighbourhood; he had been greatly
struck with the bearing and conversation of Aram ; and
with the usual felicity with which the accomplished earl
adapted his nature to those with whom he was thrown,
he had succeeded in ingratiating himself with Aram in
return.   He could not, indeed, persuade the haughty

and solitary student to visit him at the castle ; but the earl did not disdain to seek any one from whom he could obtain instruction, and he had twice or thrice voluntarily encountered Aram, and effectually drawn him from his reserve. The earl now heard with some pleasure, and more surprise, that the austere recluse was about to be married to the beauty of the county, and he resolved to seize the first occasion to call at the manor-house to offer his compliments and congratulations to its inmates.

Sensible men of rank who, having enjoyed their dignity from their birth, may reasonably be expected to grow occasionally tired of it, often like mixing with those the most who are the least dazzled by the condescension : I do not mean to say, with the vulgar *parvenus* who mistake rudeness for independence—no man forgets respect to another who knows the value of respect to himself; but the respect should be paid easily; it is not every *Grand Seigneur* who, like *Louis the Fourteenth*, is only pleased when he puts those he addresses out of countenance.

There was, therefore, much in the simplicity of Lester's manners and those of his nieces, which rendered the family at the manor-house especial favourites with Lord ——— ; and the wealthier but less honoured squirearchs of the county, stiff in awkward pride, and bustling with yet more awkward veneration, heard with astonishment and anger of the numerous visits which his lordship, in his brief sojourn at the castle, always contrived to pay to the Lesters, and the constant in-

vitations which they received to his most familiar fes-
tivities.

Lord —— was no sportsman; and one morning,
when all his guests were engaged among the stubbles
of September, he mounted his quiet palfrey, and gladly
took his way to the manor-house.

It was towards the latter end of the month, and one
of the earliest of the autumnal fogs hung thinly over
the landscape. As the earl wound along the sides of
the hill on which his castle was built, the scene on
which he gazed below received from the grey mists
capriciously hovering over it, a dim and melancholy
wildness. A broader and whiter vapour, that streaked
the lower part of the valley, betrayed the course of the
rivulet; and beyond, to the left, rose, wan and spectral,
the spire of the little church adjoining Lester's abode.
As the horseman's eye wandered to this spot, the sun
suddenly broke forth, and lit up as by enchantment
the quiet and lovely hamlet, imbedded as it were
beneath—the cottages, with their gay gardens and jas-
mined porches—the streamlet half in mist, half in
light, while here and there columns of vapour rose
above its surface like the chariots of the water genii,
and broke into a thousand hues beneath the smiles of
the unexpected sun; but far to the right, the mists
around it yet unbroken, and the outline of its form
only visible, rose the lone house of the student, as if
there the sadder spirits of the air yet rallied their
broken armament of mist and shadow.

The earl was not a man peculiarly alive to scenery,

but he now involuntarily checked his horse, and gazed
for a few moments on the beautiful and singular aspect
which the landscape had so suddenly assumed.   As he
so gazed, he observed in a field at some little distance
three or four persons gathered round a bank, and
among them he thought he recognised the comely form
of Rowland Lester.   A second inspection convinced
him that he was right in his conjecture, and, turning
from the road through a gap in the hedge, he made
towards the group in question.   He had not proceeded
far, before he saw that the remainder of the party was
composed of Lester's daughters, the lover of the elder,
and a fourth, whom he recognised as a celebrated
French botanist, who had lately arrived in England,
and who was now making an amateur excursion throughout the more attractive districts of the island.

The earl guessed rightly, that Monsieur de N——
had not neglected to apply to Aram for assistance in a
pursuit which the latter was known to have cultivated
with such success, and that he had been conducted
hither as to a place affording some specimen or another
not unworthy of research.   He now, giving his horse
to his groom, joined the group.

CHAPTER III.

Wherein the Earl and the Student converse on grave but delightful matters.—The Student's notion of the only earthly Happiness.

> *Aram.* If the witch Hope forbids us to be wise,
> Yet when I turn to these—Woe's only friends,
>   [*Pointing to his books.*
> And with their weird and eloquent voices calm
> The stir and Babel of the world within,
> I can but dream that my vexed years at last
> Shall find the quiet of a hermit's cell;
> And, neighbouring not this worn and jaded world,
> Beneath the lambent eyes of the loved stars,
> And with the hollow rocks and sparry caves,
> The tides, and all the many-musicked winds,
> My oracles and co-mates;—watch my life
> Glide down the Stream of Knowledge, and behold
> Its waters with a musing stillness glass
> The thousand hues of Nature and of Heaven.
>   *From "Eugene Aram," a MS. Tragedy.*

THE earl continued with the party he had joined; and
when their occupation was concluded, and they turned
homeward, he accepted the squire's frank invitation to
partake of some refreshment at the manor-house. It
so chanced, or perhaps the earl so contrived it, that
Aram and himself, in their way to the village, lingered
a little behind the rest, and that their conversation was
thus, for a few minutes, not altogether general.

"Is it I, Mr Aram," said the earl, smiling, "or is it
Fate that has made you a convert? The last time we

sagely and quietly conferred together, you contended
that the more the circle of existence was contracted,
the more we clung to a state of pure and all self-dependent intellect, the greater our chance of happiness.
Thus you denied that we were rendered happier by our
luxuries, by our ambition, or by our affections.   Love
and its ties were banished from your solitary Utopia ;
and you asserted that the true wisdom of life lay solely
in the cultivation—not of our feelings, but our faculties.   You know, I held a different doctrine ; and it is
with the natural triumph of a hostile partisan that I
hear you are about to relinquish the practice of one of
your dogmas ;—in consequence, may I hope, of having
forsworn the theory ? "

"Not so, my lord," answered Aram, colouring
slightly ; "my weakness only proves that my theory
is difficult—not that it is wrong.   I still venture to
think it true.   More pain than pleasure is occasioned
us by others—banish others, and you are necessarily
the gainer.   Mental activity and moral quietude are
the two states which, were they perfected and united,
would blend into happiness.   It is such a union which
constitutes all we imagine of heaven, or conceive of the
majestic felicity of a God."

"Yet, while you are on earth you will be (believe
me) happier in the state you are about to choose," said
the earl.   "Who could look at that enchanting face"
(the speaker directed his eyes towards Madeline) "and
not feel that it gave a pledge of happiness that could
not be broken ? "

It was not in the nature of Aram to like any allusion to himself, and still less to his affections; he turned aside his head and remained silent: the wary earl discovered his indiscretion immediately.

"But let us put aside individual cases," said he— "the *meum* and the *tuum* forbid all general argument: and confess that there is for the majority of human beings a greater happiness in love than in the sublime state of passionless intellect to which you would so chillingly exalt us. Has not Cicero said wisely, that we ought no more to subject too slavishly our affections, than to elevate them too imperiously into our masters? *Neque se nimium erigere, nec subjacere serviliter.*"

"Cicero loved philosophising better than philosophy," said Aram, coldly; "but surely, my lord, the affections give us pain as well as pleasure? The doubt, the dread, the restlessness of love—surely these prevent the passion from constituting a happy state of mind? To me, one knowledge alone seems sufficient to imbitter all its enjoyments—the knowledge that the object beloved must die. What a perpetuity of fear that knowledge creates! The avalanche that may crush us depends upon a single breath!"

"Is not that too refined a sentiment? Custom surely blunts us to every chance, every danger, that may happen to us hourly. Were the avalanche over you for a day, I grant your state of torture; but had an avalanche rested over you for years, and not yet fallen, you would forget that it could ever fall; you would eat, sleep, and make love, as if it were not!"

"Ha! my lord, you say well—you say well," said Aram, with a marked change of countenance; and, quickening his pace, he joined Lester's side, and the thread of the previous conversation was broken off.

The earl afterwards, in walking through the garden (an excursion which he proposed himself, for he was somewhat of a horticulturist), took an opportunity to renew the subject.

"You will pardon me," said he, "but I cannot convince myself that man would be happier were he without emotions; and that to enjoy life he should be solely dependent on himself."

"Yet it seems to me," said Aram, "a truth easy of proof. If we love, we place our happiness in others. The moment we place our happiness in others, comes uncertainty, but uncertainty is the bane of happiness. Children are the source of anxiety to their parents; his mistress to the lover. Change, accident, death, all menace us in each person whom we regard. Every new affection opens new channels by which grief can invade us; but, you will say, by which joy also can flow in:—granted! But in human life is there not more grief than joy? What is it that renders the balance even? What makes the staple of our happiness—endearing to us the life at which we should otherwise repine? It is the mere passive, yet stirring consciousness of life itself!—of the sun and the air—of the physical being; but this consciousness every emotion disturbs. Yet could you add to its tranquillity an excitement that never exhausts itself—that becomes refreshed, not sated, with every new possession—then you would obtain happiness. There is only one excitement of this divine order—that of intellectual culture. Behold now my theory! Examine it—it contains no flaw. But if," renewed Aram, after a pause, "a man is subject to fate solely in himself, not in others, he soon hardens his mind against all fear, and prepares it for all events. A little philosophy enables him to bear bodily pain, or the common infirmities of flesh : by a philosophy somewhat deeper, he can conquer the ordinary reverses of fortune, the dread of shame, and the last calamity of death. But what philosophy could ever thoroughly console him for the ingratitude of a friend, the worthlessness of a child, the death of a mistress ? Hence, only, when he stands alone, can a man's soul say to Fate, 'I defy thee.'"

"You think, then," said the earl, reluctantly diverting the conversation into a new channel, " that in the pursuit of knowledge lies our only *active* road to *real* happiness. Yet here how eternal must be the disappointments even of the most successful! Does not Boyle tell us of a man who, after devoting his whole life to the study of one mineral, confessed himself, at last, ignorant of all its properties ?"

" Had the object of his study been himself, and not the mineral, he would not have been so unsuccessful a student," said Aram, smiling. " Yet," added he, in a graver tone, " we do indeed cleave the vast heaven of Truth with a weak and crippled wing; and often we are appalled in our way by a dread sense of the immensity around us, and of the inadequacy of our own strength. But there is a rapture in the breath of the pure and difficult air, and in the progress by which we compass earth, the while we draw nearer to the stars, that again exalts us beyond ourselves, and reconciles the true student unto all things, even to the hardest of them all—the conviction how feebly our performance can ever imitate the grandeur of our ambition ! As you see the spark fly upwards—sometimes not falling to earth till it be dark and quenched—thus soars, whither it recks not, so that the direction be *above,* the luminous spirit of him who aspires to Truth; nor will it back to the vile and heavy clay from which it sprang, until the light which bore it upward be no more ! "

CHAPTER IV.

A deeper Examination into the Student's Heart.—The Visit to the
Castle.—Philosophy put to the Trial.

I weigh not Fortune's frown or smile,
I joy not much in earthly joys,
I seek not state, I seek not style,
I am not fond of Fancy's toys;
I rest so pleased with what I have,
I wish no more, no more I crave.—JOSHUA SYLVESTER.

THE reader will pardon me if I somewhat clog his interest in my tale by the didactic character of brief conversations I have just given, and which I am compelled
to renew. It is not only the history of his life, but the
character and tone of Aram's mind, that I wish to
stamp upon my page. Fortunately, however, the path
my story assumes is of such a nature that, in order to
effect this object, I shall never have to desert, and
scarcely again even to linger by, the way.

Every one knows the magnificent moral of Goethe's
"Faust." Every one knows that sublime discontent
—that chafing at the bounds of human knowledge—
that yearning for the intellectual paradise beyond,

which "the sworded angel" forbids us to approach
—that daring, yet sorrowful state of mind—that sense
of defeat, even in conquest, which Goethe has embodied—a picture of the loftiest grief of which the
soul is capable, and which may remind us of the profound and august melancholy which the great sculptor
breathed into the repose of the noblest of mythological
heroes, when he represented the god resting after his
labours, as if more convinced of their vanity than elated
with their extent!

In this portrait, the grandeur of which the wild
scenes that follow in the drama we refer to do not
(strangely wonderful as they are) perhaps altogether
sustain, Goethe has bequeathed to the gaze of a calmer
and more practical posterity the burning and restless
spirit—the feverish desire for knowledge more vague
than useful which characterised the exact epoch in the
intellectual history of Germany in which the poem was
inspired and produced.

At these bitter waters, the Marah of the streams of
wisdom, the soul of the man whom we have made the
hero of these pages had also, and not lightly, quaffed.
The properties of a mind, more calm and stern than
belonged to the visionaries of the Hartz and the Dan-
ube, might indeed have preserved him from that thirst
for the Impossible, which gives so peculiar a romance,
not only to the poetry, but the philosophy, of the Ger-
man people. But if he rejected the superstitions, he
did not also reject the bewilderments, of the mind. He
loved to plunge into the dark and metaphysical subtle-

ties which human genius has called daringly forth
from the realities of things—

> "to spin
> A shroud of *thought*, to hide him from the sun
> Of this familiar life, which seem's to be,
> But is not—or is but quaint mockery
> Of all we would believe ; or sadly blame
> The jarring and inexplicable frame
> Of this wrong world : and then anatomise
> The purposes and thoughts of man, whose eyes
> Were closed in distant years ; or widely guess
> The issue of the earth's great business,
> When we shall be, as we no longer are ;—
> Like babbling gossips, safe, who hear the war
> Of winds, and sigh !—but tremble not ! "

Much in him was a type, or rather forerunner, of
the intellectual spirit that broke forth among our coun-
trymen when *we* were children, and is now slowly
dying away amidst the loud events and absorbing
struggles of the awakening world.   But in one respect
he stood aloof from all his tribe—in his hard indifference to worldly ambition and his contempt of fame.
As some sages have considered the universe a dream,
and self the only *reality*, so in his austere and collected
reliance upon his own mind—the gathering in, as it
were, of his resources—he appeared to regard the pomps
of the world as shadows, and the life of his own spirit
the only substance.   He had built a city and a tower
within the Shinar of his own heart, whence he might
look forth, unscathed and unmoved, upon the deluge
that broke over the rest of the earth.

Only in one instance, and that, as we have seen,
after much struggle, he had given way to the emotions

that agitate his kind, and had surrendered himself to
the dominion of another. This was against his theories
—but what theories ever resist love? In yielding,
however, thus far, he seemed more on his guard than
ever against a broader encroachment.   He had admitted one " fair spirit" for his "minister," but it was
only with a deeper fervour to invoke "the desert" as
his "dwelling-place."   Thus, when the earl—who, like
most practical judges of mankind, loved to apply to
each individual the motives that actuate the mass, and
who only unwillingly, and somewhat sceptically, assented to the exceptions, and was driven to search for
peculiar clues to the eccentric instance,—finding, to
his secret triumph, that Aram had admitted one in-
truding emotion into his boasted circle of indifference—
imagined that he should easily induce him (the spell
once broken) to receive another, he was surprised and
puzzled to discover himself in the wrong.

Lord —— at that time had been lately called into
the administration, and he was especially anxious to
secure the support of all the talent that he could
enlist on his behalf. The times were those in which
party ran high, and in which individual political writings were honoured with an importance which the
periodical press in general has now almost wholly
monopolised.   On the side opposed to government,
writers of great name and high attainments had shone
with peculiar effect, and the earl was naturally desirous
that they should be opposed by an equal array of intellect on the side espoused by himself. The name alone

of Eugene Aram, at a day when scholarship was renown, would have been no ordinary acquisition to the
cause of the earl's party; but that judicious and penetrating nobleman perceived that Aram's abilities, his
various research, his extended views, his facility of
argument, and the heat and energy of his eloquence,
might be rendered of an importance which could not
have been anticipated from the name alone, however
eminent, of a retired and sedentary scholar: he was
not, therefore, without an interested motive in the
attentions he now lavished upon the student, and in
his curiosity to put to the proof the disdain of all
worldly enterprise and worldly temptation which
Aram affected. He could not but think that, to a
man poor and lowly of circumstance, conscious of
superior acquirements, about to increase his wants by
admitting to them a partner, and arrived at that age
when the calculations of interest and the whispers of
ambition have usually most weight:—he could not but
think that to such a man the dazzling prospects of
social advancement, the hope of the high fortunes, and
the powerful and glittering influence which political
life, in England, offers to the aspirant, might be rendered altogether irresistible.

He took several opportunities, in the course of the
next week, of renewing his conversation with Aram,
and of artfully turning it into the channels which he
thought most likely to produce the impression he desired to create. He was somewhat baffled, but by no
means dispirited, in his attempts; but he resolved to

defer his ultimate proposition until it could be made
to the fullest advantage. He had engaged the Lesters
to promise to pass a day at the castle ; and with great
difficulty, and at the earnest intercession of Madeline,
Aram was prevailed upon to accompany them. So
extreme was his distaste to general society, and, from
some motive or another more powerful than mere con-
stitutional reserve, so invariably had he for years refused all temptations to enter it, that, natural as this
concession was rendered by his approaching marriage
to one of the party, it filled him with a sort of terror
and foreboding of evil. It was as if he were passing
beyond the boundary of some law, on which the very
tenure of his existence depended. After he had consented, a trembling came over him ; he hastily left the
room, and, till the day arrived, was observed by his
friends of the manor-house to be more gloomy and
abstracted than they ever had known him, even at the
earliest period of acquaintance.

On the day itself, as they proceeded to the castle,
Madeline perceived, with a tearful repentance of her
interference, that he sat by her side cold and rapt ;
and that, once or twice, when his eyes dwelt upon her,
it was with an expression of reproach and distrust.

It was not till they entered the lofty hall of the
castle, when a vulgar diffidence would have been most
abashed, that Aram recovered himself. The earl was
standing—the centre of a group in the recess of a window in the saloon, opening upon an extensive and
stately terrace. He came forward to receive them with

the polished and warm kindness which he bestowed
upon all his inferiors in rank., He complimented the
sisters ; he jested with Lester; but to Aram only
he manifested less the courtesy of kindness than of
respect. He took his arm, and, leaning on it with a
light touch, led him to the group at the window. It
was composed of the most distinguished public men in
the country, and among them (the earl himself was
connected, through an illegitimate branch, with the
reigning monarch) was a prince of the blood-royal. :

To these, whom he had prepared for the introduction,
he severally, and with an easy grace, presented Aram,
and then, falling back a few steps, he watched, with a
keen but seemingly careless eye, the effect which so
sudden a contact with royalty itself would produce on
the mind of the shy and secluded student, whom it was
his object to dazzle and overpower. It was at this
moment that the native dignity of Aram, which his
studies, unworldly as they were, had certainly tended
to increase, displayed itself, in a trial which, poor as it
was in abstract theory, was far from despicable in the
eyes of the sensible and practised courtier. He received
with his usual modesty, but not with his usual shrinking and embarrassment on such occasions, the compliments he received ; a certain and far from ungraceful
pride was mingled with his simplicity of demeanour; no
fluttering of manner betrayed that he was either dazzled
or humbled by the presence in which he stood; and the
earl could not but confess, that there was never a more
favourable opportunity for comparing the aristocracy of

genius with that of birth; it was one of those homely
every-day triumphs of intellect which please us more
than they ought to do, for, after all, they are more
common than the men of courts are willing to believe.

Lord —— did not, however, long leave Aram to the
support of his own unassisted presence of mind and
calmness of nerve; he advanced and led the conversation, with his usual tact, into a course which might at
once please Aram, and afford him the opportunity to
shine. The earl had imported from Italy some of the
most beautiful specimens of classic sculpture which this
country now possesses. These were disposed in niches
around the magnificent apartment in which the guests
were assembled; and as the earl pointed them out, and
illustrated each from the beautiful anecdotes and golden
allusions of antiquity, he felt that he was affording to
Aram a gratification he could never have experienced
before, and in the expression of which the grace and
copiousness of his learning would find vent. Nor was
he disappointed. The cheek, which till then had retained its steady paleness, now caught the glow of
enthusiasm; and in a few moments there was not a
person in the group who did not feel, and cheerfully
feel, the superiority of the one who, in birth and fortune, was immeasurably the lowest of all.

The English aristocracy, whatever be the faults of
their education, have at least the merit of being alive
to the possession, and easily warmed to the possessor,
of classical attainments: perhaps too much so; for

they are thus apt to judge all talent by a classical
standard, and all theory by classical experience.
Without—save in very rare instances—the right to
boast of any deep learning, they are far more susceptible than the nobility of any other nation to the *spiritum
Camœnæ*.   They are easily and willingly charmed back
to the studies which, if not eagerly pursued in their
youth, are still entwined with all their youth's brightest
recollections ; the schoolboy's prize, and the master's
praise, the first ambition, and its first reward.   A felicitous quotation, a delicate allusion, are never lost upon
their ear ; and the veneration which, at Eton, they
bore to the best verse-maker in the school, tinctures
their judgment of others throughout life, mixing, I
know not what, both of liking and esteem, with their
admiration of one who uses his classical weapons with
a scholar's dexterity, not a pedant's inaptitude : for
such a one there is a sort of agreeable confusion in
their respect; they are inclined, unconsciously, to believe
that he must necessarily be a high gentleman—ay, and
something of a good fellow into the bargain.

It happened, then, that Aram could not have dwelt
upon a theme more likely to arrest the spontaneous
interest of those with whom he now conversed—men
themselves of more cultivated minds than usual, and
more capable than most (from that acute perception of
real talent, which is produced by habitual political
warfare) of appreciating not only his endowments, but
his facility in applying them.

" You are right, my lord," said Sir ——, the whipper-in of the —— party, taking the earl aside ; " he would be an inestimable pamphleteer." ·

" Could you get him to write us a sketch of the state of parties ; luminous, eloquent ?" whispered a lord of the bedchamber.

The earl answered by a *bon mot*, and turned to a bust of Caracalla.

The hours at that time were (in the country at least) not late, and the earl was one of the first introducers of the polished fashion of France, by which we testify a preference of the society of the women to that of our own sex ; so that, in leaving the dining-room, it was not so late but that the greater part of the guests walked out upon the terrace, and admired the expanse of country which it overlooked, and along which the thin veil of the twilight began now to hover.

Having safely deposited his royal guest at a whist table, and thus left himself a free agent, the earl, inviting Aram to join him, sauntered among the loiterers on the terrace for a few moments, and then descended a broad flight of steps which brought them into a more shaded and retired walk, on either side of which rows of orange-trees gave forth their fragrance, while, to the right, sudden and numerous vistas were cut amidst the more regular and dense foliage, affording glimpses— now of some rustic statue—now of some lonely temple —now of some quaint fountain, on the play of whose waters the first stars had begun to tremble.

It was one of those magnificent gardens, modelled from the stately glories of Versailles, which it is now the mode to decry, but which breathe so unequivocally of the palace. I grant that they deck Nature with somewhat too prolix a grace ; but is Beauty always best seen in *déshabille ?* And with what associations of the brighest traditions connected with Nature they link her more luxuriant loveliness ! Must we breathe only the *malaria* of Rome to be capable of feeling the interest attached to the fountain or the statue ?

"I am glad," said the earl, "that you admired my bust of Cicero—it is from an original very lately discovered. What grandeur in the brow !—what energy in the mouth and downward bend of the head ! It is pleasant even to imagine we gaze upon the likeness of so bright a spirit ;—and confess, at least of Cicero, that in reading the aspirations and outpourings of his mind, you have felt your apathy to fame melting away ; you have shared the desire to live in the future age,—' the longing after immortality !'"

"Was it not that longing," replied Aram, "which gave to the character of Cicero its poorest and most frivolous infirmity ? Has it not made him, glorious as he is despite of it, a byword in the mouth of every schoolboy ? Whenever you mention his genius, do you not hear an appendix on his vanity ?"

"Yet without that vanity, that desire for a name with posterity, would he have been equally great—would he equally have cultivated his genius ?"

"Probably, my lord, he would not have equally cultivated his genius, but in reality he might have been equally great. A man often injures his mind by the

means that increase his genius. You think this, my
lord, a paradox; but examine it. How many men of
genius have been but ordinary men, take them from
the particular objects in which they shine! Why is
this, but that in cultivating one branch of intellect,
they neglect the rest? Nay, the very torpor of the
reasoning faculty has often kindled the imaginative.
Lucretius is said to have composed his sublime poem
under the influence of a delirium. The susceptibilities
that we create or refine by the pursuit of one object
weaken our general reason; and I may compare with
some justice the powers of the mind to the faculties of
the body, in which squinting is occasioned by an inequality of strength in the eyes, and discordance of
voice by the same inequality in the ears."

"I believe you are right," said the earl; "yet I own
I willingly forgive Cicero for his vanity, if it contri-
buted to the production of his orations and his essays.
And he is a greater man, even with his vanity un-
conquered, than if he had conquered his foible, and, in
doing so, taken away the incitements to his genius."

"A greater man in the world's eye, my lord, but
scarcely in reality. Had Homer written his *Iliad* and
then burned it, would his genius have been less? The
world would have known nothing of him; but would
he have been a less extraordinary man on that account?
We are too apt, my lord, to confound greatness and
fame."

"There is one circumstance," added Aram, after a
pause, "that should diminish our respect for renown.

Errors of life, as well as foibles of character, are often the real enhancers of celebrity. Without his errors, I doubt whether *Henri Quatre* would have become the idol of a people. How many Whartons has the world known, who, deprived of their frailties, had been inglorious! The light that you so admire, reaches you only through the distance of time, on account of the angles and unevenness of the body whence it emanates. Were the surface of the moon smooth it would be invisible."

" I admire your illustrations," said the earl; " but I reluctantly submit to your reasonings. You would then neglect your powers, lest they should lead you into errors ? "

" Pardon me, my lord ; it is because I think *all* the powers should be cultivated, that I quarrel with the exclusive cultivation of one. And it is only because I would strengthen the whole mind that I dissent from the reasonings of those who tell you to consult your genius."

" But your genius may serve mankind more than this general cultivation of intellect ? "

" My lord," replied Aram, with a mournful cloud upon his countenance, " that argument may have weight with those who think mankind *can* be effectually served, though they may be often dazzled, by the labours of an individual. But, indeed, this perpetual talk of 'mankind' signifies nothing : each of us consults his proper happiness, and we consider him a madman who ruins his own peace of mind by an everlasting fretfulness of philanthropy."

This was a doctrine that half pleased, half displeased the earl : it shadowed forth the most dangerous notions which Aram entertained.

"Well, well," said the noble host, as, after a short contest on the ground of his guest's last remark, they left off where they began, "let us drop these general discussions ; I have a particular proposition to unfold. We have, I trust, Mr Aram, seen enough of each other to feel that we can lay a sure foundation for mutual esteem. For my part, I own frankly, that I have never met with one who has inspired me with a sincerer admiration. I am desirous that your talents and great learning should be known in the widest sphere. You may despise fame, but you must permit your friends the weakness to wish *you* justice, and themselves triumph. You know my post in the present administration : the place of my secretary is one of great trust, some influence, and fair emolument. I offer it to you—accept it, and you will confer upon me an honour and an obligation. You will have your own separate house ; or apartments in mine, solely appropriated to your use. Your privacy will never be disturbed. Every arrangement shall be made for yourself and your bride, that either of you can suggest. Leisure for your own pursuits you will have, too, in abundance—there are others who will perform all that is toilsome in the mere details of your office. In London, you will see around you the most eminent living men of all nations, and in all pursuits. If you contract (which believe me is possible—it is a tempting game !)

any inclination towards public life, you will have the most brilliant opportunities afforded you, and I foretell you the most signal success. Stay yet one moment :— for this you will owe me no thanks. Were I not sensible that I consult my own interests in this proposal, I should be courtier enough to suppress it."

"My lord," said Aram, in a voice which, in spite of its calmness, betrayed that he was affected, "it seldom happens to a man of my secluded habits and lowly pursuits to have the philosophy he affects put to so severe a trial. I am grateful to you—deeply grateful for an offer so munificent—so undeserved. I am yet more grateful that it allows me to sound the strength of my own heart, and to find that I did not too highly rate it. Look, my lord, from the spot where we now stand" (the moon had risen, and they had now returned to the terrace); "in the vale below, and far among those trees, lies my home. More than two years ago I came thither to fix the resting-place of a sad and troubled spirit. There have I centred all my wishes and my hopes; and there may I breathe my last! My lord, you will not think me ungrateful that my choice is made; and you will not blame my motive, though you may despise my wisdom."

"But," said the earl, astonished, "you cannot foresee all the advantages you would renounce? At your age—with your intellect—to choose the living sepulchre of a hermitage—it was wise to *reconcile* yourself to it, but it is not wise to *prefer* it! Nay, nay; consider—pause. I am in no haste for your decision;

and what advantages have you in your retreat, that you
will not possess in a greater degree with me? Quiet?
—I pledge it to you under my roof. Solitude?—you
shall have it at your will. Books?—what are those
which you, which any individual, may possess, to the
public institutions, the magnificent collections, of the
metropolis? What else is it you enjoy yonder, and
cannot enjoy with me?"

"Liberty!" said Aram, energetically.—"Liberty!
the wild sense of independence. Could I exchange
the lonely stars and the free air for the poor lights
and feverish atmosphere of worldly life? Could I
surrender my mood, with its thousand eccentricities
and humours—its cloud and shadow—to the eyes of
strangers, or veil it from their gaze by the irksomeness
of an eternal hypocrisy? No, my lord! I am too
old to turn disciple to the world! You promise me
solitude and quiet. What charm would they have
for me if I felt they were held from the generosity
of another? The attraction of solitude is only in its
independence. You offer me the circle, but not the
magic which made it holy. Books! *They*, years
since, would have tempted me; but those whose wisdom I have already drained, have taught me now almost enough: and the two books whose interest can
never be exhausted—Nature and my own heart—will
suffice for the rest of life. My lord, I require no time
for consideration."

"And you positively refuse me?"

"Gratefully refuse you."

The earl peevishly walked away for one moment; but it was not in his nature to lose himself for more.

"Mr Aram," said he, frankly, and holding out his hand, "you have chosen nobly, if not wisely; and though I cannot forgive you for depriving me of such a companion, I thank you for teaching me such a lesson. Henceforth I will believe that philosophy may exist in practice, and that a contempt for wealth and for honours is not the mere profession of discontent. This is the first time, in a various and experienced life, that I have found a man sincerely deaf to the temptations of the world—and that man of such endowments! If ever you see cause to alter a theory that I still think erroneous, though lofty—remember me; and at all times, and on all occasions," he added, with a smile, "when a friend becomes a necessary evil, call to mind our starlight walk on the castle terrace."

Aram did not mention to Lester, or even Madeline, the above conversation. The whole of the next day he shut himself up at home; and when he again appeared at the manor-house he heard, with evident satisfaction, that the earl had been suddenly summoned on state affairs to London.

There was an unaccountable soreness in Aram's mind, which made him feel a resentment—a suspicion against all who sought to lure him from his retreat. "Thank Heaven!" thought he, when he heard of the earl's departure; "we shall not meet for another year!" He was mistaken.—*Another year!*

CHAPTER V.

Being got out of town in the road to Penaflor, master of my own action and forty good ducats, the first thing I did was to give my mule her head, and to go at what pace she pleased.

.   .   .   .

I left them in the inn, and continued my journey; I was hardly got half a mile farther, when I met a cavalier very genteel, &c.—*Gil Blas.*

IT was broad and sunny noon on the second day of their journey, as Walter Lester, and the valorous attendant with whom it had pleased Fate to endow him, rode slowly into a small town, in which the corporal, in his own heart, had resolved to bait his Roman-nosed horse and refresh himself. Two comely inns had the younger traveller of the two already passed with an indifferent air, as if neither bait nor refreshment made any part of the necessary concerns of this habitable world. And in passing each of the said hostelries, the Roman-nosed horse had uttered a snort of indignant surprise, and the worthy corporal had responded to the quadrupedal remonstrance by a loud hem. It seemed, however, that Walter heard neither

of the above significant admonitions; and now the
town was nearly passed, and a steep hill, that seemed
winding away into eternity, already presented itself to
the rueful gaze of the corporal.

"The boy's clean mad," grunted Bunting to himself
—"must do my duty to him—give him a hint."

Pursuant to this notable and conscientious determination, Bunting jogged his horse into a trot, and
coming alongside of Walter, put his hand to his hat
and said—

"Weather warm, your honour—horses knocked up
—next town far as hell !—halt a bit here—augh !"

"Ha! that is very true, Bunting; I had quite forgotten the length of our journey.   But see, there is a
signpost yonder; we will take advantage of it."

"Augh ! and your honour's right—fit for the forty-
second," said the corporal, falling back; and in a few
moments he and his charger found themselves, to their
mutual delight, entering the yard of a small but com-
fortable-looking inn.

The host, a man of a capacious stomach and a rosy
cheek—in short, a host whom your heart warms to
see—stepped forth immediately, held the stirrup for
the young squire (for the corporal's movements were
too stately to be rapid), and ushered him, with a bow,
a smile, and a flourish of his napkin, into one of those
little quaint rooms, with cupboards bright with high
glasses and old china, that it pleases us still to find
extant in the old-fashioned inns, in our remoter roads
and less Londonised districts.

Mine host was an honest fellow, and not above his profession; he stirred the fire, dusted the table, brought the bill of fare, and a newspaper seven days old, and then bustled away to order the dinner, and chat with the corporal. That accomplished hero had already thrown the stables into commotion, and, frightening the two ostlers from their attendance on the steeds of more peaceable men, had set them both at leading his own horse and his master's to and fro the yard, to be cooled into comfort and appetite.

He was now busy in the kitchen, where he had seized the reins of government, sent the scullion to see if the hens had laid any fresh eggs, and drawn upon himself the objurgations of a very thin cook with a squint.

"Tell you, ma'am, you are wrong—quite wrong—seen the world—old soldier—and know how to fry eggs better than any she in the three kingdoms—hold jaw—mind your own business—where's the frying-pan?—baugh!"

So completely did the corporal feel himself in his element, while he was putting everybody else out of the way, and so comfortable did he find his new quarters, that he resolved that the "bait" should be at all events prolonged until his good cheer had been deliberately digested, and his customary pipe duly enjoyed.

Accordingly, but not till Walter had dined—for our man of the world knew that it is the tendency of that meal to abate our activity, while it increases our good humour—the corporal presented himself to his master, with a grave countenance.

" Greatly vexed, your honour—who'd have thought it ?—But those large animals are bad on long march."

" Why, what's the matter now, Bunting ? "

" Only, sir, that the brown horse is so done up, that I think it would be as much as life's worth to go any farther for several hours."

" Very well ; and if I propose staying here till the evening ?—We have ridden far, and are in no great hurry."

" To be sure not—sure and certain not," cried the corporal.   " Ah, master, you know how to command, I see.   Nothing like discretion—discretion, sir, is a jewel.   Sir, it is more than a jewel—it's a pair of stirrups ! "

" A what, Bunting ? "

" Pair of stirrups, your honour.   Stirrups help us to get on, so does discretion ; to get off, ditto discretion.   Men without stirrups look fine, ride bold, tire soon : men without discretion cut dash, but knock up all of a crack.   Stirrups—— but what signifies ? Could say much more, your honour, but don't love chatter."

" Your simile is ingenious enough, if not poetical," said Walter ; " but it does not hold good to the last. When a man falls, his discretion should preserve him ; but he is often dragged in the mud by his stirrups."

" Beg pardon—you're wrong," quoth the corporal, nothing taken by surprise ; " spoke of the new-fangled

stirrups that open, crank, when we fall, and let us out
of the scrape."*

Satisfied with his repartee, the corporal now (like
an experienced jester) withdrew to leave its full effect
on the admiration of his master.　A little before sun-
set the two travellers renewed their journey.

"I have loaded the pistols, sir," said the corporal,
pointing to the holsters on Walter's saddle.　"It is
eighteen miles off to the next town—will be dark long
before we get there."

"You did very right, Bunting, though I suppose
there is not much danger to be apprehended from the
gentlemen of the highway."

"Why, the landlord do say the revarse, your honour—been many robberies lately in these here parts."

"Well, we are fairly mounted, and you are a for-
midable-looking fellow, Bunting."

"Oh! your honour," quoth the corporal, turning
his head stiffly away, with a modest simper, "you
makes me blush; though, indeed, bating that I have
the military air, and am more in the prime of life,
your honour is wellnigh as awkward a gentleman as
myself to come across."

"Much obliged for the compliment!" said Walter,
pushing his horse a little forward: the corporal took
the hint and fell back.

It was now that beautiful hour of twilight when
lovers grow especially tender.　The young traveller

* Of course the corporal does not speak of the patent stirrup:
that would be an anachronism.

every instant threw his dark eyes upward, and thought
—not of Madeline, but her sister.   The corporal himself grew pensive, and in a few moments his whole
soul was absorbed in contemplating the forlorn state
of the abandoned Jacobina.

In this melancholy and silent mood, they proceeded
onward till the shades began to deepen : and by the
light of the first stars Walter beheld a small, spare
gentleman riding before him on an ambling nag, with
cropped ears and mane.   The rider, as he now came up
to him, seemed to have passed the grand climacteric,
but looked hale and vigorous ; and there was a certain
air of staid and sober aristocracy about him, which involuntarily begat your respect.

He looked hard at Walter as the latter approached,
and still more hard at the corporal.   He seemed satisfied with the survey.

" Sir," said he, slightly touching his hat to Walter,
and with an agreeable though rather sharp intonation
of voice, " I am very glad to see a gentleman of your
appearance travelling my road.   Might I request the
honour of being allowed to join you so far as you go ?
To say the truth, I am a little afraid of encountering
those industrious gentlemen who have been lately somewhat notorious in these parts ; and it may be better for
all of us to ride in as strong a party as possible."

" Sir," replied Walter, eyeing in his turn the speaker,
and in his turn also feeling satisfied with the scrutiny,
" I am going to ——, where I shall pass the night on my
way to town, and shall be very happy in your company."

The corporal uttered a loud hem; that penetrating man of the world was not too well pleased with the advances of a stranger.

"What fools them boys be!" thought he, very discontentedly. "Howsomever, the man does seem like a decent country gentleman, and we are two to one: besides, he's old, little, and—augh baugh—I daresay we are safe enough, for all that *he* can do."

The stranger possessed a polished and well-bred demeanour; he talked freely and copiously, and his conversation was that of a shrewd and cultivated man. He informed Walter, that not only the roads had been infested by those more daring riders common at that day, and to whose merits we ourselves have endeavoured to do justice in a former work of blessed memory, but that several houses had been lately attempted, and two absolutely plundered.

"For myself," he added, "I have no money to signify, about my person: my watch is only valuable to me for the time it has been in my possession: and if the rogues robbed one civilly, I should not so much mind encountering them; but they are a desperate set, and offer violence when there is nothing to be got by it. Have you travelled far to-day, sir?"

"Some six or seven-and-twenty miles," replied Walter. "I am proceeding to London, and not willing to distress my horses by too rapid a journey."

"Very right, very good; and horses, sir, are not now what they used to be when I was a young man. Ah, what wagers I used to win then! Horses galloped, sir,

when I was twenty; they trotted when I was thirty-
five; but they only amble now. Sir, if it does not tax
your patience too severely, let us give our nags some
hay and water at the half-way house yonder."

Walter assented; they stopped at a little solitary inn
by the side of the road, and the host came out with
great obsequiousness when he heard the voice of Walter's companion.

"Ah, Sir Peter!" said he, "and how be'st your
honour?—fine night, Sir Peter—hope you'll get home
safe, Sir Peter."

"Safe—ay! indeed, Jock, I hope so too. Has all
been quiet here this last night or two?"

"Whish, sir!" whispered my host, jerking his thumb
back towards the house; "there be two ugly customers
within I does not know: they have got famous good
horses, and are drinking hard. I can't say as I knows
anything agen 'em, but I think your honours had better
be jogging."

"Aha! thank ye, Jock, thank ye. Never mind the
hay now," said Sir Peter, pulling away the reluctant
mouth of his nag; and turning to Walter, "Come, sir,
let us move on. Why, zounds! where is that servant
of yours?"

Walter now perceived, with great vexation, that the
corporal had disappeared within the alehouse; and,
looking through the casement, on which the ruddy
light of the fire played cheerily, he saw the man of the
world lifting a little measure of "the pure creature" to
his lips: and close by the hearth, at a small round

table, covered with glasses, pipes, &c., he beheld two
men eyeing the tall corporal very wistfully, and of no
prepossessing appearance themselves. One, indeed, as
the fire played full on his countenance, was a person of
singularly rugged and sinister features ; and this man,
he now remarked, was addressing himself with a grim
smile to the corporal, who, setting down his little
" noggin," regarded him with a stare, which appeared
to Walter to denote recognition. This survey was the
operation of a moment ; for Sir Peter took it upon himself to despatch the landlord into the house, to order forth
the unseasonable carouser ; and presently the corporal
stalked out, and having solemnly remounted, the whole
trio set onward in a brisk trot. As soon as they were
without sight of the alehouse, the corporal brought the
aquiline profile of his gaunt steed on a level with his
master's horse.

"Augh, sir ! " said he, with more than his usual
energy of utterance, " I seed him ! "

" Him ! whom ? "

" Man with ugly face what drank at Peter Dealtry's,
and went to Master Aram's,—knew him in a crack—
sure he's a Tartar ! "

"What ! does your servant recognise one of those
suspicious fellows whom Jock warned us against ? "
cried Sir Peter, pricking up his ears.

" So it seems, sir," said Walter : " he saw him once
before, many miles hence ; but I fancy he knows
nothing really to his prejudice."

"Augh!" cried the corporal; "he's d—d ugly, anyhow!"

"That's a tall fellow of yours," said Sir Peter, jerking up his chin with that peculiar motion common to the brief in stature, when they are covetous of elongation. "He looks military :—has he been in the army? —Ay, I thought so; one of the King of Prussia's grenadiers, I suppose? Faith, I hear hoofs behind!"

"Hem!" cried the corporal, again coming alongside of his master. "Beg pardon, sir—served in the forty-second—nothing like regular line—stragglers always cut off;—had rather not straggle just now—enemy behind!"

Walter looked back and saw two men approaching them at a hand-gallop. "We are a match at least for them, sir," said he, to his new acquaintance.

"I am devilish glad I met you," was Sir Peter's rather selfish reply.

"'Tis he! 'tis the devil!" grunted the corporal, as the two men now gained their side and pulled up; and Walter recognised the faces he had remarked in the alehouse.

"Your servant, gentlemen," quoth the uglier of the two; "you ride fast——"

"And ready—bother—baugh!" chimed in the corporal, plucking a gigantic pistol from his holster, without any further ceremony.

"Glad to hear it, sir!" said the hard-featured stranger, nothing dashed. "But I can tell *you* a secret!"

"What's that—augh!" said the corporal, cocking his pistol.

"Whoever hurts you, friend, cheats the gallows!" replied the stranger, laughing, and spurring on his horse, to be out of reach of any practical answer with which the corporal might favour him. But Bunting was a prudent man, and not apt to be choleric.

"Bother!" said he, and dropped his pistol, as the other stranger followed his ill-favoured comrade.

"You see we are too strong for them!" cried Sir Peter, gaily; "evidently highwaymen! How very fortunate that I should have fallen in with you!"

A shower of rain now began to fall. Sir Peter looked serious — he halted abruptly—unbuckled his cloak, which had been strapped before his saddle—wrapped himself up in it—buried his face in the collar—muffled his chin with a red handkerchief, which he took out of his pocket, and then turning to Walter, he said to him, "What! no cloak, sir? no wrapper even? Upon my soul I am very sorry I have not another handkerchief to lend you!"

"Man of the world—baugh!" grunted the corporal, and his heart quite warmed to the stranger he had at first taken to be a robber.

"And now, sir," said Sir Peter, patting his nag, and pulling up his cloak-collar still higher, "let us go gently; there is no occasion for hurry. Why distress our horses?"

"Really, sir," said Walter, smiling, "though I have a great regard for my horse, I have some for myself;

and I should rather like to be out of this rain as soon
as possible."

"Oh, ah! *you* have no cloak. I forgot that; to
be sure—to be sure, let us trot on, gently—though—
gently. Well, sir, as I was saying, horses are not so
swift as they were. The breed is bought up by the
French! I remember once, Johnny Courtland and I,
after dining at my house till the champagne had played
the dancing-master to our brains, mounted our horses,
and rode twenty miles for a cool thousand the winner.
I lost it, sir, by a hair's-breadth; but I lost it on purpose: it would have half ruined Johnny Courtland to
have paid me, and he had that delicacy, sir—he had
that delicacy, that he would not have suffered me to
refuse taking his money—so what could I do, but lose
on purpose? You see I had no alternative!"

"Pray, sir," said Walter, charmed and astonished at
so rare an instance of the generosity of human friend-
ships—"pray, sir, did I not hear you called Sir Peter
by the landlord of the little inn? Can it be, since
you speak so familiarly of Mr Courtland, that I have
the honour to address Sir Peter Hales?"

"Indeed *that* is my name," replied the gentleman,
with some surprise in his voice. "But I have never
had the honour of seeing you before."

"Perhaps my name is not unfamiliar to you," said
Walter. "And among my papers I have a letter addressed to you from my uncle, Rowland Lester."

"God bless me!" cried Sir Peter. "What! Rowy?
—well, indeed, I am overjoyed to hear of him. So

you are his nephew? Pray tell me all about him—a wild, gay, rollicking fellow still, eh? Always fencing, sa—sa! or playing at billiards, or hot in a steeple-chase; there was not a jollier, better-humoured fellow in the world than Rowy Lester."

"You forget, Sir Peter," said Walter, laughing at a description so unlike his sober and steady uncle, "that some years have passed since the time you speak of."

"Ah, and so there have," replied Sir Peter. "And what does your uncle say of *me?*"

"That when he knew you, you were all generosity, frankness, hospitality."

"Humph, humph!" said Sir Peter, looking ex-tremely disconcerted, a confusion which Walter im-puted solely to modesty. "I was a hairbrained, foolish fellow then—quite a boy, quite a boy: but bless me, it rains sharply, and you have no cloak. But we are close on the town now. An excellent inn is the 'Duke of Cumberland's Head;' you will have charming ac-commodation there."

"What, Sir Peter, you know this part of the coun-try well!"

"Pretty well, pretty well; indeed, I live near, that is to say, not *very* far from, the town. This turn, if you please. We separate here. I have brought you a little out of your way—not above a mile or two, for fear the robbers should attack me if I was left alone. I had quite forgot you had no cloak. That's your road —this mine. Aha! so Rowy Lester is still alive and hearty!—the same excellent, wild fellow, no doubt.

Give my kindest remembrance to him when you write. Adieu, sir."

This latter speech having been delivered during a halt, the corporal had heard it : he grinned delightedly as he touched his hat to Sir Peter, who now trotted off, and muttered to his young master,—

" Most sensible man, that, sir ! "

CHAPTER VI.

Sir Peter displayed.—One man of the world suffers from another.
—The Incident of the Bridle begets the Incident of the Saddle.—
The Incident of the Saddle begets the Incident of the Whip.—The
Incident of the Whip begets what the Reader must read to see.

Nihil est allud magnum quam multa minuta.* —*Vet. Auct.*

" AND so," said Walter, the next morning, to the head
waiter, who was busied about their preparations for
breakfast—"and so Sir Peter Hales, you say, lives
within a mile of the town ? "

" *Scarcely* a mile, sir—black or green ?—you passed
the turn to his house last night ;—sir, the eggs are
quite fresh this morning.   This inn belongs to Sir
Peter."

" Oh !—Does Sir Peter see much company ? "

The waiter smiled.

" Sir Peter gives very handsome dinners, sir ; twice
a-year !   A most clever gentleman, Sir Peter !   They
say he is the best manager of property in the whole
county.   Do you like Yorkshire cake ?—toast ! yes,
sir !"

* Nor is there anything that hath so great a power as the aggre-
gate of small things.

"So, so," said Walter to himself, "a pretty true description my uncle gave me of this gentleman. 'Ask me too often to dinner, indeed !'—'offer me money if I want it !'—'spend a month at his house !'—'most hospitable fellow in the world !'—My uncle must have been dreaming."

Walter had yet to learn, that the men most prodigal when they have nothing but expectations, are often most thrifty when they know the charms of absolute possession. Besides, Sir Peter had married a Scotch lady, and was blessed with eleven children ! But was Sir Peter Hales much altered? Sir Peter Hales was exactly the same man in reality that he always had been. Once he was selfish in extravagance ; he was now selfish in thrift. He had always pleased himself, and forgot other people ; that was exactly what he valued himself on doing now. But the most absurd thing about Sir Peter was, that while he was for ever extracting use from every one else, he was mightily afraid of being himself put to use. He was in parliament, and noted for never giving a frank out of his own family. Yet withal, Sir Peter Hales was still an agreeable fellow ; nay, he was more liked and much more esteemed than ever. There is something conciliatory in a saving disposition ; but people put themselves in a great passion when a man is too liberal with his own. It is an insult on their own prudence. "What right has he to be so extravagant ? What an example to our servants !" But your close neighbour does not humble you. You love your close neighbour ; you

respect your close neighbour ; you have your harmless jest against him—but he is a most respectable
man.

"A letter, sir, and a parcel from Sir Peter Hales,"
said the waiter, entering.

The parcel was a bulky, angular, awkward packet of
brown paper, sealed once and tied with the smallest
possible quantity of string : it was addressed to Mr
James Holwell, Saddler, —— Street, ——. The letter
was to —— Lester, Esq., and ran thus, written in a
very neat, stiff, Italian character :—

"D^r S^r,

"I trust you had no difficulty in find^g y^e 'Duke of
Cumberland's Head ;' it is an excellent I^n.

"I greatly reg^t y^t you are unavoid^y oblig'd to go on
to Lond^n ; for, otherwise, I sh^d have had the sincerest
pleas^e in seeing you here at din^r, & introducing you to
L^y Hales. Anoth^r time I trust we may be more fortunate.

"As you pass thro' ye litt^e town of ——, exactly 21
miles hence, on the road to Lond^n, will you do me the
fav^r to allow your serv^t to put the little parcel I send,
into his pock^t, & drop it as direct^d. It is a bridle I am
forc'd to return. Country work^n are such bung^n.

"I sh^d most certain^y have had ye hon^r to wait on you
person^y, but the rain has given me a m^o sev^e cold ;—
hope you have escap'd, tho' by y^e by, you had no cloke,
nor wrapp^r !

"My kindest regards to your m^o excellent unc^e. I

am quite sure he's the same fine merr' fell" he always was !—tell him so !

"D' S', Yours faith',

"PETER GRINDLESCREW HALES.

"P.S. You know perh' y' poor Jn° Court⁴, your uncle's m° intim° friend, lives in ——, the town in which your serv' will drop y° brid°. He is much alter'd, poor Jn° !"

"Altered ! alteration then seems the fashion with my uncle's friends !" thought Walter, as he rang for the corporal, and consigned to his charge the unsightly parcel.

"It is to be carried twenty-one miles at the request of the gentleman we met last night—a most sensible man, Bunting !"

"Augh—waugh—your honour !" grunted the corporal, thrusting the bridle very discontentedly into his pocket, where it annoyed him the whole journey by incessantly getting between his seat of leather and his seat of honour. It is a comfort to the inexperienced, when one man of the world smarts from the sagacity of another ; we resign ourselves more willingly to our fate. Our travellers resumed their journey, and in a few minutes, from the cause we have before assigned, the corporal became thoroughly out of humour.

"Pray, Bunting," said Walter, calling his attendant to his side, "do you feel sure that the man we met yesterday at the alehouse, is the same you saw at Grassdale some months ago ?"

"D—n it!" cried the corporal quickly, and clapping his hand behind.

"How, sir?"

"Beg pardon, your honour—slip tongue, but this confounded parcel!—augh—bother."

"Why don't you carry it in your hand?"

"'Tis so ungainsome, and be d—d to it! And how can I hold parcel and pull in this beast, which requires two hands? his mouth's as hard as a brickbat—augh!"

"You have not answered my question yet?"

"Beg pardon, your honour. Yes, certain sure the man's the same; phiz not to be mistaken."

"It is strange," said Walter, musing, "that Aram should know a man who, if not a highwayman as we suspected, is at least of rugged manner and disreputable appearance; it is strange, too, that Aram always avoided recurring to the acquaintance, though he confessed it." With this he broke into a trot, and the corporal into an oath.

They arrived by noon at the little town specified by Sir Peter, and in their way to the inn (for Walter resolved to rest there), passed by the saddler's house. It so chanced that Master Holwell was an adept in his craft, and that a newly-invented hunting-saddle at the window caught Walter's notice. The artful saddler persuaded the young traveller to dismount and look at "the most convenientest and handsomest saddle that ever was seen:" and the corporal having lost no time in getting rid of his encumbrance, Walter dismissed

him to the inn with the horses, and after purchasing
the saddle in exchange for his own, he sauntered into
the shop to look at a new snaffle. A gentleman's
servant was in the shop at the time, bargaining for a
riding-whip; and the shop-boy, among others, showed
him a large old-fashioned one, with a tarnished silver
handle. Grooms have no taste for antiquity, and in
spite of the silver handle, the servant pushed it aside
with some contempt. Some jest he uttered at the time
chanced to attract Walter's notice to the whip; he took
it up carelessly, and perceived with great surprise that
it bore his own crest, a bittern, on the handle. He
examined it now with attention, and underneath the
crest were the letters G. L., his father's initials.

"How long have you had this whip?" said he to
the saddler, concealing the emotion which this token
of his lost parent naturally excited.

"Oh, a 'nation long time sir," replied Mr Holwell.
"It is a queer old thing, but really is not amiss, if the
silver was scrubbed up a bit, and a new lash put on;
you may have it a bargain, sir, if so be you have taken
a fancy to it."

"Can you at all recollect how you came by it?"
said Walter, earnestly. "The fact is, that I see by
the crest and initials that it belonged to a person
whom I have some interest in discovering."

"Why, let me think," said the saddler, scratching
the tip of his right ear; "'tis so long ago sin' I had it,
I quite forget how I came by it."

"Oh, is it that whip, John?" said the wife, who had been attracted from the back parlour by the sight of the handsome young stranger. "Don't you remember, it's a many year ago, a gentleman who passed a day with Squire Courtland, when he first came to settle here, called and left the whip to have a new thong put to it? But I fancies he forgot it, sir" (turning to Walter), "for he never called for it again; and the squire's people said as how he was agone into Yorkshire; so there the whip's been ever sin'. I remembers it, sir, 'cause I kept it in the little parlour nearly a year, to be in the way like."

"Ah! I thinks I do remember it now," said Master Holwell. "I should think it's a matter of twelve yearn ago. I suppose I may sell it without fear of the gentleman's claiming it again."

"Not more than twelve years!" said Walter, anxiously; for it was some seventeen years since his father had been last heard of by his family.

"Why, it may be thirteen, sir, or so, more or less; I can't say exactly."

"More likely fourteen," said the dame; "it can't be much more, sir, we have only been married fifteen year come next Christmas. But my old man here is ten years older nor I."

"And the gentleman, you say, was at Mr Courtland's?"

"Yes, sir, that I'm sure of," replied the intelligent Mrs Holwell; "they said he had come lately from Ingee."

Walter now despairing of hearing more, purchased the whip; and blessing the worldly wisdom of Sir Peter Hales, that had thus thrown him on a clue, which, however slight, he resolved to follow up, he inquired the way to Squire Courtland's, and proceeded thither at once.

CHAPTER VII.

Gad's my life, did you ever hear the like ? what a strange man is this !
What you have possessed me withal, I'll discharge it amply.
            BEN JONSON : *Every Man in his Humour.*

MR COURTLAND's house was surrounded by a high wall, and stood at the outskirts of the town. A little wooden door, buried deep within the wall, seemed the only entrance. At this Walter paused, and after twice applying to the bell, a footman of a peculiarly grave and sanctimonious appearance opened the door.

In reply to Walter's inquiries, he informed him that Mr Courtland was very unwell, and never saw "company." Walter, however, producing from his pocket-book the introductory letter given him by his uncle, slipped it into the servant's hand, accompanied by half-a-crown, and begged to be announced as a gentleman on very particular business.

"Well sir, you can step in," said the servant, giving way ; "but my master is very poorly—very poorly, indeed."

"Indeed; I am sorry to hear it: has he been long so?"

"Going on for ten —— years, sir!" replied the servant, with great gravity; and opening the door of the house, which stood within a few paces of the wall, on a singularly flat and bare grass-plot, he showed him into a room, and left him alone.

The first thing that struck Walter in this apartment was its remarkable *lightness*. Though not large, it had no less than seven windows. Two sides of the wall seemed indeed all window! Nor were these admittants of the celestial beam shaded by any blind or curtain;—

> "The gaudy, babbling, and remorseless day,"

made itself thoroughly at home in this airy chamber. Nevertheless, though so light, it seemed to Walter anything but cheerful. The sun had blistered and discoloured the painting of the wainscot, originally of a pale sea-green; there was little furniture in the apartment; one table in the centre, some half-a-dozen chairs, and a very small Turkey carpet, which did not cover one-tenth part of the clean, cold, smooth oak boards, constituted all the goods and chattels visible in the room. But what particularly added effect to the bareness of all within, was the singular and laborious bareness of all without. From each of these seven windows, nothing but a forlorn green flat of some extent was to be seen; there was neither tree, nor shrub, nor flower, in the whole expanse, although, by several stumps of trees near the house, Walter perceived that the place had not always been so destitute of vegetable life.

While he was yet looking upon this singular baldness of scene, the servant re-entered with his master's compliments, and a message that he should be happy to see any relation of Mr Lester.

Walter accordingly followed the footman into an apartment possessing exactly the same peculiarities as the former one—viz., a most disproportionate plurality of windows, a commodious scantiness of furniture, and a prospect without, that seemed as if the house had been built in the middle of Salisbury Plain.

Mr Courtland himself, a stout man, still preserving the rosy hues and comely features, though certainly not the hilarious expression, which Lester had attributed to him, sat in a large chair, close by the centre window, which was open. He rose and shook Walter by the hand with great cordiality.

"Sir, I am delighted to see you! How is your worthy uncle? I only wish he were with you—you dine with me of course. Thomas, tell the cook to add a tongue and chicken to the roast beef—no, young gentleman, I will have no excuse: sit down, sit down; pray come near the window; do you not find it dreadfully close? not a breath of air? This house is so choked up; don't you find it so, eh? Ah, I see, you can scarcely gasp."

"My dear sir, you are mistaken: I am rather cold, on the contrary: nor did I ever in my life see a more airy house than yours."

"I try to make it so, sir, but I can't succeed; if you had seen what it was when I first bought it! A garden here, sir; a copse there; a wilderness, God wot! at the back; and a row of chestnut-trees in the front! You may conceive the consequence, sir; I had not been long here, not two years, before my health was gone, sir, gone—the d—d vegetable life sucked it out of me. The trees kept away all the air; I was nearly suffocated, without, at first, guessing the cause. But at length, though not till I had been withering away for five years, I discovered the origin of my malady. I went to work, sir; I plucked up the cursed garden, I cut down the infernal chestnuts, I made a bowling-green of the diabolical wilderness, but I fear it is too late. I am dying by inches—have been dying ever since. The malaria has effectually tainted my constitution."

Here Mr Courtland heaved a deep sigh, and shook his head with a most gloomy expression of countenance.

"Indeed, sir," said Walter, "I should not, to look at you, imagine that you suffered under any complaint. You seem still the same picture of health that my uncle describes you to have been when you knew him so many years ago."

"Yes, sir, yes; the confounded malaria fixed the colour to my cheeks: the blood is stagnant, sir. Would to Heaven I could see myself a shade paler!—the blood does not flow; I am like a pool in a citizen's garden, with a willow at each corner;—but a truce to

my complaints.   You see, sir, I am no hypochondriac,
as my fool of a doctor wants to persuade me : a hypochondriac shudders at every breath of air, trembles
when a door is open, and looks upon a window as the
entrance of death.   But I, sir, never can have enough
air ; thorough draught or east wind, it is all the same
to me, so that I do but breathe.   Is that like hypo-
chondria ?—pshaw !   But tell me, young gentleman,
about your uncle : is he quite well,—stout—hearty,—
does he breathe easily,—no oppression ? "

"Sir, he enjoys exceedingly good health ; he did
please himself with the hope that I should give him
good tidings of yourself, and another of his old friends,
whom I accidentally saw yesterday—Sir Peter Hales."

"Hales !   Peter Hales !—ah ! a clever little fellow
that.   How delighted Lester's good heart will be to
hear that little Peter is so improved ;—no longer a
dissolute harum-scarum fellow, throwing away his
money, and always in debt.   No, no ; a respectable,
steady character, an excellent manager, an active
member of parliament, domestic in private life—oh !
a very worthy man, sir ; a very worthy man ! "

"He seems altered, indeed, sir," said Walter, who
was young enough in the world to be surprised at this
eulogy ; " but is still agreeable and fond of anecdote.
He told me of his race with you for a thousand
guineas."

"Ah, don't talk of those days," said Mr Courtland,
shaking his head, pensively ; "it makes me melancholy.   Yes, Peter ought to recollect that, for he has

never paid me to this day; affected to treat it as a jest, and swore he could have beat me if he would. But indeed it was my fault, sir; Peter had not then a thousand farthings in the world; and when he grew rich, he became a steady character, and I did not like to remind him of our former follies. Aha! can I offer you a pinch of snuff?—You look feverish, sir; surely this room must affect you, though you are too polite to say so. Pray open that door, and then this window, and put your chair right between the two. You have no notion how refreshing the draught is."

Walter politely declined the proffered ague; and, thinking he had now made sufficient progress in the acquaintance of this singular non-hypochondriac to introduce the subject he had most at heart, hastened to speak of his father.

" I have chanced, sir," said he, " very unexpectedly upon something that once belonged to my poor father;" here he showed the whip. " I find from the saddler of whom I bought it, that the owner was at your house some twelve or fourteen years ago. I do not know whether you are aware that our family have heard nothing respecting my father's fate for a considerably longer time than that which has elapsed since you appear to have seen him, if at least I may hope that he was your guest, and the owner of this whip; and any news you can give me of him, any clue by which he can possibly be traced, would be to us all—to me in particular—an inestimable obligation."

" Your father!" said Mr Courtland. " Oh—ay,

your uncle's brother.   What was his Christian name?
—Henry?"

"Geoffrey."

"Ay, exactly; Geoffrey!   What! not been heard
of?—his family not know where he is?   A sad thing,
sir; but he was always a wild fellow; now here, now
there, like a flash of lightning.   But it is true, it is
true, he did stay a day here, several years ago, when I
first bought the place.   I can tell you all about it;
but you seem agitated—do come nearer the window:—
there, that's right.   Well, sir, it is, as I said, a great
many years ago—perhaps fourteen—and I was speaking
to the landlord of the 'Greyhound' about some hay
he wished to sell, when a gentleman rode into the yard
full tear, as your father always did ride, and in getting
out of his way I recognised Geoffrey Lester.   I did
not know him well—far from it; but I had seen him
once or twice with your uncle, and though he was a
strange pickle, he sang a good song, and was deuced
amusing.   Well, sir, I accosted him; and, for the sake
of your uncle, I asked him to dine with me, and take
a bed at my new house.   Ah! I little thought what a
dear bargain it was to be!   He accepted my invitation;
for I fancy—no offence, sir—there were few invitations
that Mr Geoffrey Lester ever refused to accept.   We
dined *tête-à-tête*—I am an old bachelor, sir—and very
entertaining he was, though his sentiments seemed to
me broader than ever.   He was capital, however, about
the tricks he had played his creditors—such manœuvres—such escapes!   After dinner he asked me if I

ever corresponded with his brother. I told him no ;
that we were very good friends, but never heard from
each other ; and he then said, ' Well, I shall surprise
him with a visit shortly : but in case you *should* unexpectedly have any communication with him, don't
mention having seen me ; for, to tell you the truth, I
am just returned from India, where I should have
scraped up a little money, but that I spent it as fast
as I got it.   However, you know that I was always
proverbially the luckiest fellow in the world [and so,
sir, your father was !], and while I was in India, I
saved an old colonel's life at a tiger-hunt : he went
home shortly afterwards, and settled in Yorkshire ;
and the other day, on my return to England, to which
my ill-health drove me, I learned that my old colonel
had died recently, and left me a handsome legacy, with
his house in Yorkshire.   I am now going down to
Yorkshire to convert the chattels into gold—to receive
my money ; and I shall then seek out my good-brother,
my household gods, and, perhaps, though it's not likely,
settle into a sober fellow for the rest of my life.'   I
don't tell you, young gentleman, that those were your
father's exact words—one can't remember verbatim so
many years ago ; but it was to that effect.   He left me
the next day, and I never heard anything more of him :
to say the truth, he was looking wonderfully yellow,
and fearfully reduced.   And I fancied at the time he
could not live long : he was prematurely old, and de-
crepit in body, though gay in spirit ; so that I had

tacitly imagined, in never hearing of him more, that he had departed life. But, good heavens! did you never hear of this legacy?"

"Never: not a word!" said Walter, who had listened to these particulars in great surprise. "And to what part of Yorkshire did he say he was going?"

"That he did not mention."

"Nor the colonel's name?"

"Not as I remember; he might, but I think not. But I am certain that the county was Yorkshire; and the gentleman, whatever his name, was a colonel. Stay: I recollect one more particular, which it is lucky I do remember. Your father, in giving me, as I said before, in his own humorous strain, the history of his adventures, his hairbreadth escapes from his duns, the various disguises and the numerous *aliases* he had assumed, mentioned that the name he had borne in India—and by which, he assured me, he had made quite a good character—was Clarke: he also said, by the way, that he still kept to that name, and was very merry on the advantages of having so common a one—'By which,' he observed, wittily, 'he could father all his old sins on some other Mr Clarke, at the same time that he could seize and appropriate all the *merits* of all his other namesakes.' Ah, no offence, but he was a sad dog, that father of yours! So you see that, in all probability, if he ever reached Yorkshire, it was under the name of Clarke that he claimed and received his legacy."

"You have told me more," said Walter, joyfully,

" than we have heard since his disappearance ; and I
shall turn my horses' heads northward to-morrow by
break of day. But you say, ' If he ever reached Yorkshire.' What should prevent him ? "

" His health ! " said the non-hypochondriac. " I
should not be greatly surprised if—if ;—in short, you
had better look at the gravestones, by the way, for the
name of Clarke."

"Perhaps you can give me the dates, sir," said
Walter, somewhat cast down by that melancholy
admonition.

" Ay ! I'll see—I'll see after dinner ; the common-
ness of the name has its disadvantages now. Poor
Geoffrey ! I daresay there are fifty tombs to the
memory of fifty Clarkes between this and York. But
come, sir, there's the dinner-bell."

Whatever might have been the maladies entailed
upon the portly frame of Mr Courtland by the vegetable life of the departed trees, a want of appetite was
not among the number. Whenever a man is not ab-
stinent from rule, or from early habit, solitude makes
its votaries particularly fond of their dinner. They
have no other event wherewith to mark their day ;
they think over it, they anticipate it, they nourish its
soft idea in their imagination : if they do look forward
to anything else more than dinner, it is—supper.

Mr Courtland deliberately pinned the napkin to his
waistcoat, ordered all the windows to be thrown open,
and set to work like the good canon in *Gil Blas*.
He still retained enough of his former self to preserve

an excellent cook ; and though most of his viands were
of the plainest, who does not know what skill it requires to produce an unexceptionable roast or a blame-
less boil ?

Half a tureen of strong soup—three pounds, at least,
of stewed carp—all the *under part* of a sirloin of beef,
—three quarters of a tongue—the moiety of a chicken
—six pancakes, and a tartlet, having severally disappeared down the jaws of the invalid,

> " Et cuncta terrarum subacta
> Præter atrocem animum Catonis," *

he still called for two devilled biscuits and an anchovy !

When these were gone, he had the wine set on a
little table by the window, and declared that the air
seemed closer than ever. Walter was no longer surprised at the singular nature of the non-hypochondriac's complaint.

Walter declined the bed that Mr Courtland offered
him—though his host kindly assured him that it had
no curtains, and that there was not a shutter to the
house—upon the plea of starting the next morning at
daybreak, and his consequent unwillingness to disturb
the regular establishment of the invalid ; and Courtland, who was still an excellent, hospitable, friendly
man, suffered his friend's nephew to depart with regret. He supplied him, however, by a reference to an
old notebook, with the date of the year, and even
month, in which he had been favoured by a visit from

* And everything of earth subdued, except the resolute mind of
Cato.

Mr Clarke, who, it seemed, had also changed his Christian name from Geoffrey to one beginning with D; but whether it was David or Daniel, the host remembered not. In parting with Walter, Courtland shook his head, and observed,—

" *Entre nous*, sir, I fear this may be a wild-goose chase. Your father was too facetious to confine himself to fact—excuse me, sir; and perhaps the colonel and the legacy were merely inventions *pour passer le temps;* there was only one reason, indeed, that made me fully believe the story."

"What was that, sir?" asked Walter, blushing deeply at the universality of that estimation his father had obtained.

" Excuse me, my young friend."

"Nay, sir, let me press you."

" Why, then, Mr Geoffrey Lester did not ask me to lend him any money!"

The next morning, instead of repairing to the gaieties of the metropolis, Walter had, upon this dubious clue, altered his journey northward; and with an unquiet yet sanguine spirit, the adventurous son commenced his search after the fate of a father evidently so unworthy of the anxiety he had excited.

CHAPTER VIII.

Walter's Meditations.—The Corporal's Grief and Anger.—The Corporal personally described.—An Explanation with his Master.—The Corporal opens himself to the young Traveller. —His Opinions on Love;—on the World;—on the Pleasure and Respectability of Cheating;—on Ladies—and a Particular Class of Ladies;—on Authors;—on the Value of Words;—on Fighting;—with sundry other matters of equal delectation and improvement.—An Unexpected Event.

Quale per incertam Lunam sub luce malignâ
Est iter.*—VIRGIL.

THE road prescribed to our travellers by the change in their destination led them back over a considerable portion of the ground they had already traversed; and since the corporal took care that they should remain some hours in the place where they dined, night fell upon them as they found themselves in the midst of the same long and dreary stage in which they had encountered Sir Peter Hales and the two suspected highwaymen.

Walter's mind was full of the project on which he was bent. The reader can fully comprehend how vivid

* Even as a journey by the unpropitious light of the uncertain moon.

were the emotions called up by the hope of a solution
to the enigma of his father's fate ; and sanguinely did
he now indulge those intense meditations with which
the imaginative minds of the young always brood over
every more favourite idea, until they exalt the hope
into a passion.   Everything connected with this strange
and roving parent had possessed for the breast of his
son not only an anxious, but indulgent interest.   The
judgment of a young man is always inclined to sympathise with the wilder and more enterprising order
of spirits ; and Walter had been at no loss for secret
excuses wherewith to defend the irregular life and
reckless habits of his parent.   Amidst all his father's
evident and utter want of principle, Walter clung with
a natural and self-deceptive partiality to the few traits
of courage or generosity which relieved, if they did not
redeem, his character : traits which, with a character
of that stamp, are so often, though always so unprofit-
ably blended, and which generally cease with the
commencement of age.   He now felt elated by the conviction, as he had always been inspired by the hope,
that it was to be his lot to discover one whom he still
believed living, and whom he trusted to find amended.
The same intimate persuasion of the "good-luck" of
Geoffrey Lester, which all who had known him appeared to entertain, was felt even in a more credulous
and earnest degree by his son.   Walter gave way now,
indeed, to a variety of conjectures as to the motives
which could have induced his father to persist in the
concealment of his fate after his return to England ;

but such of those conjectures as, if the more rational, were also the more despondent, he speedily and resolutely dismissed. Sometimes he thought that his father, on learning the death of the wife he had abandoned, might have been possessed with a remorse which rendered him unwilling to disclose himself to the rest of his family, and a feeling that the main tie of home was broken ; sometimes he thought that the wanderer had been disappointed in his expected legacy, and, dreading the attacks of his creditors, or unwilling to throw himself once more on the generosity of his brother, had again suddenly quitted England, and entered on some enterprise or occupation abroad. It was also possible, to one so reckless and changeful, that even, after receiving the legacy, a proposition from some wild comrade might have hurried him away on any Continental project at the mere impulse of the moment, for the impulse of the moment had always been the guide of his life ; and once abroad, he might have returned to India, and in new connections forgotten the old ties at home. Letters from abroad, too, miscarry ; and it was not improbable that the wanderer might have written repeatedly, and, receiving no answer to his communications, imagined that the dissoluteness of his life had deprived him of the affections of his family ; and, deserving so well to have the proffer of renewed intercourse rejected, believed that it actually was so. These, and a hundred similar conjectures, found favour in the eyes of the young traveller ; but the chances of a fatal accident, or sudden death, he

pertinaciously refused at present to include in the
number of probabilities. Had his father been seized
with a mortal illness on the road, was it not likely that,
in the remorse occasioned in the hardiest by approaching death, he would have written to his brother, and,
recommending his child to his care, have apprised him
of the addition to his fortune? Walter, then, did not
meditate embarrassing his present journey by those
researches among the dead which the worthy Courtland had so considerately recommended to his prudence: should his expedition, contrary to his hopes,
prove wholly unsuccessful, it might then be well to
retrace his steps and adopt the suggestion. But what
man, at the age of twenty-one, ever took much precaution on the darker side of a question in which his
heart was interested?

With what pleasure, escaping from conjecture to a
more ultimate conclusion, did he, in recalling those
words, in which his father had more than hinted to
Courtland of his future amendment, contemplate recovering a parent made wise by years and sober by
misfortunes, and restoring him to a hearth of tranquil
virtues and peaceful enjoyments! He imaged to himself a scene of that domestic happiness which is so perfect in our dreams, because in our dreams monotony is
always excluded from the picture. And in this creation of Fancy the form of Ellinor, his bright-eyed
and gentle cousin, was not the least conspicuous.
Since his altercation with Madeline, the love he had
once thought so ineffaceable had faded into a dim and

sullen hue ; and, in proportion as the image of Madeline grew indistinct, that of her sister became more brilliant. Often now, as he rode slowly onward, in the quiet of the deepening night, and the mellow stars softening all on which they shone, he pressed the little token of Ellinor's affection to his heart, and wondered that it was only within the last few days he had discovered that her eyes were more beautiful than Madeline's, and her smile more touching. Meanwhile the redoubted corporal, who was by no means pleased with the change in his master's plans, lingered behind, whistling the most melancholy tune in his collection. No young lady, anticipative of balls or coronets, had ever felt more complacent satisfaction in a journey to London than that which had cheered the athletic breast of the veteran on finding himself, at last, within one day's gentle march of the metropolis. And no young lady, suddenly summoned back in the first flush of her *début* by an unseasonable fit of gout or economy in papa, ever felt more irreparably aggrieved than now did the dejected corporal. His master had not yet even acquainted him with the cause of the countermarch ; and in his own heart he believed it nothing but the wanton levity and unpardonable fickleness "common to all them ere boys afore they have seen the world." He certainly considered himself a singularly ill-used and injured man, and drawing himself up to his full height, as if it were a matter with which heaven should be acquainted at the earliest possible opportunity, he indulged, as we before said, in the melancholy consolation of a whistled death-dirge, occasionally interrupted by a long-drawn interlude, half-sigh, half-snuffle, of his favourite *augh—baugh.*

And here we remember that we have not as yet given to our reader a fitting portrait of the corporal on horseback. Perhaps no better opportunity than the present may occur; and perhaps, also, Corporal Bunting, as well as Melrose Abbey, may seem a yet more interesting picture when viewed by the pale moonlight.

The corporal, then, wore on his head a small cocked-hat, which had formerly belonged to the colonel of the Forty-second—the prints of my uncle Toby may serve to suggest its shape; it had once boasted a feather—that was gone: but the gold lace, though tarnished, and the cockade, though battered, still remained. From under this shade the profile of the corporal assumed a particular aspect of heroism: though a good-looking man in the main, it was his air, height, and complexion which made him so; and, unlike Lucian's one-eyed prince, a side view was not the most favourable point in which his features could be regarded. His eyes, which were small and shrewd, were half hid by a pair of thick, shaggy brows, which, while he whistled, he moved to and fro, as a horse moves his ears when he gives warning that he intends to shy; his nose was straight—so far so good—but then it did not go far enough; for though it seemed no despicable proboscis in front, somehow or another it appeared exceedingly short in profile: to make up for this, the upper lip was of a length the more striking from being

exceedingly straight ;—it had learned to hold itself
upright, and make the most of its length as well as its
master! his under-lip, alone protruded in the act of
whistling, served yet more markedly to throw the nose
into the background; and as for the chin—talk of the
upper-lip being long indeed!—the chin would have
made two of it; such a chin! so long, so broad, so
massive, had it been put on a dish it might have passed,
without discredit, for a round of beef! and it looked
yet larger than it was from the exceeding tightness of
the stiff black-leather stock below, which forced forth
all the flesh it encountered into another chin—a
remove to the round! The hat, being somewhat too
small for the corporal, and being cocked knowingly in
front, left the hinder half of the head exposed. And
the hair, carried into a club, according to the fashion,
lay thick, and of a grizzled black, on the brawny shoulders below. The veteran was dressed in a blue coat,
originally a frock ; but the skirts having once, to the
imminent peril of the place they guarded, caught fire
as the corporal stood basking himself at Peter Dealtry's, had been so far amputated as to leave only the
stump of a tail, which just covered, and no more, that
part which neither Art in bipeds nor Nature in quad-
rupeds loves to leave wholly exposed. And that part,
ah, how ample ! Had Liston seen it, he would have
hid for ever his diminished—opposite to *head!* No
wonder the corporal had been so annoyed by the parcel of the previous day, a coat so short, and a——;
but no matter, pass we to the rest ! It was not only
in its skirts that this wicked coat was deficient ; the

corporal, who had within the last few years thriven
lustily in the inactive serenity of Grassdale, had out-
grown it prodigiously across the chest and girth;
nevertheless he managed to button it up. And thus
the muscular proportions of the wearer bursting forth
in all quarters, gave him the ludicrous appearance of
a gigantic schoolboy. His wrists, and large sinewy
hands, both employed at the bridle of his hard-
mouthed charger, were markedly visible; for it was
the corporal's custom, whenever he came to an obscure
part of the road, carefully to take off, and prudently to
pocket, a pair of scrupulously clean white leather
gloves, which smartened up his appearance prodigiously
in passing through the towns in their route. His
breeches were of yellow buckskin, and ineffably tight;
his stockings were of grey worsted; and a pair of laced
boots, that reached the ascent of a very mountainous
calf, but declined any further progress, completed his
attire.

Fancy then this figure, seated with laborious and
unswerving perpendicularity on a demi-pique saddle,
ornamented with a huge pair of well-stuffed saddle-
bags, and holsters revealing the stocks of a brace of
immense pistols, the horse with its obstinate mouth
thrust out, and the bridle drawn as tight as a bow-
string! its ears laid sullenly down, as if, like the corporal, it complained of going to Yorkshire; and its
long thick tail, not set up in a comely and well-edu-
cated arch, but hanging sheepishly down, as if resolved
that its buttocks should at least be better covered than
its master's!

And now, reader, it is not our fault if you cannot form some conception of the physical perfections of the corporal and his steed.

The reverie of the contemplative Bunting was interrupted by the voice of his master calling upon him to approach.

" Well, well," muttered he, " the younker can't expect one as close at his heels as if we were trotting into Lunnun, which we might be at this time, sure enough, if he had not been so d—d flighty—augh!"

" Bunting, I say, do you hear?"

" Yes, your honour, yes; this ere horse is so 'nation sluggish."

" Sluggish! why, I thought he was too much the reverse, Bunting. I thought he was one rather requiring the bridle than the spur."

" Augh! your honour, he's slow when he should not, and fast when he should not; change his mind from pure whim, or pure spite: new to the world, your honour, that's all; a different thing if properly broke. There be a many like him!"

" You mean to be personal, Mr Bunting," said Walter, laughing at the evident ill-humour of his attendant.

" Augh! indeed and no!—I daren't—a poor man like me—go for to presume to be parsonal—unless I get hold of a poorer!"

" Why, Bunting, you do not mean to say that you would be so ungenerous as to affront a man because he was poorer than you? Fie!"

" Whaugh, your honour, and is not that the very

reason why I'd affront him? Surely, it is not my betters I should affront : that would be ill-bred, your honour—quite want of discipline."

"But we owe it to our great commander," said Walter, " to love all men."

"Augh ! sir, that's very good maxim—none better —but shows ignorance of the world, sir—great !"

" Bunting, your way of thinking is quite disgraceful. Do you know, sir, that it is the Bible you were speaking of?"

" Augh, sir ! but the Bible was addressed to them Jew creturs ! Howsomever, it's an excellent book for the poor; keeps 'em in order, favours discipline—none more so."

" Hold your tongue. I called you, Bunting, because I think I heard you say you had once been at York. Do you know what towns we shall pass on our road thither?"

"Not I, your honour; it's a mighty long way. What would the squire think?—just at Lunnun, too ! Could have learned the whole road, sir, inns and all, if you had but gone on to Lunnun first. Howsomever, young gentlemen will be hasty—no confidence in those older, and who are experienced in the world. I knows what I knows," and the corporal recommenced his whistle.

" Why, Bunting, you seem quite discontented at my change of journey. Are you tired of riding, or were you very eager to get to town?"

" Augh, sir ! I was only thinking of what's best for

your honour. I! 'Tis not for me to like or dislike. Howsomever, the horses, poor creturs, must want rest for some days. Them dumb animals can't go on for ever, bumpety, bumpety, as your honour and I do. Whaugh!"

"It is very true, Bunting; and I have had some thoughts of sending you home again with the horses, and travelling post."

"Eh!" grunted the corporal, opening his eyes, "hopes your honour ben't serious."

"Why, if *you* continue to look so serious, I must be serious too. You understand, Bunting?"

"Augh! and that's all, your honour," cried the corporal, brightening up; "shall look merry enough to-morrow, when one's in, as it were, like, to the change of the road. But you see, sir, it took me by surprise. Said I to myself, says I, it is an odd thing for you, Jacob Bunting, on the faith of a man, it is! to go tramp here, tramp there, without knowing why or wherefore, as if you were still a private in the Forty-second, 'stead of a retired corporal. You see, your honour, my pride was a-hurt; but it's all over now; only spites those beneath me—I knows the world at my time o' life."

"Well, Bunting, when you learn the reason of my change of plan, you'll be perfectly satisfied that I do quite right. In a word, you know that my father has been long missing; I have found a clue by which I yet hope to trace him. This is the reason of my journey to Yorkshire."

"Augh!" said the corporal, "and a very good reason: you're a most excellent son, sir;—and Lunnun
so nigh!"

"The thought of London seems to have bewitched
you. Did you expect to find the streets of gold since
you were there last?"

"A—well, sir, I hears they *be* greatly improved."

"Pshaw! you talk of knowing the world, Bunting,
and yet you pant to enter it with all the inexperience
of a boy. Why, even I could set you an example."

"'Tis 'cause I knows the world," said the corporal,
exceedingly nettled, "that I wants to get back to it.
I have heard of some spoonies as never kissed a girl,
but never heard of any one who had kissed a girl once
that did not long to be at it again."

"And I suppose, Mr Profligate, it is that longing
which makes you so hot for London?"

"There have been worse longings nor that," quoth
the corporal, gravely.

"Perhaps you meditate marrying one of the London
belles; an heiress—eh?"

"Can't but say," said the corporal, very solemnly,
"but that might be 'ticed to marry a fortin, if so be
she was young, pretty, good-tempered, and fell des-
perately in love with *me*—best quality of all."

"You're a modest fellow."

"Why, the longer a man lives, the more knows his
value; would not sell myself a bargain now, whatever
might at twenty-one."

"At that rate you would be beyond all price at seventy," said Walter. "But now tell me, Bunting, were you ever in love—really and honestly in love?"

"Indeed, your honour," said the corporal, "I have been over head and ears; but that was afore I learnt to swim. Love's very like bathing. At first we go souse to the bottom, but if we're not drowned then, we gather pluck, grow calm, strike out gently, and make a deal pleasanter thing of it afore we've done. I'll tell you, sir, what I thinks of love: 'twixt you and me, sir, 'tis not that great thing in life boys and girls want to make it out to be: if 'twere one's dinner, that would be summut, for one can't do without that; but lauk, sir, love's all in the fancy. One does not eat it, nor drink it; and as for the rest—why, it's bother!"

"Bunting, you're a beast," said Walter, in a rage; for though the corporal had come off with a slight rebuke for his sneer at religion, we grieve to say that an attack on the sacredness of love seemed a crime beyond all toleration to the theologian of twenty-one.

The corporal bowed, and thrust his tongue in his cheek.

There was a pause of some moments.

"And what," said Walter, for his spirits were raised, and he liked recurring to the quaint shrewdness of the corporal—"and what, after all, is the great charm of the world that you so much wished to return to it?"

"Augh!" replied the corporal, "'tis a pleasant thing to look about un with all one's eyes open; rogue here, rogue there—keeps one alive :—life in Lunnun, life in a village—all the difference 'twixt healthy walk and a doze in arm-chair : by the faith of a man, 'tis ! "

" What ! it is pleasant to have rascals about one ? "

" Sure*ly*, yes," returned the corporal, dryly : "what so delightful-like as to feel one's cliverness and 'bility all set an end—bristling up like a porkypine ?   Nothing makes a man tread so light, feel so proud, breathe so briskly, as the knowledge that he has all his wits about him, that he's a match for any one, that the divil himself could not take him in ! "

Walter laughed.

" And to feel one is likely to be cheated is the pleasantest way of passing one's time in town, Bunting, eh ? "

" Augh ! and in cheating, too," answered the corporal ; "'cause you sees, sir, there be two ways o' living ; one to cheat—one to be cheated. 'Tis pleasant enough to be cheated for a little while, as the younkers are, and as you'll be, your honour ; but that's a pleasure don't last long — t'other lasts all your life ; daresay your honour's often heard rich gentlemen say to their sons, ' You ought, for your own happiness' sake, like, my lad, to have summut to do ; ought to have some profession, be you niver so rich : ' very true, your honour, and what does that mean ?—why, it means that 'stead of being idle and cheated, the boy ought to be busy, and cheat—augh ! "

" Must a man who follows a profession necessarily cheat, then ? "

" Baugh ! can your honour ask that ? Does not the lawyer cheat, and the doctor cheat, and the parson cheat, more than any ? And that's the reason they all takes so much int'rest in their profession—bother ! "

" But the soldier ? you say nothing of him."

" Why, the soldier," said the corporal, with dignity —" the *private* soldier, poor fellow, is only cheated ; but when he comes for to get for to be as high as a corp'ral or a sargent, he comes for to get to bully others, and to cheat. Augh ! then, 'tis not for the privates to cheat ; that would be 'sumption, indeed—save us ! "

" The general, then, cheats more than any, I suppose ? "

" 'Course, your honour ; he talks to the world 'bout honour an' glory, and love of his country, and suchlike ! Augh ! that's proper cheating ! "

" You're a bitter fellow, Mr Bunting. And pray what do you think of the ladies—are they as bad as the men ? "

" Ladies—augh ! when they're married—yes ! but of all them ere creturs I respects the kept ladies the most ; on the faith of a man, I do ! Gad ! how well they knows the world—one quite envies the she-rogues : they beats the wives hollow ! Augh ! and your honour should see how they fawns, and flatters, and butters up a man, and makes him think they loves him like winkey, all the time they ruins him ! They kisses money out of the miser, and sits in their

satins, while the wife—'drot her !—sulks in a ging-
ham. Oh, they be clivir creturs, and they'll do what
they likes with Old Nick, when they gets there, for
'tis the old gentlemen they cozens the best; and
then," continued the corporal, waxing more and more
loquacious — for his appetite in talking grew with
that it fed on—"then there be another set o' queer
folks you'll see in Lunnun, sir, that is, if you falls in
with 'em—hang all together, quite in a clink. I seed
lots on 'em when lived with the colonel — Colonel
Dysart, you knows—augh !"

" And what are they ? "

" Rum ones, your honour; what they calls authors."

" Authors ! what the deuce had you or the colonel
to do with authors ? "

" Augh, then ! the colonel was a very fine gentleman, what the larned calls a my-seen-ass ; wrote little
songs himself—'crossticks, you knows, your honour :
once he made a play—'cause why ?—he lived with an
actress !"

" A very good reason, indeed, for emulating Shakespeare : and did the play succeed ? "

" Fancy it did, your honour ; for the colonel was a
dab with the scissors."

" Scissors ! the pen, you mean ? "

" No ! that's what the dirty authors make plays
with ; a lord and a colonel, my-seen-asses, always takes
the scissors."

" How !"

" Why, the colonel's lady had lots of plays, and she

marked a scene here, a jest there, a line in one place, a bit of blarney in t'other ; and the colonel sat by with a great paper book, cut 'em out, pasted them in book. Augh ! but the colonel pleased the town mightily."

" Well, so he saw a great many authors : and did not they please you ? "

" Why, they be so d——d quarrelsome," said the corporal ; " wringle, wrangle, wrongle, snap, growl, scratch ; that's not what a man of the world does ; man of the world nivir quarrels : then, too, these creturs always fancy you forgets that their father was a clargyman ; they always thinks more of their family, like, than their writings ; and if they does not get money when they wants it, they bristles up and cries, ' Not treated like a gentleman, by G— !' Yet, after all, they've a deal of kindness in 'em, if you knows how to manage 'em—augh ! but cat-kindness—paw to-day, claw to-morrow. And, then, they always marries young—the poor things !—and have a power of children, and live on the fame and fortin they *are* to get one of these days ; for, my eye ! they be the most sanguinest folks alive ? "

" Why, Bunting, what an observer you have been ! Who could ever have imagined that you had made yourself master of so many varieties in men ! "

" Augh, your honour, I had nothing to do, when I was the colonel's valley, but to take notes to ladies and make use of my eyes. Always a 'flective man."

" It is odd that, with all your abilities, you did not provide better for yourself."

"'Twas not my fault," said the corporal, quickly; "but, somehow, do what will, 'tis not always the cliverest as foresees the best. But I be young yet, your honour!"

Walter stared at the corporal, and laughed outright: the corporal was exceedingly piqued.

"Augh! mayhap you thinks, sir, that 'cause not so young as you, not young at all; but what's forty, or fifty, or fifty-five, in public life? Never hear much of men afore then. 'Tis the autumn that reaps, spring sows, augh!—bother!"

"Very true and very poetical. I see you did not live among authors for nothing."

"I knows summut of language, your honour," quoth the corporal, pedantically.

"It is evident."

"For, to be a man of the world, sir, must know all the ins and outs of speechifying; 'tis words, sir, that makes another man's mare go your road. Augh! that must have been a cliver man as invented language; wonders who 'twas—mayhap Moses, your honour?"

"Never mind who it was," said Walter, gravely; "use the gift discreetly."

"Humph!" said the corporal. "Yes, your honour," renewed he, after a pause, "it be a marvel to think on how much a man does in the way of cheating as has the gift of the gab. Wants a missis, talks her over; wants your purse, talks you out on it; wants a place, talks himself into it. What makes the parson?— words; the lawyer?—words; the parliament-man?

—words ! Words can ruin a country in the big house ; words save souls in the pulpits ; words make even them ere authors, poor creturs ! in every man's mouth. Augh ! sir, take note of the *words*, and the *things* will take care of themselves—bother !"

" Your reflections amaze me, Bunting," said Walter, smiling. " But the night begins to close in : I trust we shall not meet with any misadventure."

" 'Tis an ugsome bit of road !" said the corporal, looking round him.

" The pistols ? "

" Primed and loaded, your honour."

" After all, Bunting, a little skirmish would be no bad sport—eh ? especially to an old soldier like you."

" Augh, baugh ! 'tis no pleasant work, fighting, without pay at least ; 'tis not like love and eating, your honour, the better for being what they calls 'gratis !'"

" Yet I have heard you talk of the pleasure of fighting ; not for pay, Bunting, but for your king and country !"

" Augh ! and that's when I wanted to cheat the poor creturs at Grassdale, your honour ; don't take the liberty to talk stuff to my master !"

They continued thus to beguile the way till Walter again sank into a reverie, while the corporal, who began more and more to dislike the aspect of the ground they had entered on, still rode by his side.

The road was heavy, and wound down the long hill which had stricken so much dismay into the corporal's

stout heart on the previous day, when he had beheld
its commencement at the extremity of the town, where
but for him they had *not* dined. They were now a
little more than a mile from the said town; the whole
of the way was taken up by this hill; and the road,
very different from the smoothened declivities of the
present day, seemed to have been cut down the very
steepest part of its centre; loose stones and deep ruts
increased the difficulty of the descent, and it was with
a slow pace and a guarded rein that both our travellers
now continued their journey. On the left side of the
road was a thick and lofty hedge; to the right, a wild,
bare, savage heath, sloped downward, and just afforded
a glimpse of the spires and chimneys of the town,
at which the corporal was already supping in idea!
That incomparable personage was, however, abruptly
recalled to the present instant by a most violent
stumble on the part of his hard-mouthed Roman-
nosed horse. The horse was all but down, and the
corporal all but over.

"D—n it," said the corporal, slowly recovering his
perpendicularity; "and the way to Lunnun was as
smooth as a bowling-green!"

Ere this rueful exclamation was well out of the
corporal's mouth, a bullet whizzed past him from the
hedge; it went so close to his ear that but for that
lucky stumble Jacob Bunting had been as the grass
of the field, which flourisheth one moment and is cut
down the next!

Startled by the sound, the corporal's horse made off

full tear down the hill, and carried him several paces
beyond his master ere he had power to stop its career.
But Walter, reining up his better-managed steed,
looked round for the enemy, nor looked in vain.

Three men started from the hedge with a simultan-
eous shout.   Walter fired, but without effect; ere he
could lay hand on the second pistol his bridle was
seized, and a violent blow from a long double-handed
bludgeon brought him to the ground.

BOOK III.

CHAPTER I.

Fraud and Violence enter even Grassdale.—Peter's News.—
The Lovers' Walk.—The Reappearance.

Auf. Whence comest thou?—What wouldest thou?—*Coriolanus.*

ONE evening Aram and Madeline were passing through
the village in their accustomed walk, when Peter
Dealtry sallied forth from the "Spotted Dog," and
hurried up to the lovers with a countenance full of
importance, and a little ruffled by fear.

"Oh, sir, sir (miss, your servant!),—have you heard
the news? Two houses at Checkington" (a small town,
some miles distant from Grassdale) "were forcibly
entered last night — robbed, your honour, robbed.
Squire Tibson was tied to his bed, his bureau rifled,
himself shockingly *confused* on the head; and the
maid-servant, Sally—her sister lived with me, a very
good girl—was locked up in the cupboard. As to the
other house, they carried off all the plate. There were
no less than four men, all masked, your honour, and
armed with pistols. What if they should come here!

such a thing was never heard of before in these parts.
But, sir—but, miss—do not be afraid; do not ye, now,
for I may say with the psalmist—

> 'But wicked men shall drink the dregs
> Which they in wrath shall wring;
> For *I* will lift my voice, and make
> Them flee while I do sing.'"

"You could not find a more effective method of putting them to flight, Peter," said Madeline, smiling;
"but go and talk to my uncle. I know we have a
whole magazine of blunderbusses and guns at home;
they may be useful now. But you are well provided
in case of attack. Have you not the corporal's famous
cat, Jacobina?—surely a match for fifty robbers!"

"Ay, miss, on the principle of set a thief to catch a
thief, perhaps she may be; but really it is no jesting
matter. I don't say as how I am timbersome; but,
tho' flesh is grass, I does not wish to be cut down afore
my time. Ah, Mr Aram, your house is very lonesome
like; it is out of reach of all your neighbours. Hadn't
you better, sir, take up your lodgings at the squire's
for the present?"

Madeline pressed Aram's arm, and looked up fearfully in his face. "Why, my good friend," said he to
Dealtry, "robbers will have little to gain in my house,
unless they are given to learned pursuits. It would be
something new, Peter, to see a gang of housebreakers
making off with a telescope, or a pair of globes, or a
great folio covered with dust."

"Ay, your honour, but they may be the more savage
for being disappointed."

"Well, well, Peter, we will see," replied Aram, impatiently; "meanwhile we may meet you again at the hall. Good evening for the present."

"Do, dearest Eugene—do, for Heaven's sake," said Madeline, with tears in her eyes, as, turning from Dealtry, they directed their steps towards the quiet valley, at the end of which the student's house was situated, and which was now more than ever Madeline's favourite walk; "do, dearest Eugene, come up to the manor-house till these wretches are apprehended. Consider how open *your* house is to attack; and surely there can be no necessity to remain in it now."

Aram's calm brow darkened for a moment. "What, dearest," said he, "can you be affected by the foolish fears of yon dotard? How do we know as yet, whether this improbable story have any foundation in truth? At all events, it is evidently exaggerated. Perhaps an invasion of the poultry-yard, in which some hungry fox was the real offender, may be the true origin of this terrible tale. Nay, love—nay, do not look thus reproachfully; it will be time enough for us, when we have sifted the grounds of alarm, to take our precautions; meanwhile, do not blame me if in your presence I cannot admit fear. Oh, Madeline—dear, dear Madeline, could you guess, could you dream, how different life has become to me since I knew you! Formerly, I will frankly own to you, that dark and boding apprehensions were wont to lie heavy at my heart; the cloud was more familiar to me than the sunshine. But now I have grown a child, and can see around me nothing but hope; my life was winter—your love has breathed it into spring."

"And yet, Eugene—yet——"

"Yet what, my Madeline?"

"There are still moments when I have no power over your thoughts; moments when you break away from me; when you mutter to yourself feelings in which I have no share, and which seem to steal the consciousness from your eye and the colour from your lip."

"Ah, indeed!" said Aram, quickly; "what! you watch me so closely?"

"Can you wonder that I do!" said Madeline, with an earnest tenderness in her voice.

"You must not, then—you must not," returned her lover, almost fiercely. "I cannot bear too nice and sudden a scrutiny; consider how long I have clung to a stern and solitary independence of thought, which allows no watch, and forbids account of itself to any one. Leave it to time and your love to win their inevitable way. Ask not too much from me now. And mark—mark, I pray you, whenever, in spite of myself, these moods you refer to darken over me, heed not—listen not—*leave me!*—solitude is their only cure! Promise me this, love—promise."

"It is a harsh request, Eugene; and I do not think I will grant you so complete a monopoly of thought," answered Madeline, playfully, yet half in earnest.

"Madeline," said Aram, with a deep solemnity of

manner, "I ask a request on which my very love for you depends. From the depths of my soul, I implore you to grant it; yea, to the very letter."

"Why, why, this is——" began Madeline, when, encountering the full, the dark, the inscrutable gaze of her strange lover, she broke off in a sudden fear, which she could not analyse; and only added, in a low and subdued voice—"I promise to obey you."

As if a weight were lifted from his heart, Aram now brightened at once into himself in his happiest mood. He poured forth a torrent of grateful confidence, of buoyant love, that soon swept from the remembrance of the blushing and enchanted Madeline the momentary fear, the sudden chillness, which his look had involuntarily stricken into her mind. And as they now wound along the most lonely part of that wild valley, his arm twined round her waist, and his low but silver voice giving magic to the very air she breathed—she felt, perhaps, a more entire and unruffled sentiment of present, and a more credulous persuasion of future happiness, than she had ever experienced before. And Aram himself dwelt with a more lively and detailed fulness than he was wont on the prospects they were to share, and the security and peace which retirement would bestow upon their life.

"Shall it not," he said—"shall it not be, that we shall look from our retreat upon the shifting passions and the hollow loves of the distant world? We can have no petty object, no vain allurement, to distract the unity of our affection; we must be all in all to each other; for what else can there be to engross our thoughts and occupy our feelings *here?*

"If, my beautiful love, you have selected one whom the world might deem a strange choice for youth and loveliness like yours, you have, at least, selected one who *can* have no idol but yourself. The poets tell you, and rightly, that solitude is the fit sphere for love; but how few are the lovers whom solitude does not fatigue! They rush into retirement, with souls unprepared for its stern joys and its unvarying tranquillity: they weary of each other, because the solitude itself to which they fled palls upon and oppresses them. But to me, the freedom which low minds call obscurity, is the aliment of life: I do not enter the temples of Nature as a stranger, but the priest: nothing can ever tire me of the lone and august altars on which I sacrificed my youth: and now, what nature, what wisdom once were to me—no, no, more, immeasurably more than these—you are! Oh, Madeline! methinks there is nothing under heaven like the feeling which puts us apart from all that agitates, and fevers, and degrades the herd of men; which grants us to control the tenor of our future life, because it annihilates our dependence upon others; and while the rest of earth are hurried on, blind and unconscious, by the hand of Fate, leaves us the sole lords of our destiny; and able, from the Past, which we have governed, to become the prophets of our Future!"

At this moment Madeline uttered a faint shriek, and clung trembling to Aram's arm. Amazed, and aroused from his enthusiasm, he looked up, and on seeing the cause of her alarm, seemed himself transfixed, as by a sudden terror, to the earth.

But a few paces distant, standing amidst the long and rank fern that grew on either side of their path, quite motionless, and looking on the pair with a sarcastic smile, stood the ominous stranger, whom the second chapter of our first Book introduced to the reader.

For one instant Aram seemed utterly appalled and overcome; his cheek grew the colour of death; and Madeline felt his heart beat with a loud, a fearful force beneath the breast to which she clung. But his was not the nature any earthly dread could long daunt. He whispered to Madeline to come on; and slowly, and with his usual firm but gliding step, continued his way.

"Good evening, Eugene Aram," said the stranger; and as he spoke, he touched his hat slightly to Madeline.

"I thank you," replied the student, in a calm voice; "do you want aught with me?"

"Humph!—yes, if it so please you."

"Pardon me, dear Madeline," said Aram, softly, and disengaging himself from her, "but for one moment."

He advanced to the stranger; and Madeline could not but note that, as Aram accosted him, his brow fell, and his manner seemed violent and agitated: but she could not hear the words of either; nor did the con-

ference last above a minute.   The stranger bowed, and
turning away, soon vanished among the shrubs.   Aram
regained the side of his mistress.

"Who," cried she, eagerly, "*is* that fearful man?
What is his business?   What his name?"

"He is a man whom I knew well some fourteen
years ago," replied Aram, coldly, and with ease; "I
did not then lead quite so lonely a life; and we were
thrown much together.   Since that time he has been
in unfortunate circumstances—rejoined the army—he
was in early life a soldier, and had been disbanded—
entered into business, and failed; in short, he has par-
taken of those vicissitudes inseparable from the life of
one driven to seek the world.   When he travelled this
road some months ago, he accidentally heard of my
residence in the neighbourhood, and naturally sought
me.   Poor as I am, I was of some assistance to him.
His route brings him hither again, and he again seeks
me: I suppose, too, that I must again aid him."

"And is that, *indeed*, all?" said Madeline, breathing more freely.   "Well, poor man, if he be your
friend, he must be inoffensive — I have done him
wrong.   And does he want money?   I have some to
give him—here, Eugene!"   And the simple-hearted
girl put her purse into Aram's hand.

"No, dearest," said he, shrinking back, "no, we
shall not require *your* contribution : I can easily spare
him enough for the present.   But let us turn back, it
grows chill."

"And why did he leave us, Eugene?"

" Because I desired him to visit me at home an hour hence."

" An hour ! then you will not sup with us to-night ? "

" No, not this night, dearest."

The conversation now ceased; Madeline in vain endeavoured to renew it. Aram, though without relapsing into one of his frequent reveries, answered her only in monosyllables. They arrived at the manor-house, and Aram at the garden-gate took leave of her for the night, and hastened backward towards his home. Madeline, after watching his form through the deepening shadows until it disappeared, entered the house with a listless step ; a nameless and thrilling presentiment crept to her heart ; and she could have sat down and wept, though without a cause.

CHAPTER II.

The Interview between Aram and the Stranger.

The spirits I have raised abandon me;
The spells which I have studied baffle me.—*Manfred.*

MEANWHILE Aram strode rapidly through the village, and not till he had regained the solitary valley did he relax his step.

The evening had already deepened into night. Along the sere and melancholy woods the autumnal winds crept with a lowly but gathering moan. Where the water held its course, a damp and ghostly mist clogged the air; but the skies were calm, and checkered only by a few clouds, that swept in long, white, spectral streaks, over the solemn stars. Now and then the bat wheeled swiftly round, almost touching the figure of the student, as he walked musingly onward. And the owl,* that before the month waned many days would be seen no more in that region, came heavily from the trees, like a guilty thought that deserts its shade. It was one of those nights half-dim, half-glorious, which

* That species called the short-eared owl.

mark the early decline of the year. Nature seemed restless and instinct with change ; there were those signs in the atmosphere which leave the most experienced in doubt whether the morning may rise in storm or sunshine. And in this particular period, the skyey influences seem to tincture the animal life with their own mysterious and wayward spirit of change. The birds desert their summer haunts ; an unaccountable disquietude pervades the brute creation ; even men in this unsettled season have considered themselves, more than at others, stirred by the motion and whisperings of their genius. And every creature that flows upon the tide of the Universal Life of things, feels upon the ruffled surface the mighty and solemn change which is at work within its depths.

And now Aram had nearly threaded the valley, and his own abode became visible on the opening plain, when the stranger emerged from the trees to the right, and suddenly stood before the student. " I tarried for you here, Aram," said he, " instead of seeking you at home, at the time you fixed ; for there are certain private reasons which make it prudent I should keep as much as possible among the owls, and it was therefore safer, if not more pleasant, to lie here amidst the fern, than to make myself merry in the village yonder."

" And what," said Aram, " again brings you hither ? Did you not say, when you visited me some months since, that you were about to settle in a different part of the country with a relation ? "

" And so I intended ; but Fate, as you would say, or

the Devil, as I should, ordered it otherwise. I had
·not long left you, when I fell in with some old friends,
bold spirits and true ; the brave outlaws of the road
and the field. Shall I have any shame in confessing
that I preferred their society—a society not unfamiliar
to me—to the dull and solitary life that I might have
led in tending my old bedridden relation in Wales,
who, after all, may live these twenty years, and at the
end can scarcely leave me enough for a week's ill-luck
at the hazard-table ? In a word, I joined my gallant
friends, and intrusted myself to their guidance. Since
then, we have cruised around the country, regaled ourselves cheerily, frightened the timid, silenced the frac-
tious, and by the help of your fate, or my devil, have
found ourselves, by accident, brought to exhibit our
valour in this very district, honoured by the dwelling-
place of my learned friend Eugene Aram."

"Trifle not with me, Houseman," said Aram, sternly,
"I scarcely yet understand you. Do you mean to imply that yourself, and the lawless associates you say you
have joined, are lying out now for plunder in these
parts ? "

"You say it : perhaps you heard of our exploits,
last night, some four miles hence ? "

" Ha ! was that villany yours ? "

"Villany !" repeated Houseman, in a tone of sullen
offence. " Come, Master Aram, these words must not
pass between you and me, friends of such date, and on
such a footing."

" Talk not of the past," replied Aram, with a livid

lip, "and call not those whom Destiny once, in despite of Nature, drove down her dark tide in a momentary companionship, by the name of friends. Friends we are not; but while we live there is a tie between us stronger than that of friendship."

"You speak truth and wisdom," said Houseman, sneeringly; "for my part, I care not what you call us, friends or foes."

"Foes, foes!" exclaimed Aram, abruptly; "not that. Has life no medium in its ties?—Pooh—pooh! not foes; *we* may not be foes to each other."

"It *were* foolish, at least at present," said Houseman, carelessly.

"Look you, Houseman," continued Aram, drawing his comrade from the path into a wilder part of the scene, and, as he spoke, his words were couched in a more low and inward voice than heretofore. "Look you, I cannot live and have my life darkened thus by your presence. Is not the world wide enough for us both? Why haunt each other? What have you to gain from me? Can the thoughts that my sight recalls to you be brighter, or more peaceful, than those which start upon me when I gaze on you? Does not a ghastly air, a charnel breath, hover about us both? Why perversely incur a torture it is so easy to avoid? Leave me—leave these scenes. All earth spreads before you—choose your pursuits and your resting-place elsewhere, but grudge me not this little spot."

"I have no wish to disturb you, Eugene Aram, but I must live; and in order to live, I must obey my

companions: if I deserted them, it would be to starve.
They will not linger long in this district; a week, it
may be; a fortnight at most: then, like the Indian
animal, they will strip the leaves and desert the tree.
In a word, after we have swept the country, we are
gone."

"Houseman, Houseman!" said Aram, passionately,
and frowning till his brows almost hid his eyes; but
that part of the orb which they did not hide seemed
as living fire; "I now implore, but I can threaten—
beware!—silence, I say" (and he stamped his foot
violently on the ground, as he saw Houseman about
to interrupt him); "listen to me throughout. Speak
not to me of tarrying here—speak not of days, of
weeks—every hour of which would sound upon my
ear like a death-knell. Dream not of a sojourn in
these tranquil shades, upon an errand of dread and
violence—the minions of the law aroused against you,
girt with the chances of apprehension and a shameful
death——"

"And a full confession of my past sins," interrupted
Houseman, laughing wildly.

"Fiend! devil!" cried Aram, grasping his comrade
by the throat, and shaking him with a vehemence that
Houseman, though a man of great strength and sinew,
impotently attempted to resist. "Breathe but another word of such import; dare to menace me with
the vengeance of such a thing as thou, and by the
heaven above us I will lay thee dead at my feet!"

"Release my throat, or you will commit murder,"

gasped Houseman, with difficulty, and growing already black in the face.

Aram suddenly relinquished his gripe, and walked away with a hurried step, muttering to himself. He then returned to the side of Houseman, whose flesh still quivered either with rage or fear, and, his own self-possession completely restored, stood gazing upon him with folded arms, and his usual deep and passion- less composure of countenance; and Houseman, if he could not boldly confront, did not altogether shrink from, his eye. So there and thus they stood, at a little distance from each other, both silent, and yet with something unutterably fearful in their silence.

"Houseman," said Aram, at length, in a calm, yet a hollow voice, "it may be that I was wrong; but there lives no man on earth, save you, who could thus stir my blood—nor you with ease. And know, when you menace me, that it is not your menace that sub- dues or shakes my spirit; but that which robs my veins of their even tenor is, that you should deem your menace *could* have such power, or that you—that any man—should arrogate to himself the thought that he could, by the prospect of whatsoever danger, humble the soul and curb the will of Eugene Aram. And now I am calm; say what you will, I cannot be vexed again."

"I have done," replied Houseman, coldly. "I have *nothing* to say; farewell!" and he moved away among the trees.

"Stay," cried Aram, in some agitation—"stay; we

must not part thus. Look you, Houseman, you say you would starve, should you leave your present associates. That may not be; quit them this night—this moment: leave the neighbourhood, and the little in my power is at your will."

"As to that," said Houseman, dryly, "what is in your power is, I fear me, so little, as not to counterbalance the advantages I should lose in quitting my companions. I expect to net some three hundreds before I leave these parts."

"Some three hundreds!" repeated Aram, recoiling; "that were indeed beyond me. I told you when we last met, that it is only from an annual payment I draw the means of subsistence."

"I remember it. I do not ask you for money, Eugene Aram; these hands can maintain me," replied Houseman, smiling grimly. "I told you at once the sum I expected to receive *somewhere*, in order to prove that you need not vex your benevolent heart to afford me relief. I knew well the sum I named was out of your power; unless, indeed, it be part of the marriage-portion you are about to receive with your bride. Fie, Aram! what, secrets from your old friend! You see I pick up the news of the place without your confidence."

Again Aram's face worked, and his lip quivered; but he conquered his passion with a surprising self-command, and answered mildly—

"I do not know, Houseman, whether I shall receive any marriage-portion whatsoever; if I do, I am willing to make some arrangement by which I could *engage* you to molest me no more. But it yet wants several days to my marriage; quit the neighbourhood now, and a month hence let us meet again. Whatever at that time may be my resources, you shall frankly know them."

"It cannot be," said Houseman. "I quit not these districts without a certain sum, not in hope, but possession. But why interfere with me? I seek not my hoards in your coffer. Why so anxious that I should not breathe the same air as yourself?"

"It matters not," replied Aram, with a deep and ghastly voice; "but when you are near me, I feel as if I were with the dead: it is a spectre I would exorcise in ridding me of your presence. Yet this is not what I now speak of. You are engaged, according to your own lips, in lawless and midnight schemes, in which you may (and the tide of chances runs towards that bourne) be seized by the hand of Justice."

"Ho!" said Houseman, sullenly; "and was it not for saying that you feared this, and its probable consequences, that you wellnigh stifled me but now? So truth may be said one moment with impunity, and the next at peril of life! These are the subtleties of you wise schoolmen, I suppose. Your Aristotles and your Zenos, your Platos and your Epicuruses, teach you notable distinctions, truly!"

"Peace!" said Aram; "are we at all times ourselves? Are the passions never our masters? You maddened me into anger; behold, I am now calm: the

subjects discussed between myself and you are of life
and death; let us approach them with our senses collected and prepared. What, Houseman, are you bent
upon your own destruction as well as mine, that you
persevere in courses which *must* end in a death of
shame ? "

"What else can I do ? I will not work, and I
cannot live like you in a lone wilderness on a crust of
bread. Nor is my name like yours, mouthed by the
praise of honest men : my character is marked; those
who once welcomed me shun now. I have no resource
for society (for *I* cannot face myself alone), but in the
fellowship of men like myself, whom the world has
thrust from its pale. I have no resource for bread,
save in the pursuits that are branded by justice, and
accompanied with snares and danger. What would
you have me do ? "

"Is it not better," said Aram, "to enjoy peace and
safety upon a small but certain pittance, than to live
thus from hand to mouth ?—vibrating from wealth to
famine, and the rope around your neck sleeping and
awake ? Seek your relation; in that quarter you yourself said your character was not branded : live with
him, and know the quiet of easy days, and I promise
you, that if aught be in my power to make your lot
more suitable to your wants, so long as you lead the
life of honest men, it shall be freely yours. Is not
this better, Houseman, than a short and sleepless career
of dread ? "

"Aram," answered Houseman, "are you in truth

calm enough to hear me speak? I warn you, that if again you forget yourself, and lay hands on me——"

"Threaten not, threaten not," interrupted Aram, "but proceed; all within me is now still and cold as ice. Proceed without fear or scruple."

"Be it so; we do not love one another; you have affected contempt for me—and I—I—no matter—I am not a stone or a stick, that I should not feel. You have scorned me—you have outraged me—you have not used towards me even the decent hypocrisies of prudence—yet now you would ask of me the conduct, the sympathy, the forbearance, the concession of friendship. You wish that I should quit these scenes, where, to my judgment, a certain advantage awaits me, solely that I may lighten your breast of its selfish fears. You dread the dangers that await me on your own account. And in my apprehension you forebode your own doom. You ask me, nay, not ask, you would command, you would awe me to sacrifice my will and wishes, in order to soothe your anxieties and strengthen your own safety. Mark me! Eugene Aram, I have been treated as a tool, and I will not be governed as a friend. I will not stir from the vicinity of your home till my designs be fulfilled—I enjoy, I hug myself in your torments, I exult in the terror with which you will hear of each new enterprise, each new daring, each new triumph of myself and my gallant comrades. And now I am avenged for the affront you put upon me."

Though Aram trembled with suppressed passions,

from limb to limb, his voice was still calm, and his lip
even wore a smile as he answered—

"I was prepared for this, Houseman; you utter
nothing that surprises or appals me. You hate me;
it is natural: men united as we are rarely look on
each other with a friendly or a pitying eye.   But,
Houseman, I KNOW YOU!—you are a man of vehement passions, but interest with you is yet stronger
than passion. If not, our conference is over.   Go—
and do your worst."

"You are right, most learned scholar; I can fetter
the tiger within, in his deadliest rage, by a golden
chain."

"Well, then, Houseman, it is not your interest to
betray me—my destruction is your own."

"I grant it; but if I am apprehended, and to be
hung for robbery?"

"It will be no longer an object to you to care for
my safety. Assuredly I comprehend this. But my
interest induces me to wish that you be removed from
the peril of apprehension, and your interest replies,
that if you can obtain equal advantages in security,
you would forego advantages accompanied by peril.
Say what we will, wander as we will, it is to this
point that we must return at last."

"Nothing can be clearer; and were you a rich man,
Eugene Aram, or could you obtain your bride's dowry
(no doubt a respectable sum) in advance, the arrangement might at once be settled."

Aram gasped for breath, and, as usual with him in

emotion, made several strides, muttering rapidly and indistinctly to himself, and then returned.

"Even were this possible, it would be but a short reprieve: I could not trust you; the sum would be spent, and I again in the state to which you have compelled me now, but without the means again to relieve myself. No, no! if the blow must fall, be it so one day as another."

"As you will," said Houseman; "but——" Just at that moment a long shrill whistle sounded below, as from the water. Houseman paused abruptly— "That signal is from my comrades; I must away. Hark, again! Farewell, Aram."

"Farewell, if it must be so," said Aram, in a tone of dogged sullenness; "but, to-morrow, should you know of any means by which I could feel secure, beyond the security of your own word, from your future molestation, I might—yet how?"

"To-morrow," said Houseman, "I cannot answer for myself; it is not always that I can leave my comrades: a natural jealousy makes them suspicious of the absence of their friends. Yet hold; *the night* after to-morrow, the Sabbath night, most virtuous Aram, I can meet you—but not here—some miles hence. You know the foot of the Devil's Crag, by the waterfall; it is a spot quiet and shaded enough in all conscience for our interview; and I will tell you a secret I would trust to no other man (hark, again!)— it is close by our present lurking-place. Meet me there! —it would, indeed, be pleasanter to hold our conference under shelter—but just at present I would rather not trust myself beneath any honest man's roof in this neighbourhood. Adieu! on Sunday night, one hour before midnight."

The robber, for such then he was, waved his hand, and hurried away in the direction from which the signal seemed to come.

Aram gazed after him, but with vacant eyes; and remained for several minutes rooted to the spot, as if the very life had left him.

"The Sabbath night!" said he, at length, moving slowly on; "and I must spin forth my existence in trouble and fear till then—*till* then! what remedy can I *then* invent? It is clear that I can have no dependence on his word, if won; and I have not even aught wherewith to buy it. But courage, courage, my heart: and work thou my busy brain! Ye have never failed me yet!"

CHAPTER III.

Not my own fears, nor the prophetic soul
Of the wide world, dreaming on things to come,
Can yet the lease of my true love control.
Shakespeare's Sonnets.

Commend me to their love, and I am proud, say,
That my occasions have found time to use them,
Toward a supply of money; let the request
Be fifty talents.—*Timon of Athens.*

THE next morning the whole village was alive and
bustling with terror and consternation. Another, and
a yet more daring robbery had been committed in the
neighbourhood, and the police of the county town had
been summoned, and were now busy in search of the
offenders. Aram had been early disturbed by the
officious anxiety of some of his neighbours; and it
wanted yet some hours of noon when Lester himself
came to seek and consult with the student.

Aram was alone in his large and gloomy chamber,
surrounded, as usual, by his books, but not, as usual,
engaged in their contents. With his face leaning on

his hand, and his eyes gazing on a dull fire, that crept heavily upward through the damp fuel, he sat by his hearth listless, but wrapped in thought.

"Well, my friend," said Lester, displacing the books from one of the chairs, and drawing the seat near the student's, "you have ere this heard the news; and, indeed, in a county so quiet as ours, these outrages appear the more fearful from their being so unlooked for. We must set a guard in the village, Aram, and you *must* leave this defenceless hermitage and come down to us—not for your own sake, but consider you will be an additional safeguard to Madeline. You will lock up the house, dismiss your poor old governant to her friends in the village, and walk back with me at once to the hall."

Aram turned uneasily in his chair.

"I feel your kindness," said he, after a pause, "but I cannot accept it,—Madeline——" he stopped short at that name, and added, in an altered voice—"no, I will be one of the watch, Lester; I will look to her— to your—safety; but I cannot sleep under another roof. I am superstitious, Lester—superstitious. I have made a vow, a foolish one, perhaps, but I dare not break it. And my vow binds me, not to pass a night, save on indispensable and urgent necessity, anywhere but in my own home."

"But there *is* necessity."

"My conscience says not," said Aram, smiling. "Peace, my good friend, we cannot conquer men's foibles, or wrestle with men's scruples."

Lester in vain attempted to shake Aram's resolution on this head; he found him immovable, and gave up the effort in despair.

"Well," said he, "at all events we have set up a watch, and can spare you a couple of defenders. They shall reconnoitre in the neighbourhood of your house, if you persevere in your determination; and this will serve, in some slight measure, to satisfy poor Madeline."

"Be it so," replied Aram; "and dear Madeline herself, *is* she so alarmed?"

And now, in spite of all the more wearing and haggard thoughts that preyed upon his breast, and the dangers by which he conceived himself beset, the student's face, as he listened with eager attention to every word that Lester uttered concerning his daughter, testified how alive he yet was to the least incident that related to Madeline, and how easily her innocent and peaceful remembrance could allure him from himself.

"This room," said Lester, looking round, "will be, I conclude, after Madeline's own heart; but will you always suffer her here? Students do not sometimes like even the gentlest interruption."

"I have not forgotten that Madeline's comfort requires some more cheerful retreat than this," said Aram, with a melancholy expression of countenance. "Follow me, Lester; I meant this for a little surprise to her. But Heaven only knows if I shall ever show it to herself."

"Why? what doubt of that can even your boding temper indulge?"

" We are as the wanderers in the desert," answered Aram, " who are taught wisely to distrust their own senses : that which they gaze upon as the waters of existence is often but a faithless vapour that would lure them to destruction."

In thus speaking he had traversed the room, and, opening a door, showed a small chamber with which it communicated, and which Aram had fitted up with evident and not ungraceful care. Every article of furniture that Madeline might most fancy he had procured from the neighbouring town. And some of the lighter and more attractive books that he possessed were ranged around on shelves, above which were vases intended for flowers ; the window opened upon a little plot that had been lately broken up into a small garden, and was already intersected with walks and rich with shrubs.

There was something in this chamber that so entirely contrasted the one it adjoined, something so light and cheerful and even gay in its decoration and general aspect, that Lester uttered an exclamation of delight and surprise. And indeed it did appear to him touching that this austere scholar, so wrapped in thought, and so inattentive to the common forms of life, should have manifested so much of tender and delicate consideration. In another it would have been nothing, but in Aram it was a trait that brought involuntary tears to the eyes of the good Lester. Aram observed them ; he walked hastily away to the window, and sighed heavily. This did not escape his friend's notice, and after commenting on the attractions of the little room, Lester said—

"You seem oppressed in spirits, Eugene; can anything have chanced to disturb you · beyond, at least, these alarms, which are enough to agitate the nerves of the hardiest of us?"

"No," said Aram; "I had no sleep last night, and my health is easily affected, and with my health my mind. But let us go to Madeline; the sight of her will revive me."

They then strolled down to the manor-house, and met by the way a band of the younger heroes of the village, who had volunteered to act as a patrol, and who were now marshalled by Peter Dealtry, in a fit of heroic enthusiasm.

Although it was broad daylight, and consequently there was little cause of immediate alarm, the worthy publican carried on his shoulder a musket on full cock; and each moment he kept peeping about, as if not only every bush, but every blade of grass, contained an ambuscade, ready to spring up the instant he was off his guard. By his side the redoubted Jacobina, who had transferred to her new master the attachment she had originally possessed for the corporal, trotted peeringly along, her tail perpendicularly cocked, and her ears moving to and fro with a most incomparable air of vigilant sagacity. The cautious Peter every now and then checked her ardour, as she was about to quicken her step, and enliven the march by gambols better adapted to serener times.

"Soho, Jacobina, soho! gently, girl, gently: thou little knowest the dangers that may beset thee. Come up, my good fellows, come to the 'Spotted Dog;' I will tap a barrel on purpose for you; and we will settle the plan of defence for the night. Jacobina, come in, I say; come in,

> ' Lest, like a lion, they thee tear,
> And rend in pieces small:
> While there is none to succour thee,
> And rid thee out of thrall.'

What ho, there! Oh! I beg your honour's pardon! Your servant, Mr Aram."

"What, patrolling already?" said the squire; "your men will be tired before they are wanted; reserve their ardour for the night."

"Oh, your honour, I have only been beating up for recruits; and we are going to consult a bit at home. Ah! what a pity the corporal isn't here; he would have been a tower of strength unto the righteous. But, howsomever, I do my best to supply his place— Jacobina, child, be still: I can't say as I knows the musket-sarvice, your honour; but I fancy's as how we can do it extemporaneous-like, at a pinch."

"A bold heart, Peter, is the best preparation," said the squire.

"And," quoth Peter, quickly, "what saith the worshipful Mister Sternhold, in the 45th Psalm, 5th verse?—

> ' Go forth with godly speed, in meekness, truth, and might,
> And thy right hand shall thee instruct in works of dreadful
> might.'"

Peter quoted these verses, especially the last, with a truculent frown, and a brandishing of the musket, that surprisingly encouraged the hearts of his little armament; and with a general murmur of enthusiasm, the warlike band marched off to the "Spotted Dog."

Lester and his companion found Madeline and Ellinor standing at the window of the hall; and Madeline's light step was the first that sprang forward to welcome their return: even the face of the student brightened when he saw the kindling eye, the parted lip, the buoyant form, from which the pure and innocent gladness she felt on seeing him broke forth.

There was a remarkable *trustfulness* in Madeline's disposition. Thoughtful and grave as she was by nature, she was yet ever inclined to the more sanguine colourings of life; she never turned to the future with fear—a placid sentiment of hope slept at her heart—she was one who surrendered herself with a fond and implicit faith to the guidance of all she loved; and to the chances of life. It was a sweet indolence of the mind, which made one of her most beautiful traits of character; there is something so unselfish in tempers reluctant to despond. You see that such persons are not occupied with their own existence; they are not fretting the calm of the present life with the egotisms of care, and conjecture, and calculation; if they learn anxiety, it is for another: but in *the heart* of that other, how entire is their trust!

It was this disposition in Madeline which perpetually charmed, and yet perpetually wrung the soul of her wild lover; and as she now delightedly hung upon his arm, uttering her joy at seeing him safe, and presently forgetting that there ever had been cause for alarm, his heart was filled with the most gloomy sense of horror and desolation. "What," thought he, "if this poor unconscious girl could dream that at this moment I am girded with peril, from which I see no ultimate escape? Delay it as I will, it seems as if the blow must come at last. What, if she could think how fearful is my interest in these outrages, that in all probability, if their authors are detected, there is one who will drag me into their ruin; that I am given over, bound and blinded, into the hands of another; and that other, a man steeled to mercy, and withheld from my destruction by a thread —a thread that a blow on himself would snap. Great God! wherever I turn I see despair! And she—she clings to me; and, beholding me, thinks the whole earth is filled with hope!"

While these thoughts darkened his mind, Madeline drew him onward into the more sequestered walks of the garden, to show him some flowers she had transplanted. And when an hour afterwards he returned to the hall, so soothing had been the influence of her looks and words upon Aram, that, if he had not forgotten the situation in which he stood, he had at least calmed himself to regard with a steady eye the chances of escape.

The meal of the day passed as cheerfully as usual, and when Aram and his host were left over their abstemious potations, the former proposed a walk before the evening deepened. Lester readily consented, and they sauntered into the fields. The squire soon perceived that something was on Aram's mind, of which he felt evident embarrassment in ridding himself; at length the student said, rather abruptly—

"My dear friend, I am but a bad beggar, and therefore let me get over my request as expeditiously as possible. You said to me once that you intended bestowing some dowry upon Madeline—a dowry I would and could willingly dispense with; but should you of that sum be now able to spare me some portion as a loan—should you have some three hundred pounds with which you could accommodate me——"

"Say no more, Eugene, say no more," interrupted the squire; "you can have double that amount. I ought to have foreseen that your preparations for your approaching marriage must have occasioned you some inconvenience: you can have six hundred pounds from me to-morrow."

Aram's eyes brightened. "It is too much, too much, my generous friend," said he; "the half suffices; but—but a debt of old standing presses me urgently, and to-morrow, or rather Monday morning, *is* the time fixed for payment."

"Consider it arranged," said Lester, putting his hand on Aram's arm; and then leaning on it gently, he added, "and now that we are on this subject, let me tell you what I intended as a gift to you and my dear Madeline ; it is but small, but my estates are rigidly entailed on Walter, and of poor value in themselves, and it is half the savings of many years."

The squire then named a sum, which, however small it may seem to our reader, was not considered a despicable portion for the daughter of a small country squire at that day, and was in reality a generous sacrifice for one whose whole income was scarcely, at the most, seven hundred a-year.   The sum mentioned doubled that now to be lent, and which was of course a part of it ; an equal portion was reserved for Ellinor.

"And to tell you the truth," said the squire, "you must give me some little time for the remainder—for, not thinking some months ago, it would be so soon wanted, I laid out eighteen hundred pounds in the purchase of Winclose farm, six of which (the remainder of your share) I can pay off at the end of the year : the other twelve, Ellinor's portion, will remain a mortgage on the farm itself.   And between us," added the squire, "I do hope that I need be in no hurry respecting her, dear girl.   When Walter returns, I trust matters may be arranged in a manner and through a channel that would gratify the most cherished wish of my heart.   I am convinced that Ellinor is exactly suited to him ; and, unless he should lose his senses for some one else in the course of his travels, I trust that he will not be long returned

before he will make the same discovery. I think of
writing to him very shortly after your marriage, and
making him promise, at all events, to revisit us at
Christmas. Ah! Eugene, we shall be a happy party
then, I trust. And be assured that we shall beat up
your quarters and put your hospitality and Madeline's
housewifery to the test."

Therewith the good squire ran on for some minutes
in the warmth of his heart, dilating on the fireside
prospects before them, and rallying the student on
those secluded habits, which he promised him he
should no longer indulge with impunity.

"But it is growing dark," said he, awakening from
the theme which had carried him away, "and by this
time Peter and our patrol will be at the hall. I told
them to look up in the evening, in order to appoint
their several duties and stations—let us turn back.
Indeed, Aram, I can assure you that I, for my own
part, have some strong reasons to take precautions
against any attack; for, besides the old family plate
(though that's not much), I have—you know the
bureau in the parlour to the left of the hall?—well,
I have in that bureau three hundred guineas, which
I have not as yet been able to take to safe hands
at ——, and which, by the way, will be yours to-
morrow. So, you see, it would be no light misfor-
tune to me to be robbed."

"Hist!" said Aram, stopping short; "I think I
heard steps on the other side of the hedge."

The squire listened, but heard nothing; the senses

of his companion were, however, remarkably acute, more especially that of hearing.

"There is certainly some one; nay, I catch the steps of *two* persons," whispered he to Lester.

"Let us come round the hedge by the gap below."

They both quickened their pace; and gaining the other side of the hedge, did indeed perceive two men in carter's frocks, strolling on towards the village.

"They are strangers, too," said the squire, suspiciously; "not Grassdale men. Humph! could they have overheard us, think you?"

"If men whose business it is to overhear their neighbours—yes; but not if they be honest men," answered Aram, in one of those shrewd remarks which he often uttered, and which seemed almost incompatible with the tenor of those quiet and abstruse pursuits that generally deaden the mind to worldly wisdom.

They had now approached the strangers, who, however, appeared mere rustic clowns, and who pulled off their hats with the wonted obeisance of their tribe.

"Holla, my men," said the squire, assuming his magisterial air; for the mildest squire in Christendom can play the bashaw when he remembers he is a justice of the peace. "Holla! what are you doing here this time of day You are not after any good, I fear."

"We ax pardon, your honour," said the elder clown, in the peculiar accent of the country, "but we be come from Gladsmuir, and be going to work at Squire Nixon's, at Mowhall, on Monday; so as I has a brother living on the green afore the squire's, we be agoing to sleep at his house to-night and spend the Sunday there, your honour."

"Humph! humph! What's your name?"

"Joe Wood, your honour! and this here chap is Will Hutchings."

"Well, well, go along with you," said the squire, "and mind what you are about. I should not be surprised if you snared one of Squire Nixon's hares by the way."

"Oh, well and indeed, your honour——"

"Go along, go along," said the squire, and away went the men.

"They seem honest bumpkins enough," observed Lester.

"It would have pleased me better," said Aram, "had the speaker of the two particularised less; and you observed that he seemed eager not to let his companion speak; that is a little suspicious."

"Shall I call them back?" asked the squire.

"Why, it is scarcely worth while," said Aram; "perhaps I over-refine. And now I look again at them, they seem really what they affect to be. No, it is useless to molest the poor wretches any more. There is something, Lester, humbling to human pride in a rustic's life. It grates against the heart to think of the tone in which we unconsciously permit ourselves to address him. We see in him humanity in its simple state: it is a sad thought to feel that we despise it; that all we respect in our species is what

has been created by art; the gaudy dress, the glittering equipage, or even the cultivated intellect; the
mere and naked material of nature we eye with indifference or trample on with disdain. Poor child of
toil, from the grey dawn to the setting sun, one long
task!—no idea elicited, no thought awakened, beyond
those that suffice to make him the machine of others
—the serf of the hard soil. And then, too, mark how
we scowl upon his scanty holidays, how we hedge in
his mirth with laws, and turn his hilarity into crime!
We make the whole of the gay world, wherein we
walk and take our pleasure, to him a place of snares
and perils. If he leave his labour for an instant, in
that instant how many temptations spring up to him!
And yet we have no mercy for *his* errors; the jail—
the transport-ship—the gallows; those are the illustrations of our lecture-books—those the bounds of
every vista that we cut through the labyrinth of our
laws. Ah, fie on the disparities of the world! They
cripple the heart, they blind the sense, they con-
centrate the thousand links between man and man
into the two basest of earthly ties—servility and
pride. Methinks the devils laugh out when they
hear us tell the boor that his soul is as glorious and
eternal as our own; and yet when, in the grinding
drudgery of his life, not a spark of that soul can be
called forth; when it sleeps, walled around in its
lumpish clay, from the cradle to the grave, without
a dream to stir the deadness of its torpor."

"And yet, Aram," said Lester, "the lords of science

have their ills. Exalt the soul as you will, you cannot raise it above pain. Better, perhaps, to let it sleep, since in waking it looks only upon a world of trial."

"You say well, you say well," said Aram, smiting his heart; "and I suffered a foolish sentiment to carry me beyond the . sober boundaries of our daily sense."

CHAPTER IV.

Military preparations.—The Commander and his Men.—Aram
persuaded to pass the night at the Manor-house.

Falstaff. Bid my lieutenant Peto meet me at the town's end.
. . . . I pressed me none but such toasts and butter,
with hearts in their bellies no bigger than pins' heads.—*First
Part of King Henry IV.*

THEY had scarcely reached the manor-house before the
rain, which the clouds had portended throughout the
whole day, began to descend in torrents, and, to use
the strong expression of the Latin poet, the night
rushed down, black and sudden, over the face of the
earth.

The new watch were not by any means the hardy
and experienced soldiery by whom rain and darkness
are unheeded. They looked with great dismay upon
the character of the night in which their campaign
was to commence. The valorous Peter, who had sus-
tained his own courage by repeated applications to a
little bottle, which he never failed to carry about
him in all the more bustling and enterprising occasions of life, endeavoured, but with partial success, to
maintain the ardour of his band. Seated in the ser-

vants' hall of the manor-house, in a large arm-chair, Jacobina on his knee, and his trusty musket, which, to the great terror of the womankind, had never been uncocked all day, still grasped in his right hand, while the stock was grounded on the floor, he indulged in martial harangues, plentifully interlarded with plagiarisms from the worshipful translations of Messrs Sternhold and Hopkins, and psalmodic versions of a more doubtful authorship. And when, at the hour of ten, which was the appointed time, he led his warlike force, which consisted of six rustics, armed with sticks of incredible thickness, three guns, one pistol, a broadsword, and a pitchfork (the last a weapon likely to be more effectively used than all the rest put together);—when, at the hour of ten, he led them up to the room above, where they were to be passed in review before the critical eye of the squire, with Jacobina leading the on-guard, you could not fancy a prettier picture for a hero, in a little way, than mine host of the " Spotted Dog."

His hat was fastened tight on his brows by a blue pocket-handkerchief; he wore a spencer of a light brown drugget, a world too loose, above a leather jerkin; his breeches of corduroy were met all of a sudden, half way up the thigh, by a detachment of Hessians, formerly in the service of the corporal, and bought some time since by Peter Dealtry to wear when employed in shooting snipes for the squire, to whom he occasionally performed the office of gamekeeper;

suspended round his wrist by a bit of black ribbon
was his constable's baton : he shouldered his musket
gallantly, and he carried his person as erect as if the
least deflection from its perpendicularity were to cost
him his life.   One may judge of the revolution that
had taken place in the village, when so peaceable a
man as Peter Dealtry was thus metamorphosed into a
commander-in-chief!   The rest of the regiment hung
sheepishly back, each trying to get as near to the door
and as far from the ladies as possible.   But Peter, having made up his mind that a hero should only look
straight forward, did not condescend to turn round to
perceive the irregularity of his line.   Secure in his
own existence, he stood truculently forth, facing the
squire, and prepared to receive his plaudits.

Madeline and Aram sat apart at one corner of the
hearth, and Ellinor leaned over the chair of the former;
the mirth that she struggled to suppress from being
audible mantling over her arch face and laughing eyes;
while the squire, taking the pipe from his mouth,
turned round on his easy-chair, and nodded compla-
cently to the little corps and the great commander.

"We are all ready now, your honour," said Peter, in
a voice that did not seem to belong to his body, so big
did it sound,—"all hot, all eager."

"Why, you yourself are a host, Peter," said Ellinor,
with affected gravity; "your sight alone would frighten
an army of robbers : who could have thought you could
assume so military an air?   The corporal himself was
never so upright !"

"I have practised my present *n*attitude all the day, miss," said Peter, proudly; "and I believe I may now say, as Mr Sternhold says or sings in the 26th Psalm, verse 12th,—

> "'My foot is stayed for all essays,
> It standeth well and right;
> Wherefore to God will I give praise
> In all the people's sight!'

Jacobina, behave yourself, child. I don't think, your honour, that we miss the corporal so much as I fancied at first, for we all does very well without him."

"Indeed, you are a most worthy substitute, Peter. And now, Nell, just reach me my hat and cloak: I will set you at your posts: you will have an ugly night of it."

"Very, indeed, your honour," cried all the army, speaking for the first time.

"Silence—order—discipline," said Peter, gruffly. "March!"

But, instead of *marching* across the hall, the recruits huddled up one after the other, like a flock of geese, whom Jacobina might be supposed to have set in motion, and each scraping to the ladies, as they shuffled, sneaked, bundled, and bustled out at the door.

"We are well guarded now, Madeline," said Ellinor. "I fancy we may go to sleep as safely as if there were not a housebreaker in the world."

"Why," said Madeline, "let us trust they will be more efficient than they seem, though I cannot persuade myself that we shall really need them. One

might almost as well conceive a tiger in our arbour as
a robber in Grassdale.   But, dear, dear Eugene, do not
—do not leave us this night : Walter's room is ready
for you, and if it were only to walk across that valley
in such weather, it would be cruel to leave us.   Let me
beseech you ; come, you cannot, you dare not, refuse
me such a favour."

Aram pleaded his vow, but it was overruled ; Madeline proved herself a most exquisite casuist in setting
it aside.   One by one, his objections were broken
down ; and how, as he gazed into those eyes, could he
keep any resolution that Madeline wished him to
break ? The power she possessed over him seemed
exactly in proportion to his impregnability to every
one else.   The surface on which the diamond cuts its
easy way will yield to no more ignoble instrument ; it
is easy to shatter it, but by only one pure and precious
gem can it be shaped.   But if Aram remained at the
house this night, how could he well avoid a similar
compliance the next ?   And on the next was his interview with Houseman.   This reason for resistance
yielded to Madeline's soft entreaties ; he trusted to
the time to furnish him with excuses ; and when
Lester returned, Madeline, with a triumphant air,
informed him that Aram had consented to be their
guest for the night.

"Your influence is, indeed, greater than mine," said
Lester, wringing his hat as the delicate fingers of Ellinor loosened his cloak ; " yet one can scarely think our
friend sacrifices much in concession, after proving the

weather without. I should pity our poor patrol most exceedingly, if I were not thoroughly assured that within two hours every one of them will have quietly slunk home ; and even Peter himself, when he has exhausted his bottle, will be the first to set the example. However, I have stationed two of the men near our house, and the rest at equal distances along the village."

"Do you really think they will go home, sir?" said Ellinor, in a little alarm ; "why, they would be worse than I thought them, if they were driven to bed by the rain. I knew they could not stand a pistol, but a shower, however hard, I did imagine would scarcely quench their valour."

"Never mind, girl," said Lester, gaily chucking her under the chin, "we are quite strong enough now to resist them. You see Madeline has grown as brave as a lioness.—Come, girls, come, let's have supper, and stir up the fire. And, Nell, where are my slippers?"

And thus on the little family scene—the cheerful wood-fire flickering against the polished wainscot ; the supper-table arranged, the squire drawing his oak chair towards it, Ellinor mixing his negus ; and Aram and Madeline, though three times summoned to the table, and having three times answered to the summons, still lingering apart by the hearth—let us drop the curtain.

We have only, ere we close our chapter, to observe, that when Lester conducted Aram to his chamber he placed in his hands an order, payable at the county-town, for three hundred pounds. "The rest," he said, in a whisper, "is below, where I mentioned; and there, in my secret drawer, it had better rest till the morning."

The good squire then, putting his finger to his lip, hurried away, to avoid the thanks, which, indeed, whatever gratitude he might feel, Aram was ill able to express.

CHAPTER V.

Juliet. My true love is grown to such excess,
I cannot sum up half my sum of wealth.—*Romeo and Juliet.*

Eros. Oh, a man in arms';
His weapon drawn, too !—*The False One.*

It was a custom with the two sisters, when they re-
paired to their chamber for the night, to sit conversing,
sometimes even for hours, before they finally retired to
bed. This, indeed, was the usual time for their little
confidences, and their mutual dilations over those hopes
and plans for the future which always occupy the
larger share of the thoughts and conversation of the
young. I do not know anything in the world more
lovely than such conferences between two beings who
have no secrets to relate but what arise, all fresh, from
the springs of a guiltless heart—those pure and beautiful mysteries of an unsullied nature which warm us to
hear ; and we think with a sort of wonder when we
feel how arid experience has made ourselves, that so
much of the dew and sparkle of existence still linger
in the nooks and valleys, which are as yet virgin of the
sun and of mankind.

The sisters this night were more than commonly indifferent to sleep. Madeline sat by the small but bright hearth of the chamber, in her night-dress, and Ellinor, who was much prouder of her sister's beauty than her own, was employed in knotting up the long and lustrous hair which fell in rich luxuriance over Madeline's throat and shoulders.

"There certainly never *was* such beautiful hair!" said Ellinor, admiringly. "And, let me see—yes—on Thursday fortnight I may be dressing it, perhaps, for the last time—heigho!"

"Don't flatter yourself that you are so near the end of your troublesome duties," said Madeline, with her pretty smile, which had been much brighter and more frequent of late than it was formerly wont to be; so that Lester had remarked, "That Madeline really appeared to have become the lighter and gayer of the two."

"You will often come to stay with us for weeks together, at least till—till you have a double right to be mistress here. Ah! my poor hair—you need not pull it so hard."

"Be quiet, then," said Ellinor, half laughing and wholly blushing.

"Trust me, I have not been in love myself without learning its signs; and I venture to prophesy that within six months you will come to consult me whether or not—for there is a great deal to be said on both sides of the question—you can make up your mind to sacrifice your own wishes and marry Walter Lester. Ah!—gently, gently! Nell——"

" Promise to be quiet."

" I will—I will ; but you began it."

As Ellinor now finished her task, and kissed her sister's forehead, she sighed deeply.

" Happy Walter !" said Madeline.

" I was not sighing for Walter, but for you."

" For me ?—impossible !   I cannot imagine any part of my *future* life that can cost you a sigh.   Ah ! that I were more worthy of my happiness !"

" Well, then," said Ellinor, " I sighed for myself ;— I sighed to think we should so soon be parted, and that the continuance of your society would then depend, not on our mutual love, but on the will of another."

" What, Ellinor, and can you suppose that Eugene —my Eugene—would not welcome you as warmly as myself ?   Ah ! you misjudge him ; I know you have not yet perceived how tender a heart lies beneath all that melancholy and reserve."

" I feel, indeed," said Ellinor, warmly, " as if it were impossible that one whom you love should not be all that is good and noble : yet if this reserve of his should increase, as is at least possible, with increasing years ; if our society should become again, as it once was, distasteful to him, should I not lose you, Madeline ? "

" But his reserve cannot increase : do you not perceive how much it is softened already ?   Ah ! be assured that I will charm it away."

" But what is the cause of the melancholy that even now, at times, evidently preys upon him ?   Has he never revealed it to you ? "

"It is merely the early and long habit of solitude and study, Ellinor," replied Madeline; "and, shall I own to you, I would scarcely wish *that* away? His tenderness itself seems linked with his melancholy: it is like a sad but gentle music, that brings tears into our eyes, but who would change it for gayer airs?"

"Well, I must own," said Ellinor, reluctantly, "that I no longer wonder at your infatuation; I can no longer chide you as I once did: there is, assuredly, something in his voice, his look, which irresistibly sinks into the heart. And there are moments when, what with his eyes and forehead, his countenance seems more beautiful, more impressive, than any I ever beheld. Perhaps, too, for you, it is better that your lover should be no longer in the first flush of youth. Your nature seems to require something to venerate as well as to love. And I have ever observed at prayers, that you seem more especially rapt and carried beyond yourself in those passages which call peculiarly for worship and adoration."

"Yes, dearest," said Madeline, fervently. "I own that Eugene is of all beings, not only of all whom I ever knew, but of whom I ever dreamed or imagined, the one that I am most fitted to love and to appreciate. His wisdom, but, more than that, the lofty tenor of his mind, call forth all that is highest and best in my own nature. I feel exalted when I listen to him;—and yet, how gentle with all that nobleness! And to think that *he* should descend to love

me, and *so* to love me ! It is as if a star were to
leave its sphere ! "

" Hark ! one o'clock," said Ellinor, as the deep
voice of the clock told the first hour of morning.
" Heavens ! how much louder the winds rave ! And
how the heavy sleet drives against the window ! Our
poor watch without !—but you may be sure my father
was right, and they are safe at home by this time ;
nor is it likely, I should think, that even robbers
would be abroad in such weather ! "

" I have heard," said Madeline, " that robbers generally choose these dark stormy nights for their designs ;
but I confess I don't feel much alarm ; and *he* is in
the house. Draw nearer to the fire, Ellinor ; is it not
pleasant to see how serenely it burns, while the storm
howls without ? It is like my Eugene's soul, luminous
and lone amidst the roar and darkness of this unquiet
world ! "

" There spoke himself," said Ellinor, smiling to perceive how invariably women who love imitate the tone
of the beloved one. And Madeline felt it, and smiled
too.

" Hist ! " said Ellinor, abruptly ; " did you not hear
a low grating noise below ? Ah ! the winds *now* prevent your catching the sound ; but hush, hush !—the
wind pauses—there it is again ! "

" Yes, I hear it," said Madeline, turning pale ; " it
seems in the little parlour ; a continued, harsh, but
very low, noise. Good heavens ! it seems at the window below."

" It is like a file," whispered Ellinor; " perhaps———"

" You are right," said Madeline, suddenly rising ; " it is a file, and at the bars my father had fixed against the window yesterday. Let us go down and alarm the house."

" No, no ; for Heaven's sake, don't be so rash," cried Ellinor, losing all presence of mind : " hark ! the sound ceases, there is a louder noise below—and steps. Let us lock the door."

But Madeline was of that fine and high order of spirit which rises in proportion to danger, and, calming her sister as well as she could, she seized the light with a steady hand, opened the door, and (Ellinor still clinging to her) passed the landing-place, and hastened to her father's room : he slept at the opposite corner of the staircase. Aram's chamber was at the extreme end of the house. Before she reached the door of Lester's apartment, the noise below grew loud and distinct — a scuffle — voices — curses — and now the sound of a pistol !—in a minute more the whole house was stirring. Lester in his night robe, his broadsword in his hand, and his long grey hair floating behind, was the first to appear : the servants, old and young, male and female, now came thronging simultaneously round ; and in a general body, Lester several paces at their head, his daughters following next to him, they rushed to the apartment whence the noise, now suddenly stilled, had proceeded.

The window was opened, evidently by force : an instrument like a wedge was fixed in the bureau con-

taining Lester's money, and seemed to have been left
there, as if the person using it had been disturbed before the design for which it was introduced had been
accomplished, and (the only evidence of life) Aram
stood, dressed, in the centre of the room, a pistol in
his left hand, a sword in his right; a bludgeon sev-
ered in two lay at his feet, and on the floor within two
yards of him, towards the window, drops of blood yet
warm showed that the pistol had not been discharged
in vain.

"And is it you, my brave friend, whom I have to
thank for our safety?" cried Lester, in great emotion.

"You, Eugene!" repeated Madeline, sinking on his
breast.

"But thanks hereafter," continued Lester; "let us
now to the pursuit — perhaps the villain may have
perished beneath your bullet?"

"Ha!" muttered Aram, who had hitherto seemed
unconscious of all around him; so fixed had been his
eye, so colourless his cheek, so motionless his posture.
"Ha! say you so?—think you I have slain him?—
No, it cannot be—the ball did not slay; I saw him
stagger; but he rallied—not so one who receives a
mortal wound!—Ha, ha!—there is blood, you say:
that is true; but what then?—it is not the first wound
that kills; you must strike again.—Pooh, pooh! what
is a little blood?"

While he was thus muttering, Lester and the more
active of the servants had already sallied through the
window; but the night was so intensely dark that they

could not see a step beyond them. Lester returned, therefore, in a few moments, and met Aram's dark eye fixed upon him with an unutterable expression of anxiety.

"You have *found* no one?" said he, "no dying man?—Ha!—well—well—well! they must *both* have escaped : the night must favour them."

"Do you fancy the villain was severely wounded?"

"Not so—I trust not so ; he seemed able to——But stop—oh God! stop! your foot is dabbling in blood —blood shed by *me*—off! off!"

Lester moved aside with a quick abhorrence, as he saw that his feet were indeed smearing the blood over the polished and slippery surface of the oak boards, and in moving he stumbled against a dark lantern in which the light still burned, and which the robbers in their flight had left.

"Yes," said Aram, observing it, "it was by that, their own light, that I saw them—saw their faces— and—and [bursting into a loud, wild laugh] they were *both* strangers!"

"Ah, I thought so, I knew so," said Lester, pluck-ing the instrument from the bureau. "I knew they could be no Grassdale men. What did you fancy they could be? But—bless me, Madeline—what ho! help! —Aram, she has fainted at your feet."

And it was indeed true and remarkable that so utter had been the absorption of Aram's mind, that he had been not only insensible to the entrance of Madeline, but even unconscious that she had thrown herself on his breast. And she, overcome by her feelings, had slid to the ground, from that momentary resting-place, in a swoon, which Lester, in the general tumult and confusion, was now the first to perceive.

At this exclamation, at the sound of Madeline's name, the blood rushed back from Aram's heart, where it had gathered, icy and curdling; and, awakened thoroughly and at once to himself, he knelt down, and weaving his arms around her, supported her head on his breast, and called upon her with the most passionate and moving exclamations.

But when the faint bloom retinged her cheek, and her lips stirred, he printed a long kiss on that cheek— on those lips, and surrendered his post to Ellinor; who, blushingly gathering the robe over the beautiful breast from which it had been slightly drawn, now entreated all, save the women of the house, to withdraw till her sister was restored.

Lester, eager to hear what his guest could relate, therefore took Aram to his own apartment, where the particulars were briefly told.

Suspecting, which indeed was the chief reason that excused him to himself in yielding to Madeline's request, that the men Lester and himself had encountered in their evening walk might be other than they seemed, and that they might have well overheard Lester's communication as to the sum in his house and the place where it was stored, he had not undressed himself, but kept the door of his room open to listen if anything stirred. The keen sense of hearing, which we have before remarked him to possess, enabled him to catch the sound of the file at the bars even before Ellinor, notwithstanding the distance of his own chamber from the place ; and seizing the sword which had been left in his room (the pistol was his own), he had descended to the room below.

"What !" said Lester, "and without a light ? "

" The darkness is familiar to me," said Aram. " I could walk by the edge of a precipice in the darkest night without one false step, if I had but once passed it before. I did not gain the room, however, till the window had been forced ; and by the light of a dark lantern which one of them held, I perceived two men standing by the bureau—the rest you can imagine ; my victory was easy, for the bludgeon, which one of them aimed at me, gave way at once to the edge of your good sword, and my pistol delivered me of the other.—There ends the history."

Lester overwhelmed him with thanks and praises, but Aram, glad to escape them, hurried away to see after Madeline, whom he now met on the landing-place, leaning on Ellinor's arm, and still pale.

She gave him her hand, which he for one moment pressed passionately to his lips, but dropped the next, with an altered and chilled air. And hastily observing that he would not now detain her from a rest which she must so much require, he turned away and descended the stairs. Some of the servants were grouped around the place of encounter ; he entered the room, and again started at the sight of the blood.

" Bring water," said he, fiercely : " will you let the stagnant gore ooze and rot into the boards, to startle the eye and still the heart with its filthy and unutterable stain ? Water, I say ! water ! "

They hurried to obey him, and Lester, coming into the room to see the window reclosed by the help of boards, &c., found the student bending over the servants as they performed their reluctant task, and rating them with a raised and harsh voice for the hastiness with which he accused them of seeking to slur it over.

END OF THE FIRST VOLUME.